Born to
TREASON

PRAISE FOR E. B. WHEELER AND *BORN TO TREASON*

"A smartly-told story with intriguing characters. Wheeler's understanding of the tumultuous era of the Protestant Reformation and its implications is apparent in this well-crafted novel."
—Jennifer Moore, author of *Becoming Lady Lockwood*

"E. B. Wheeler expertly crafts a tale filled with angst, wit, hope, and just the right bit of romance. The historical setting and complex characters, blended with a well-paced plot, make *Born to Treason* a sure classic you'll want to visit again and again."
—Carolyn Steele, author of *Willow Springs* and *Soda Springs*

"The author beautifully captures the sights, sounds, and customs of the age. Lovers of historical fiction will be well rewarded by reading *Born to Treason*."
—Joyce DiPastena, award-winning historical romance author

"Joan Pryce is a strong, resourceful heroine who follows her heart and what she believes is right in this exciting, fast-paced historical novel that I highly recommend!"
—Loralee Evans, author of *The Shores of Bountiful*

"E. B. Wheeler takes us to a real time where fear, faith, and family were woven together in intricate and often heartbreaking ways. The emotions are real, the characters relatable and inspiring, the story thought-provoking and powerful."
—Jessilyn Stewart Peaslee, author of *Ella*

E. B. WHEELER

Born to
TREASON

SWEETWATER
BOOKS

An imprint of Cedar Fort, Inc.
Springville, Utah

This is a work of fiction. The characters, names, incidents, places, and dialogue are products of the author's imagination and are not to be construed as real. The opinions and views expressed herein belong solely to the author and do not necessarily represent the opinions or views of Cedar Fort, Inc. Permission for the use of sources, graphics, and photos is also solely the responsibility of the author.

ISBN 13: 978-1-4621-1846-5

Published by Sweetwater Books, an imprint of Cedar Fort, Inc.
2373 W. 700 S., Springville, UT 84663
Distributed by Cedar Fort, Inc., www.cedarfort.com

LIBRARY OF CONGRESS CATALOGING-IN-PUBLICATION DATA

Names: Wheeler, E. B., 1978- author.
Title: Born to treason / E.B. Wheeler.
Description: Springville, Utah : Sweetwater Books, an Imprint of Cedar Fort, Inc., [2016] |
©2016
Identifiers: LCCN 2016003639 (print) | LCCN 2016005426 (ebook) | ISBN 9781462118465
(perfect bound : alk. paper) | ISBN 9781462126415 ()
Subjects: LCSH: Catholics--Wales--History--16th century--Fiction. | Treason--Wales--History--
16th century--Fiction. | LCGFT: Historical fiction. | Romance fiction.
Classification: LCC PS3623.H42955 B67 2016 (print) | LCC PS3623.H42955 (ebook) | DDC
813/.6--dc23
LC record available at http://lccn.loc.gov/2016003639

Cover design by Michelle May Ledezma
Cover design © 2016 Cedar Fort, Inc.
Edited and typeset by Justin Greer

Printed in the United States of America

10 9 8 7 6 5 4 3 2 1

Printed on acid-free paper

To the brave men and women who

choose to chart a peaceful course

even in turbulent waters.

Chapter One

I, Joan Pryce, was born to treason. If I did not choose between betraying my country and betraying my conscience, I would betray them both. Just as my father had.

Shovelfuls of mud thumped on his coffin. Each thud resonated in my aching chest, burying me, smothering me. I pulled the hood of my cloak lower to hide my anger and grief. They were a window into my traitorous thoughts, and anyone might be a spy for Queen Elizabeth.

Her law condemned my father to a Protestant funeral—laid to rest in holy ground but unshriven, without the benefit of a priest or last rites. Some of the other mourners owned the implements to give my father a proper Catholic burial, bring peace to his soul and mine, but they were too frightened to bring the bells and candles from their hiding places. Too frightened to sing or pray. I glared at them from the safety of my hood, but none even glanced at me. Cowards, cowards: white-livered cowards, every one.

And I the greatest coward of all, for I said nothing. The thought of the gallows choked off my protests. Where was my loyalty?

Blessed Mary, forgive me.

Songs for the deceased were forbidden, but I was Welsh. I would sooner give up breathing than singing. As they dumped the last muddy earth over my father's final resting place, I quietly hummed the Requiem Mass and recited the lyrics in my mind.

Grant him eternal rest, O Lord. Let light shine upon him forever.

Tears clotted my throat. The familiar words had eased the sorrow squeezing my heart at my mother's death, but they tasted bitter now, when I saw no light.

I stood by the grave as the other mourners filtered away. A wooden slat marked the spot, declaring with terribly finality:

JAMES PRYCE

DIED 1586

The stonecutter was already at work on the tombstone, in accordance with my father's will, that would state more eloquently, "Here lies the body of James Pryce until called to stand before God at the Last Judgement. As you are, he once was. As he is, you shall be. Pray for his soul."

Even in those final words, my father showed his defiance of the queen. She forbade me from praying for my father, but that, at least, I could do without detection. The soft gray clouds and green hills of Wales huddled around the churchyard, wrapping me in their familiar comfort. New tears burned my eyes, but I blinked them back.

"Do not give up hope," I whispered, in case my father's spirit lingered near. "I'll find a way to make it right."

Holding my head high, I walked home. The long stone building blended into the gray of the day. Light filtered through the oiled linen windows. Father had planned to replace them with glass, but the fines for avoiding Protestant church services drained too many shillings. Then the queen's men arrested him as a traitor for attending a Mass.

Neighbors and distant relations gathered in the house's great hall, shuffling over the woven rush mats, avoiding the dogs, who still watched for their master to come home. A deep tension ran beneath the surface, like the prickling of your skin when a lightning storm passes over. Most of the guests spoke Welsh, though I heard English sprinkled in some of the conversations. The mourners drank my father's ale and ate his food, but the whispers around me were of matters for the living.

"They say Mary, Queen of Scots, was involved in the conspiracy."

"Queen Elizabeth might be willing to execute a cousin, but she'll not execute another queen. It could give someone ideas."

"The Lord President of Wales called up more men to patrol the coast in case the Spanish launch their armada to save the Scottish Queen. It stinks of war."

The gossip grated my raw heart, so I escaped upstairs. More people packed into the long gallery overlooking the great hall.

The word *Walsingham* caught my ear, and I slowed my steps. Who would mention the terrible name of the queen's chief spy in my father's house? I could not tell who had spoken, but a pair of unfamiliar men glanced at me and turned away to whisper.

I kept my head down and pushed past women in wide skirts and men with starched ruff collars to seek the refuge of my room.

The door was unlocked. Had I forgotten to secure it in my grief? I pushed it open and paused on the threshold. Something was amiss. The needlepoint carpet covering one of my trunks lay on the floor. I hung it back over the wooden box and dropped to my knees to pull out the small leather chest hidden beneath my bed. The latch was broken.

My hands shook as I sorted through the papers and jewels stored there. Nothing was missing, but who dared invade my room? What might they be looking for?

I bolted my door and made the sign of the cross, then returned to the chest. Setting the papers and jewels aside, I checked the false bottom. It was sealed. I sagged in relief, resting my forehead against the feather-stuffed mattress. Several strands of curly brown hair escaped my coif, and I brushed them back. With a few quick movements, I opened the box's hidden compartment. Everything was there: my book of hours, my bell, my wax Agnus Dei—all the forbidden items my mother had given me, the very possession of which could cost me what little freedom I had, and perhaps even my life.

My mother's rosary lay nestled among the other treasures. I reverently lifted the smooth amber prayer beads, remembering how her gentle hands had touched each one as she taught me—a willful, impatient little girl—to seek the God she knew and loved. Then the persecutions against Catholics had increased, and my mother's face grew more tired and more sad. With each new rumor, fine, or snub from a former friend, she had turned to the rosary with increased frequency. It had been in her hand when she died. I rolled the beads between my fingers, searching for some of her spirit—her peace—that might have lingered, trying to bring her close again.

Aching with anger and loneliness, I secured my jumbled treasures back under the false bottom and replaced the jewelry on top. I hesitated over the old letters, tracing the brittle edges of the folded paper. One of them was open. I huddled against my bed to read.

Dear Mistress Joan,

Father tells me we are to marry someday, but not until we are older. Did you know? 'Tis dull here now that you're gone, so maybe we can get married soon if you want. I found some more places in the woods that we could explore. My brother John says archery is only for boys, but I will teach you again if you want, as well as how to swim. 'Tis great sport and not as cold as you fear. I hope you come back soon. When I am older, this estate will be John's. We will have to live somewhere else. Where do you think we should go?

Your ~~obedient servant~~ friend,
Nicholas Bowen

Memories drifted back with the fragrance of the paper and ink. I had wanted to live in Spain or Italy. Nicholas liked the idea of Paris but consented to Italy if I wished it. He led our little adventures exploring his family's estate at Nant Bach with such confidence that everything seemed possible around him. If only he were here now.

I set the letter aside. It had been almost ten years since I had seen Nicholas, and five since I had heard anything of him. He probably did not even think of me anymore. Our fathers had quarreled over something and stopped speaking when I was twelve. Nicholas and I continued sending letters for a while, though our engagement was never made legally binding. I opened one of his last notes.

Mistress Pryce,

Thank you for inquiring after my health. I am fine, though very busy with my schooling. I'm glad to be going to England to continue my studies. Do you wonder why? In Wales, we are forced to speak English in our schools, but in England every scholar may only speak Latin. At least we are all on equal footing. I hope you continue to be well. Please be more careful what you say in future letters.

Nicholas Bowen

I could not recall what I wrote in my childish notes to worry him. His letters stopped soon after, though. When a year went by with no word from him, I shoved the letters aside and vowed not to think of him again.

I gently shuffled the letters into a stack. It was foolish to keep them, foolish to imagine how Nicholas's boyish charm might suit him now as a man. Still, as my father kept me sheltered from other suitors—all too Protestant for his tastes—it was hard to give up my daydreams of the smiling, headstrong boy I had once been intended for.

Voices from the long gallery called my mind back to my duties. The weight of my sorrow settled heavily on me again. I nestled the letters in with my other treasures and stowed them away. Locking my door behind me, I tiptoed down the side stairs that led to the servants' chambers and the kitchen. I had no stomach for company, so I slipped into the buttery to check on our stores.

Barrels of food and drink lined the wall, little depleted by our guests' appetites. Herbs hung from the beams overhead, and a quarter of mutton kept company with them, brought from the smokehouse for the funeral feast. I checked on my cider. The thick, sweet fragrance of apple mingled with the room's scent of herbs and vinegars. The violets I picked to preserve in sugar had sat on the oak table too long and wilted. I had intended to come back to them after nursing Father through the illness brought on by his torture at the hands of the queen's men. A new wave of misery and loneliness engulfed me.

"Joan?" Aunt Catherine's voice sounded in the hall.

I wiped the lingering tears from my face and turned to greet her. She surveyed the room, her eyes narrow, as though disappointed to find everything in order. Cousin William appeared behind her, taking in the buttery with a proprietary glance, though he was only eighteen, the same age as myself. Of course, the blackguard had been waiting for this day since my brother Richard died.

"I'll need the keys, Joan," Aunt Catherine said, speaking English.

I wrinkled my nose. The harsh sounds had little place in my father's home. "Which keys?"

"All of them, of course."

I clutched the keys hanging from my belt. "I have managed the house since my mother died. I'll happily show you—"

"'Tis my house now." Aunt Catherine held out her hand.

William watched me with the detached interest of a man at a bear-baiting trying to decide if he should bet on the wretched, teth-ered beast or the snarling dogs. I felt the weight of my chains. Aunt Catherine was the mistress here now, the mother of my father's clos-est male relative and heir.

The familiar brass of the keys bit into my palm with a sharp new pain. Give a woman a crown and scepter and she could dictate the fates of men, body and soul. A widow, even, might manage her husband's home and business, working in his stead. A single woman, though, could not be trusted with the keys to the home she had been running for years.

I held up the ring of keys and pulled off two. The rest I dropped into Aunt Catherine's outstretched hand, and she wrapped her bony fingers around them. "I'll need all the keys, Joan."

"Nay, you'll not. These keys are mine. Your son may have inher-ited my father's house, but he did not inherit me. You are not my guardians."

William smiled—a silent applause at my performance—but Aunt Catherine's wrinkled face reddened until she looked like an overcooked apple.

"You ungrateful child!" She drew a deep breath, and her face faded back to its usual yellowish hue. "You're correct. We are not your guardians, and we should not be responsible for the feeding and upkeep of someone not part of our household. We'll write to your godparents at once and tell them to expect you."

"Mother!" William interceded. "That's most inhospitable. You're throwing our cousin from her own home."

"'Tis not her home. It never was."

I glared at the prune-faced fishwife. "I'll make certain my belongings are packed. Inform my godparents that I am ready to come to them at their soonest convenience."

I pushed past her, ignoring William's whispered apology, and fled to the hallway. The guests had finally left. Maids carried off the remnants of the mourning feast, but instead of bringing them to the back door, they were moving them to the family parlor. I stopped one of the girls.

"What's going on here, Anna?"

"Mistress's orders," she mumbled with a quick glance up. The servants were watching carefully to see what their new master and mistress would be like. Some of them would already be wishing their allotted times were up.

The parade of food continued past me. "This is not done!"

William slipped into the hallway, fidgeting with his wide ruff collar. It was too large and made him look like a greedy mouse sticking its head out of a wheel of cheese. "What is it, cousin?"

"That food is meant for the servants and the poor."

"Wasteful," Aunt Catherine said, joining her son.

"The crops are doing poorly this year; 'twill be another bad harvest." How could I make them understand the suffering of people who were always on the edge of starvation? Since the queen had stripped the church of its charitable functions, they had nowhere else to turn but to the *bonheddwyr*—the ancient families of noble Welsh blood—like chicks running to their mother's wings in a storm.

Aunt Catherine raised her shrill voice. "All the more reason—"

"We are no longer in Shrewsbury, Mother," William said without looking at me directly. "Different things are expected of us, in our new position."

She pursed her lips, and I watched her with my breath held. William's words settled over her, and her expression softened. She looked at the house with new appreciation. "Of course. We have new responsibilities now. Very well, let it be taken away."

Anna shot me a grateful look, her smile barely repressed as she returned the extra food to the buttery. The servants would feast well one more time, in memory of my father, and the poor would remember him with fondness. Maybe some would even pray for his soul, make some compensation for his heretical end.

Aunt Catherine stared at the tables emptying under the servants' quick work. She cast several sidelong glances in my direction. I tried not to smile. She had no idea what food was available. I was not going to offer the information.

She stopped Anna. "We will dine simply tonight. Prepare cold meat and bread."

Anna nodded and hurried off to the kitchen, but she dashed back a moment later. "Mistress! You're needed outside!"

I ran, and Aunt Catherine followed on my heels. A ragged woman sat in the kitchen yard, clutching a young boy. He howled in pain, blood dripping from his arm.

"He fell," the woman cried, rocking back and forth with the child clutched in her arms. "He fell."

I swayed at the sight of so much blood from such a small child, but the woman was one of Father's tenants come to his funeral feast. It was our duty to help. "Anna," I croaked out.

"Anna." Aunt Catherine's commanding voice overpowered mine. "Bring me fresh water and linen. Also, I'll need some marigold and St. John's wort. Do you have those?"

Anna looked between us for a moment, but I could not find my voice. She curtseyed to Aunt Catherine and rushed off, while my aunt knelt by the stunned woman and gently took the boy from her arms. The mother cried out, and I found my senses. I rushed to her side and put my arm around her. "All will be well."

Aunt Catherine might know little about a country estate, but she was a mother who had raised children to adulthood and tended others lost in infancy. She washed and dressed the boy's wound and offered the woman and child a place to sleep in the stables until he was strong enough to walk home. The woman rose from my arms, thanking Aunt Catherine. The tenants who gathered in the yard for their share of the funeral feast nodded and whispered their approval.

She had replaced me. My home, my buttery, my cider. None of it was mine. Everything I had worked for was gone the moment my father died.

I stumbled blindly up to my room. Bolting the door behind me, I clutched the keys I would never give Aunt Catherine or anyone else. I reached under the wooden bed frame and fumbled for my rosary.

I lay on my bed, fighting tears and counting out prayers on the smooth beads. My rosary, my thoughts, my prayers. The law would even take these things from me. It would own me—body, mind, and soul—but some things it could not wrest from me without also taking my life. I was only a woman, but so was the queen. If she could rule a kingdom, I could be mistress of my own fate, even if I had to fight her for it.

Blessed Mary, holy Winifred, send me aid!

Chapter Two

A letter from my godparents, Master and Mistress Lloyd, sat open on my bed, announcing their promise to bring me to their home within the fortnight. Another restless night stretched before me. I paced, brushing my fingers over the tapestries stitched with knights and ladies, the pewter candlesticks, the washbasin painted in bright blue and green. Three wooden trunks stood open, waiting to receive the few things I could take to my new home: my clothes, my jewelry, the linens I had embroidered as part of my dowry.

A new home, a new life. My stomach fluttered. It might not be so terrible. I flung open my shutters and leaned into the cool night air. The stars painted a fiery bridge across the smooth, black night, pointing toward Conwy.

Were I a man, I would gear myself for adventure, perhaps set sail for unknown shores filled with gold and spices and strange animals. Of course, were I a man, this home would be mine. The new mourning ring for my father rested heavily on my finger. I twisted it, then touched the smooth bands I wore for my mother and brother. I already had more gold than I wanted. What I lacked was a safe harbor.

Something moved in the orchards. I squinted. The movement came again, a faint trace of light against the dark blanketing the estate. The light bobbed closer, then danced away, its glimmer trailing in the darkness. A corpse candle! Saint David, patron saint of

Wales, sent the spectral lights to warn of impending death so the doomed could prepare themselves properly. I searched for salt to throw at the fay light. It had come too late for Father.

The light wove nearer and grew more steady. It was no corpse candle, but a figure with a lantern. A thief was unlikely to announce himself thus. I peered into the dark. The figure drew close enough for me to recognize. Father William Davies approached under the veil of night, as much too late as a corpse candle to help my father, though more welcome.

He would not be welcome by my Protestant aunt and cousin, though. I pulled on my boots and threw a cloak over my dressing gown.

Holy Mary, do not let Father Davis go to the kitchen door!

I tiptoed down the side stairs, avoiding the great hall where the male servants slept on the benches. My heart thudded as I unbolted the kitchen door and slipped into the pleasant cool of the night with its heavy scent of hay and dew.

"Father Davies." I curtseyed to the priest as he came forward to greet me. He was no older than thirty, but his eyes gleamed with a fierce, unwavering determination. It gave me a fresh sense of strength, as if the warmth of his courage seeped into the air around him. "You come at a sad time."

"Mistress Pryce." He bowed and stepped back, his face gentle in the shadows of the lantern. "I heard about your father. I am sorry. I came as soon as I could."

"If only you had been here." I swallowed a sob. "He could have been laid to rest properly."

"Travel is difficult," he said, sympathy in his voice. "There are patrols everywhere, and with Sir Henry dead, everyone is on edge."

"Sir Henry?"

"Sir Henry Sidney, the Lord President of Wales. The queen has appointed the Earl of Pembroke to take his place, and I am afraid we will find him less tolerant of our beliefs."

Less tolerant? When we had to practice our faith in dark corners and secret places and be tortured or hanged for it if caught? They would crush us out of existence if we did not push back. With all the neighbors and merchants coming to greet Aunt Catherine and William, I had heard no mention of this news. Perhaps no one cared any more. Maybe the heart of the Welsh was already dying.

"I should have made more effort to be here," Father Davies said.

"In the end, 'twould have made no difference." I could not keep the bitterness from my voice. "He renounced the faith so they would end the torture and release him, yet his illness only worsened. Still, he refused last rites and forbade me from seeking a priest. He condemned himself, betrayed the faith."

He betrayed me and everything he taught me.

Father Davies lifted his face to study the stars in silence. Finally, he spoke in a low voice. "Trust in God's mercy, Mistress Pryce. Your father was a good man. We will pray for him."

A shutter creaked behind us. I glanced over my shoulder at the dark windows. "'Tis not safe for you here anymore. My cousin's family is Protestant, and there's an injured boy and his mother staying in the stables. Also, someone searched my room. It may have been my aunt, but I cannot be certain."

"You have holy objects there?"

"Well hidden."

"Keep them that way. The Queen has agents everywhere, and Walsingham's pursuivants—the priest hunters—are abroad. They can search anywhere, anytime they wish, and they use torture to gain information. Expect no mercy if you encounter them."

The breeze blew past, raising goose bumps on my shoulders. "Certainly 'tis not likely they'll search here, though."

"It is, Mistress Pryce. I have felt for the last few weeks that someone was hounding my steps, a shadow just around the corner. The danger has never been more real."

I grabbed his arm. "Then you should flee. Should my aunt catch you . . ." She might send a man to his death just out of spite. "The risk is too great."

"No matter." He gave me a rueful smile. "God is guiding me. I do not think my time has come yet."

"You sound as if you expect to be caught."

He shrugged. "I do not seek martyrdom, but it may be what

God plans for me someday. I only hope I am brave enough to face it well. Come, I will not move on without seeing to your father."

I nodded. Surely, God would protect a priest, and this was my chance to keep my promise to Father. We walked through the chilly quiet of night to the churchyard. There lay my parents, neighbors in death with those who had been their neighbors in life. Father Davies said prayers over Father's grave, and we sang. At the end, I touched the wooden grave marker.

"Farewell, Father."

Maybe he could be at peace now.

Something snapped in the trees behind the church. I tensed. If Father Davies and I were caught here, we would both be arrested. The darkness and late hour—ever friends to traitors and criminals— were our only cover.

"I will see you home, Mistress Pryce," Father Davies whispered, his gaze darting across the midnight gloom of the graveyard. "Of course, being in my company may be more dangerous than walking alone."

"Nay." I reached toward him, someone from whom I did not have to mask my thoughts and feelings. "I would like your company. 'Tis very lonely now, and . . ."

"What troubles you, child?" he asked as we passed under the canopy of trees. Their dark branches reached to shelter us.

"I am to live with my godparents, no doubt until a suitable match is made for me." Plas Lloyd would just be another temporary home for me, after all. I had my dowry: some money and land left to me by my mother. They were enough to attract a suitor, but whether the suitor would attract me was another matter. Conwy teemed with Protestants and Englishmen. I dropped my voice. "I suppose I am frightened."

"Perhaps all that is happening to you is for a reason."

"Perhaps." I wanted to be convinced by his certainty, but it was hard to see why God would take my father and my home.

"Where do your godparents live?"

"Near Conwy."

Father Davies chuckled. "Mistress Pryce, that is excellent news!"

"Is it?"

"Aye. Conwy is dear to my heart. It is near my own birthplace and the home of my good friend Robert Pugh of Penrhyn. You must seek acquaintance with him and his wife, Jane. They are staunch defenders of the faith and will make you feel welcome. I am on my way there myself."

"I am glad I'll see a friendly face at times."

"Are your godparents not friendly?"

"I suppose they are. My brother fostered with them, and I visited, but it has been many years. They are the Lloyds of Plas Lloyd."

He nodded. "They are good people. Catholic, though lukewarm in their convictions. Still, you should be secure there, and Conwy is a lovely place, so close to the sea."

A surge of excitement raced up my spine at the thought of standing on the shore, staring across the waters that could take me to all the places I had dreamed of. That reminded me. "What do you know of Nicholas Bowen of Nant Bach? 'Tis near Plas Lloyd." Nicholas was a younger son, so he was probably off making his way in the world. Still, there was a chance I would see him if he visited his family at Nant Bach. The memory of his smiling face lit the lonely corners of my heart.

"Why do you ask?"

The sudden tension in his gait sent a shock of fear through me. I almost wanted to dismiss the conversation, but now that I had ventured on the topic, there was no turning back. "Our fathers wished for us to be married."

"You are betrothed to him?"

"'Twas never made binding," I said slowly.

He relaxed. "That is well. I do not know Master Bowen personally—not many people do—except that he plays his own game. I will let you make your own judgments about him, but I cannot guarantee that he is to be trusted."

My chest tightened. There were so few people I could trust. It stung that my childhood friend might not be among them, but at least I had some warning. Despite my trepidation about Nicholas, talking to Father Davies increased my excitement to begin my journey.

"There is something else I would ask you to think on," Father Davies said.

"What is that?"

"You have a fortune, independent of your father's estate?"

"I do, my dowry."

"You might consider turning your life over to the Church. Selling whatever you are able to and settling overseas."

"You mean, taking orders?" In my imagination, the walls of a nunnery closed around me, blocking out the sunshine, the breeze, the green scent of fields and orchards. "I'm not sure I'm well suited to a confined life."

He chuckled. "I am in orders, and I hardly consider my life confined. True, you are a woman, so you would not do anything so dangerous, but you could help the poor and sick, teach, pray for those who need help. You need not take orders if you did not feel it your calling. Some godly women seek the refuge of an abbey without committing to orders, and there is still much good you could do. There are many places you might go: France, Italy—"

"Italy?" My interest picked up.

"I will not pressure you to make a decision, but I want you to consider the possibility, if other options become too onerous." He paused. "I see a spark of passion in you, Mistress Pryce, the beginning of what might become a great flame. Tended carefully it can be a force for good, but if not controlled, it may be dangerous."

I pressed my lips together. I had not known my anger and desire to burn free of my constraints were so obvious, but I would not be put in a tighter cage. "'Tis not legal to leave the country without a license, and I doubt I could obtain one."

He smiled enigmatically. "We have our own ways of dealing with that problem. The less you know, the better, for now. If the time comes, we will discuss it."

Father Davies left me at the kitchen door. He disappeared into the darkness, and I was alone again.

Chapter Three

"Look ahead, Mistress Pryce, and you'll see Conwy Castle for a moment before we turn for Plas Lloyd."

I took off my leather traveling mask and peered out of the rumbling carriage. One of the Lloyds' servants, riding outside as a guard against bandits, pointed. Dark gray towers jutted above the soft green landscape. For the past three centuries, the English had pimpled our country with their castles and walled towns to keep their settlers safe from us savage Welsh. When we won our freedom, though, we would see the stone walls come down.

Laborers with their families shuffled out of the way as our procession rattled over the dirt road. The peasants' ragged clothes hung loosely, and even the children trudged along with their sunken eyes fixed on the ground, early victims of the bad harvest. Most headed toward Conwy town, huddled in the protective shadow of the castle, and whatever hope it might offer of employment.

Ahead, half a dozen mounted men blocked the road, the hilts of the rapiers at their belts glinting in the sun. The men's fine doublets and well-fed horses did not look like those of outlaws, but the retainers of powerful lords could be just as bad. My escort inhaled sharply and reached for his own sword, motioning me back. I fell against the hard seat and clutched the rosary hidden in the folds of my skirt. The chest with my mother's treasures sat at my feet. I slid it farther back into the shadows.

"Halt in Her Majesty's name," commanded a deep voice with an English accent.

My breath caught. The queen's agents! I'd rather deal with the more honest sorts of thieves. The carriage bounced to a stop, leaving me with the feeling that the earth was moving beneath me and I could not quite keep up.

"What's your business here?" the Englishman called.

"We travel to Plas Lloyd," my escort said. "Is something amiss?"

"Aye, there are fugitives from the queen's justice abroad."

"We have none of that sort in our party. We belong to the household of Master Herbert Lloyd, a *bonheddwr* of good name in this shire."

"Just to be sure."

Spurred boots thumped onto the dirt road and jangled as they approached. I forced myself to breathe and relaxed my hands. A tall man with a scraggly beard yanked open the door. I squinted at the bright light.

"Nothing inside but a woman," Scraggle-Beard said.

"Are you certain?" asked a sharp voice in English.

Scraggle-Beard's gaze fixed on the cut of my bodice, and he laughed. "I'd be glad to verify it."

I smacked him in the nose. He howled and reeled back, clutching his face. His companions roared with laughter.

"I warned you these Welsh wenches have spirit," the sharp voice called.

"Treacherous, flit-witted harpy." Scraggle-Beard reached for me.

"She's a ward of Herbert Lloyd," my escort said through clenched teeth. "He'll not take kindly to any interference with her."

The English pig curled his hand into a fist.

"Aye, ride on!" the sharp voice said, still chuckling.

Our party creaked back into motion. I swallowed and leaned back against the seat, my hands trembling. *A pox and plague on all Englishmen!*

We put Conwy to our backs and crossed a low marsh swarming with flies and the stink of rotting plants. I clutched a silver pomander filled with orange peels and cloves to my nose until we climbed again to solid ground.

"These are tenants of Plas Lloyd, mistress," my escort announced with quiet pride.

Cultivated fields shimmering with waves of green opened from the surrounding woods, and neat little cottages faced the road at uneven intervals. The tight knot in my stomach eased a little.

We reached the Lloyds' house, a grand Welsh *plasty* three stories high. The front windows glinted with glass panes, and several chimneys rose from the walls of the stone building.

I stumbled out of the carriage, stretching stiff muscles and rubbing bruises. I felt as though the horses had dragged me along the entire rutted road. Chickens scattered out of our way, clucking and flapping, and a chorus of dogs barked a greeting.

The noise summoned the household. Stable boys hurried for the horses, and the front door swung open to reveal a huge man, so tall his head brushed the lintel of the door and with a girth straining his red doublet. His bushy gray beard framed a wide grin.

He was the Master Lloyd I recalled, though his bulk had increased greatly in the intervening years. Mistress Lloyd was plumper too, and still smiling by his side. My childhood was well beyond retrieving, but for a moment I felt safe again, as if I could rush into the sturdy walls of their home and find shelter from all my worries.

Master Lloyd strode forward to wrap me in a smothering embrace and kiss me in greeting. Mistress Lloyd smiled shyly before giving me a quick hug.

"No trouble on the road?" Master Lloyd asked, his gaze darting between his servant and me.

"Nothing extraordinary, sir," my escort replied tightly.

I frowned. Was it not extraordinary for women to be harassed on the road, treated like criminals in their own country?

"Ah, 'tis well. Do come inside, Mistress Joan." Master Lloyd guided me past the threshold into the great hall. The long room bustled with dogs, servants, and even a harper. The women of the house sat near the fireplace, with a great basket of wool in many colors. The whir of their spinning wheels hummed under the conversations of the gentlemen sitting on the benches lining the room, and the harp's chords rang to the gallery above. Scents of roasting meat and fresh-baked bread made my stomach grumble.

"I am sorry about your father," Master Lloyd said in a low tone. "Your mother too."

"Thank you," I whispered, my throat tight.

"I hope you'll feel at home here. You'll have your own chamber, a bit small, but comfortable." Master Lloyd's rumbling voice harmonized with the noise in the hall. "I installed a great many improvements these last few years. I, ah, made some Spanish investments, and they paid off handsomely."

He winked and chuckled, and I forced a smile at the joke I did not understand. He might be Catholic, but certainly he would not aid the Spanish in invading his own shores, no matter how well it paid.

"Now, to introduce you." He guided me around, rattling off a string of names. I smiled and curtseyed until my cheeks ached and my knees twinged in protest. Finally, we arrived at a group of gentlemen in the far corner, and I recognized Nicholas's profile among them.

His sandy hair was slightly disheveled, and his face clean shaven among the many trimmed beards in the company, allowing me a glimpse of my childhood friend in his strong features. I quickly smoothed back a rogue curl and put on my most charming grin. Yet he did not look at me, only stared down with his jaw tight.

My heart sank. I searched his profile for some sign of friendliness or humor, but this cold stranger was nothing like my Nicholas.

"Ah," Master Lloyd said. "Naturally, I invited Nicholas Bowen to join us. Master Nicholas, of course you have not forgotten Mistress Joan."

Nicholas turned his face to me. His left ear was missing, and a puckered red scar blighted his cheek, slanting his eye down and twisting the corner of his lips into a grotesque sneer. I dug my fingers into Master Lloyd's arm and glanced away. *What could have caused such an injury?*

I forced myself to look at Nicholas again, but my eyes locked on the maimed side of his face. I loosened my iron grip on Master Lloyd, curtseying with a tight smile. Nicholas gave me a look full of defiance and bowed, his gaze never leaving mine.

Was he angry at my shock? How was I to be anything but surprised to see him so disfigured? He had been cold to me even before I had seen him clearly, though. Perhaps it was not just my reaction that had offended him. Had I done something else wrong since entering the room, or was he bearing a grudge over something in the past?

Master Lloyd guided me to a stool near the other women, and I sat, my mind buzzing. Did Nicholas still consider us honor bound by our fathers' marriage negotiations? My stomach tightened at the thought of his hostile stare. What a husband he would be! Yet once he had been a dear friend.

A servant whispered in Master Lloyd's ear, and he nodded and cleared his throat. "Supper is ready, my friends, a feast to celebrate our new guest."

I stood amidst welcoming smiles from all in the room but one. Servants lit the candles on the table and prepared for our repast.

A rap echoed from the front door. Everyone paused, and a tension I had not been aware of rose to the surface. A servant answered the knock, and a dark-haired young man strode into the room.

"Hugh Richards!" Master Lloyd boomed, rushing forward to embrace the new arrival. The talking and laughing resumed so quickly I almost wondered if I imagined the pall that had fallen over the company.

"Master Lloyd." The young man flashed a laughing grin. "How good of you to lay a feast for me, especially since I was not expected."

Master Lloyd chuckled. "We shall celebrate you another time, Master Hugh. My goddaughter has come to stay with us, so you have her to thank for this hearty welcome."

Hugh's glance found me, and he raised his eyebrows with an appreciative grin. My cheeks warmed, and I smiled back. Hugh's bright eyes were the same color as my amber rosary, his dark beard neatly clipped to a point on his chin, and his fashionable hose showed off muscular legs.

"By all means, let me pay her my thanks," he said.

Master Lloyd gestured to him. "Joan Pryce, may I present Hugh Richards, a neighbor dear to us, if too often distant."

"Your servant," Hugh said, rising from his bow to greet me with a warm kiss.

"Careful, Master Hugh." Master Lloyd shook his finger. "She's promised to Nicholas Bowen."

"To Master Nicholas?" Hugh started back and scanned the crowd. His face lit when his gaze found Nicholas. "Bowen! This is doubly astonishing, to find you being so sociable and already making such a pretty conquest. You were always quicker in the hunt than I."

Nicholas shook his head. "No fear, Master Hugh. Master Lloyd has misspoken. Mistress Pryce is naught to me."

The room quieted as all attention pivoted to me. I gritted my teeth. *Vile knave. Cold stockfish.* He would be less than naught to me, then. Nothing I might have done warranted being discarded with such public disgrace, shamed in front of my new neighbors.

"Master Nicholas!" Master Lloyd said, "We all know 'twas your fathers' wishes, and arranged years ago."

"Too many years ago," Nicholas said. "We were children, below the legal age. 'Twas a passing fancy of two old men, a desire to join adjacent lands and nothing more."

So my lands were adjacent to his? Perhaps it would be better to sell them after all.

"Where is your honor?" Master Lloyd's voice rang in the rafters. The dogs whimpered and beat their tails on the rush mats. He rested his hand on his rapier. "I'm tempted to challenge you over this shameful behavior. Once one's word is given—"

Nicholas stepped back and folded his arms. "I have no desire to fight you, and I mean no harm to Mistress Pryce. I remain her obedient servant in this matter." His words were polite enough, but cold, and he fastened me again with his challenging gaze. What did he expect me to do? Demand that he marry me, when he made his dislike so clear?

I wished I could pick up a sword and challenge him myself, but perhaps he was too much a dove-livered coward to fight, even to defend his honor.

"We'll speak no more on this tonight," Master Lloyd said, his voice low. "For now, 'tis time to eat."

Everyone turned to the table with palpable relief. I groaned and covered my face. A gentle pressure on my arm made me jump, and I looked up into Hugh's sympathetic eyes. I would have wished him far away from such an embarrassing scene, but his smile was friendly.

"Mistress Pryce, may I escort you to your seat?"

"'Tis kind of you, Master Richards, but you do not have to—"

"I know. I wish to. Master Nicholas is a strange, knot-pated fool, and his loss is my gain, at least for the moment."

I drew a shaky breath and took Hugh's arm. I hesitated at the table, but Master Lloyd directed me to a place on the bench next to his daughter, Alice. I suspected the seating arrangement had been shuffled at the last minute, because Nicholas sat significantly further down the table, while Hugh was diagonally across from me. Nicholas did not glance in my direction. All I could see of his face was his monstrous profile.

Master Lloyd sat in the enormous, carved chair at the head of the table, a saltcellar shaped like a ship on display before him. The servants presented basins for washing our hands. Master Lloyd asked the Lord's blessing over the meal in terms so neutral they could not have offended anyone, yet I wondered if even God was a little bored by the hollow-sounding words.

Alice was a pale girl a little older than myself, but I could not coax more than a few words from her. Still, my cheeks cooled in her quiet presence. Occasionally, though, I caught Hugh watching me with a quirky smile, and the rush of warmth blossomed again on my face.

It being Friday—a fast day, as both queen and Catholic still agreed—we ate fish in place of meat, but it was fresh instead of salted. I marveled at the flavor. I had not yet visited the sea, but already it had given me a gift. That reminded me of Father Davies's encouraging speech. None of the names Master Lloyd had rattled off were *Pugh*, but the priest led me to believe my godfather might be part of the Pughs' circle of Catholic gentry.

"Master Lloyd," I said quietly, "are you acquainted with the Pughs of Plas Penrhyn?"

The conversation at our end of the table stuttered, then resumed a little more loudly.

"Aye." Master Lloyd lifted his tankard. "I know Master Pugh well."

I hesitated, choosing my words carefully. "I have heard good things of them. I hoped I might make their acquaintance."

Hugh watched me with a quizzical expression.

Master Lloyd stabbed a slice of fish from his plate with unnecessary ferocity. "Ah, I do not know when that will be possible, Mistress Joan. They are not at home currently." He did not meet my eyes.

Hugh leaned forward and cleared his throat as if to speak but shook his head and turned back to his meal.

How odd. Maybe Father Davies had been mistaken, but he had been headed to the Pughs' estate himself. There was no safe way to inquire about him. Even knowing of his existence without turning him in could get me arrested.

The servants carried the food away at the end of the meal, and we broke into smaller groups for cards and conversation. The harper struck up a lively tune in the background. I stood uncertainly in the company of strangers, but Hugh beckoned me. My heartbeat picked up as I joined him on the edge of the crowd. There was something in the way he carried himself, as tight as a harp string, so I could not help but wonder what note he would play when he was struck into action.

"Mistress Pryce," he said in a low tone, "what do you know of the Pughs?"

"I . . ." How did I answer such a question? "I have heard good spoken of them."

"By a mutual acquaintance?"

I swallowed, searching every angle of the question for hidden traps. Hugh was friendly, but he could have been one of the queen agents, sent to spy on the Lloyds' Catholic acquaintances. "My father had many friends in this part of the country."

Hugh smiled. "Wisely spoken, Mistress Pryce. I believe I can assure you that his friends are safe." He gave me a significant look. "All of them."

"I see." At least I thought I understood, but still I dared not speak openly. "Will they be returning soon?"

Hugh shuffled his thumb over the edge of a deck of cards. "That seems unlikely. They have fled their home, thanks to our new Lord President of Wales."

The blood drained from my face. "What? When?"

"The 'when' is within the last week. The rest I think you can guess."

So Father Davies had no idea what he was walking into when he returned to his friend's home. Of course, that was how he lived, and it sounded as if God had once again delivered him from the queen's hounds. The whole Pugh family driven from their home, though? Women and children turned out, the servants uprooted, the tenants without a lord to resolve their disputes and tend to their difficulties. They might not complain about the rent they did not have to pay. Nay, that would not be the way of it. Elizabeth would put someone she trusted over the lands. An Englishman.

"That's terrible," I whispered.

Hugh's face hardened, and his hands twitched. "Aye, the Queen and her agents are tyrants. Welsh Tudor blood or no, they have no place in our country. 'Twill not be long before they know that."

I leaned forward. The determination in Hugh's eyes convinced me he spoke no idle threat.

"Master Richards!" Nicholas's voice cut into our conversation. I jumped. When had he come so close behind me? "That is treasonous talk."

" 'Tis Welsh talk," Hugh snapped. "On the tongues of every son of Wales and each true bard."

"Then Wales's sons may soon find themselves without tongues," Nicholas said coldly, "and our harpers humming instead of declaiming."

I sucked in my breath. Father Davies had been right about Nicholas. Perhaps my erstwhile friend had been too long in England acquiring his fine education. He might even have been won over to spy for the queen's man, Walsingham. How much had he heard? Had I been cautious enough? Probably not.

Hugh's brow drew together; then he slapped the table and laughed. "Nicholas, you really are a devil. I had forgotten how I enjoyed our debates." Either Hugh was an excellent actor, or he truly had no fear of Nicholas. Hugh held up the cards. "More of that for another time, though. Will you join us for a game?"

Nicholas looked like he was going to agree, and then his gaze fell on me. I glanced down and flicked a piece of wool lint from my skirts.

"Perhaps later. If you'll excuse me." He sketched a quick bow and walked over to sit by Alice. She bent her head in conversation with him. Nicholas and Alice. Was that the way of it? No wonder they were cold to me. Very well, they were welcome to each other's icy company. I glanced at Hugh as he shuffled the cards. There might be other routes to my own happiness.

Chapter Four

When the Sabbath came, I donned my dressing gown, retrieved my mother's book of hours, and settled on an embroidered cushion by the fireplace in my room. Warmth seeped from the hearth. I perched the open book on my knees and turned to the pages where I'd copied my favorite scriptures and prayers. At last I had a spare moment to escape from the buzz of spinning wheels, the pressure of the sewing needle against my fingers, the constant need to watch my tongue around strangers who might wish me harm. Perfect peace.

Someone rapped at the door.

I sighed and snapped the book shut. "Aye?"

Mistress Lloyd peeked inside. "I'm sorry, Joan, 'tis time to get dressed for church."

"Church?" I pressed my fingers against the soft leather of the book. "I thought . . ."

"I know. We try to follow our conscience, but if we do not appear at the parish occasionally, we draw too much attention to ourselves." Her eyes were soft with apology. "Maud will help you dress."

I stood stiff with defiance as the maid laced me into my best bodice. So this was what Father Davies meant by lukewarm. The Lloyds paid lip service to both religions, perhaps not really believing in either. Anger and frustration slowed my fingers as I tugged at the cords tying my sleeves to my bodice. Again, I could not find the courage to speak out, despite the priests' warnings to avoid the queen's heretical services. I finished dressing by putting on my mother's necklace, a single strand of pearls. It kept her close to me, and when I ran my fingers over the smooth beads, it reminded me of her rosary hidden safely in my trunk.

The church was near enough that we avoided the bone-rattling ordeal of the carriage, hiking in silence to the old stone building settled among the rolling hills and hedge-lined fields. Parishioners gathered outside the church doors, many of whom I'd met over the last few days. Were they also here to keep up appearances, or were they sincere Protestants, ready to pounce on me for my faith? I had no way of guessing whom I could trust. Though I stood amidst a crowd, I felt far from them, small and alone, like a lost child in a marketplace. I edged back, but they surrounded me, smiling, introducing new neighbors.

I slowly relaxed in their warmth. Certainly at least some of these people were not my enemies. Maybe I could scent out the ones with Catholic sympathies. Alice Lloyd led me to join the gathering of unmarried girls that made up the parish maidens' guild. A couple of the older girls drew us aside.

"We've missed you at services of late," said Mistress Rhys, a tall girl with glossy black curls.

Alice gave her a worried glance.

"Oh, no need to fret over it." Mistress Rhys took Alice's arm, and the little jewel in the handle of her peacock feather fan glinted in the sunlight. "We all know your father is old-fashioned. My father grumbles about going too, but he hates paying the fines for staying home."

Mistress Meredith wrinkled her pointy nose. "Everything is not about money," she said, her Welsh tinted with a slight accent I could not place. "You ought to encourage your fathers to attend for the benefit of their souls."

Mistress Rhys rolled her eyes behind Mistress Meredith's back. I stifled a giggle. Mistress Meredith turned her narrow brown eyes on me.

"*Bien sûr* you are happy to attend services, Mistress Pryce."

I hid my surprise at her flawless French. If she was a Frenchwoman, she was likely to be Catholic, yet there was nothing in her critical expression to make me think I had found an ally.

I forced a smile. "I obey Master Lloyd's wishes."

"But you are not one of those Papists."

I jumped as if she'd pricked me with a needle, flushing cold then hot. It was not just the derogatory name for my Catholic beliefs, but the way she spat it, as though she had something filthy in her mouth. The most precious and sacred longings of my heart—the legacy of faith and love left to me by my mother—reduced to garbage by her tongue.

Alice gave me a quick, anxious headshake. What was I supposed to do? I would not deny my faith, but I had no desire to be arrested in the churchyard. I could equivocate. That was what the priests did: disguise the truth in a tangle of words.

"No," I said carefully, "I do not answer to that name." Because I refused to acknowledge a term so insulting. I hated the deception though.

Mistress Meredith gave a satisfied little nod and turned back to talking with Alice. My ears buzzed. I mumbled an excuse and sought refuge in the old stone chapel.

I paused at the doorway to let my eyes adjust to the dimness. Statues of saints stood at intervals along the walls, all of them smashed, their hands and faces missing. I had heard of the sacking of the churches, the great bonfires of rood screens and wooden images, but I had never been able to imagine it. How often had I prayed to Mary and the saints for comfort, especially when my mother was ill? When she died, I lit candles, asking my heavenly friends to watch over her. These statues were not the saints themselves, I knew, but still the closest I had to seeing them. Tears stung my eyes.

The villagers brushed past me, mingling and talking. I let the crowd usher me over the uneven stone floor, feeling like I was stepping through desecrated ground. How could the same people who welcomed me among them be monstrous enough to destroy such beautiful things? Some of the hands that now clutched prayer books had once wielded mallets and lit bonfires. The light of long-dead flames seemed to flicker over their faces, giving a sharp, menacing air to their smiles.

Nicholas sat alone on his family's bench. He was too young to have helped strip the church. That was a sin of our elders. Still, I wondered why he was at the Protestant services, and alone. His family had always been Catholic.

Another gentleman stopped to greet him. "Good morrow, Master Bowen."

Nicholas replied with a stiff nod.

The man fumbled with the hat in his hands. "Have you considered our request, that you take the position of warden for the poor?"

"I'm too busy with my own endeavors to take on another responsibility." Nicholas turned back to his prayer book.

The other gentleman scowled and walked away. I shook my head. It was the duty of the *bonheddwyr* like us to care for the poor, a matter of honor born of our position and privilege. Though perhaps honor meant nothing to Nicholas, nor did he care for the plights of others. Several more people walked by him without even a friendly nod. There had always been a touch of pride in Nicholas. Apparently, it had blossomed and born bitter fruit.

Alice guided me past him to the Lloyds' bench. He did not look at us until she whispered, "Good morning, Master Bowen."

He started and gave her a nod. His gaze flicked to me, but he turned away as if I were a stranger. *Let him be alone, then.*

I suffered through the sermon, but other than the commands to pray for the queen, I discovered nothing to object to. I had expected to find it as offensive as my surroundings, but it was only dull. To temper my guilt, I spent the time silently reciting my prayers, counting them on an imaginary rosary.

When we finally returned to Plas Lloyd, I tried to regain the peace of that morning, but it was shaken beyond recovery. I felt alone. A stranger in my own land. A sojourner with no refuge in sight.

Hugh arrived as we settled down for supper. He sat next to me with a smile, and my heart jumped. He had not been at church. He had his own refuge. Perhaps he would share its secrets with me.

"How are you settling in, Mistress Pryce?" he whispered while the harper sang psalms set to ancient Welsh tunes.

"I am finding it an adjustment. I came here as a child, but much has changed."

"I'll warrant it has." He gave me a sympathetic look.

"I do not think we ever met, when I visited before."

"Nay." He smiled. "I would have remembered a face as fair as yours."

I blushed and straightened my sleeve. "How long have you lived here, then?"

"My brother brought me here several years ago. His wife owns an estate down the road, and they divide their time between their two homes. They find this convenient when things get too uncomfortable in one location."

So that was his secret, to be always on the move. Perhaps I truly was a sojourner, then, but I longed for a welcoming hearth and a smiling face to tell me I was home. When supper ended and the guests left, I took a candle up to the cold sanctuary of my little chamber to prepare for bed.

Having survived the ordeal of my first Sunday, I settled back into the daily routine of Plas Lloyd, though I felt my mind would burst from tedium and my heart from loneliness.

A few days later, as I sat at the spinning wheel, Mistress Lloyd quietly announced, "I'll be going to the market this week in Conwy. Would you like to join us, Joan?"

"I would." I hated those gray English walls scarring the beautiful green of Wales, but I itched for a change of scene. I thought I could hold up to any kind of torture, but the trial of boredom and confinement drove away all my principles.

I put extra time into dressing before setting out with Mistress Lloyd and Alice for the market. I wanted to show those Englishmen that the Welsh could be fashionable too. As our carriage creaked and bumped along the road, a fine layer of dust settled over my blue skirt. I sighed and gave up trying to brush it clean. At least it was not raining, or we would have been too bogged down to move.

We climbed out of the carriage and crossed the Conwy River

on the ferry. The towers of Conwy Castle loomed above us, with the walled town stretching up the hillside overlooking the river. I pressed back against Mistress Lloyd. This might have been a mistake. I felt as if, once swallowed by the maw of the town's gates, I would never escape.

I passed under the shadow of the narrow, arched entrance, my heart pounding, and came to the sunshine on the other side. The crowd jostled me, and I kept one hand on my pouch. The Lloyds' manservant stayed close to us, his fingers on his dagger hilt and his glare catching anyone who got too close.

Narrow roads wound upward through a maze of stone and timber buildings. Brightly painted wood signs swung in the breeze, advertising tailors, barbers, glovers, butchers, smiths, and every other shop I could imagine. Vendors strolled the streets, calling their wares in singsong chants to gentlemen and ladies in black velvet and merchants with starched white ruffs. A ballad writer waved song sheets, reciting samples of his verses in English and Welsh. Laborers shuffled through the mix, nibbling on pasties stuffed with meat and onion. Above it all rose the gray battlements of Conwy Castle and, in the heart of the town, a tall, white tower.

"What's that?" I asked Alice.

She squinted up at the tower's many small windows. "It's Plas Mawr—the great hall of Robert Wynn. He was part of Elizabeth's court, and one of the first Welshmen allowed to live in the town walls."

A Welshman had been allowed to settle in an English town, then, but only because of whom he served. I glanced at the tower again, and its dark windows seemed to watch us. From its great height, it left no place to hide, like an eagle hunting its prey.

"Joan?" Mistress Lloyd caught my arm, breaking me out of my reverie.

"I'm sorry." I grinned, feeling like the foolish country girl I was. "I have been to fairs, but I have never seen so many people in one place."

She smiled. "The whole countryside turns out for market days."

I could not get enough of it as we strolled along. The scent of bread, meat pies, fish, and fresh herbs kept my head turning one way and the other as I played with the coins in my purse and thought of supper.

"Mistress Pryce! Mistress Alice!" Mistress Rhys surprised us from behind and grabbed our arms. Her peacock feather fan flapped against my sleeve, and she gave me a bright, breathless smile. "I have just seen a woman wearing a hat she got in London. You will not believe what it cost her, but 'tis the latest fashion at court, patterned after Her Majesty's."

"Oh." Knowing who else wore the fashion quenched my interest.

Two men tumbled out of a tavern in front of us, already at blows. Alice pulled Mistress Rhys back, breaking her grip on me. The crowd cleared a space for the scuffling men, cheering and shouting out bets on the outcome. The men's wide swings testified to the amount of time they had spent in the tavern. I rolled my eyes and tried to scoot away, but the crowd pushed me forward. I had an ideal view to watch the drunken louts make fools of themselves. One of their fists finally connected.

"Welsh brute!" the victim spat in English, wiping blood from his lip.

The crowd hissed, and the Welshman landed another punch. I joined my voice in the general huzzah. Here was a fight worth watching after all.

The clay-brained Englishman yanked out his sword, whipping it in a drunken circle. We booed, and the Welshman swore and fumbled for his own weapon. I pressed back against the shouting, sweating crowd. A fistfight was one thing, but I did not wish to see them kill each other.

The Englishman lunged, but a tall figure with a wide-brimmed hat stepped in. Nicholas! He grabbed the Englishman's arm and spun him off balance. The Englishman stumbled to the ground. The crowd laughed. The Welshman, finally having sword in hand, charged his opponent. Nicholas caught him and pushed him back.

One section of the crowd took the opportunity to mob the Englishman, kicking him as he shouted for help. Nicholas pushed his way in front of the Englishman and put his hand on his rapier. The attackers backed off, muttering rude remarks.

Nicholas caught my pale stare and gave me a twisted frown. He shoved the Welshman on his way and helped the Englishman from the ground. I folded my arms. I would have left the English rogue on the street amidst the flies and dung.

The Englishman spat at Nicholas. Nicholas snarled, his face like some hellish creature's, but he just turned his back on the man.

The men standing next to me shook their heads, and one of them muttered, "Coward."

The word jolted my conscience. I had cheered for the fight, but what was I doing against our English enemies? Nothing. It gnawed at me. Nicholas truly had no sense of honor, though, to let the Englishman abuse him like that, especially after Nicholas had saved him from the crowd.

"Come away, Joan." Mistress Lloyd took my arm. She glared at the stumbling Englishman, her lips pressed into a thin line.

Alice stared after Nicholas, her face ashen. Mistress Rhys patted her arm gently and guided her away. Mistress Lloyd silently led us up the street to buy lace and order fish. At one building, she glanced around cautiously, and finding Mistress Rhys distracted by a strand of pearls, she accepted a parcel of red silk. She hid it among her other purchases and quietly ordered one of her servants to drop the wine cask he carried at the back door.

I tilted my head, and she gave me a wan smile. Only very fine wine would be a reasonable trade for such silk, but why the secrecy?

My eyes widened. Mistress Lloyd was trading smuggled goods!

"Is that not dangerous?" I whispered to Alice.

She toyed with her silk folding fan, flicking it open and closed. "I suppose, but everyone drinks smuggled wine. The coast is right here, with plenty of caves for pirates to hide in, and the queen is very far away. It brings a good profit."

So that was Master Lloyd's Spanish investment. He, a smuggler, a friend of pirates.

My gaze darted around the crowded street. "Could we be caught?"

"The queen's agents try, but some of them are local men, and they all want the smuggled wine and silk as much as we do. I'm not sure they care very much to stop it, especially not when money changes hands with the right people."

How far could you go, though, before bribes would not be enough to save you? I watched over my shoulder as we continued shopping, and once I caught a man staring at us a little too long. He turned his head and ducked into a shop, yet a few minutes later, I saw the red plume of his hat again, not far behind us. I pulled my cloak closer. Surely he was not actually following us.

"Oh, 'tis Master Rhys!" Alice hurried over to gossip with Mistress Rhys's ruddy-faced brother. I was astonished at Alice's laugh and chatter—more words than I usually heard from her in a day.

I stepped back and scanned the crowd. There was no more sign of the red plume, but I still itched like someone was watching me.

"Alice! Joan! Come." Mistress Lloyd curtseyed to the Rhyses and shepherded us away.

We strolled past the castle, and a stench arose to mingle with the smell of cooking meat and the damp scent of the river. I covered my mouth and nose, and Mistress Lloyd and Alice held little nosegays made of sweet flowers to their faces.

"What is that?" I asked.

"Do they not have jails in the country?" Mistress Lloyd asked.

"Of course," I muttered past my hand. My father had caught his death and eternal condemnation in one.

Country jails were nothing like this, though. The stench of human waste drifted down the street, and we turned a corner to avoid it lest we catch the plague or sweating sickness. On our way, we passed a cart filled with what I took for filthy clothing. The tiny hand of a child hung over the edge. I turned to stare. The cart was piled with bodies hardly more than rags and bones, victims of plague, prison, or poverty. Tears welled in my eyes, and I crossed myself.

Mother Mary, give their souls rest.

"Please, mistresses!" A woman padded after us, her arms extended. At first I took her careworn face for middle aged, but when

I glanced back again, I realized she was little older than I. She caught my gaze and dropped to her knees. "A few coins to buy food for my husband in prison? He's starving."

I dropped my coins into her hands, all thought of meat pies gone. My heart ached for the bodies piled on that cart and the poor woman able to do nothing but beg for the life of her husband. I shivered and wondered how many people were in the jail for being Catholic. Would they die for their faith, or betray it as my father had?

Another stark reminder of the dangers of defiance greeted me on our way out of the town. We came around a corner, nearly face to face with a row of bodies dangling from the gallows, their eyes gone from their pasty faces, and birds plucking at their hair. I gagged into my sleeve. Mistress Lloyd and Alice kept their eyes down, and I followed their lead as we hurried past the gruesome display of the queen's justice. I did not have the heart to ask what the men's crimes had been.

Once we were past the walls, I breathed more freely, as if I'd loosened the ties on my corset. We crossed the great river again on the ferry. I watched to the north, where the slow, wide river opened into the sea beyond. Waves crept endlessly over its surface, sparkling when they caught the sun's rays. Seabirds soared and dove over the rolling waters, their mournful songs piercing the quiet. The wind blew past me, bringing the smell of wild, salty air and whispering of possibilities I had only dreamed of, now suddenly close enough to grasp.

I was not certain what I wanted, though. Adventure? A new life in Italy? The sea would take me there. What about home, family? A place I belonged, where I could relax and not always be on guard, afraid to let anyone see into my heart. Freedom? Perhaps those things waited for me across the waters as well.

Someday, someday, the waves called with a thousand ageless voices.

Alice glanced toward the sea then looked away, appearing bored. I wanted to shout at her. Did she not hear, not see the opportunities in front of us? Did no one see? Was I alone in the world?

We reached the far shore. I watched over my shoulder until the glittering blue-gray water vanished behind the gentle green swell of the hills. The word *someday* sounded in my ears long after we climbed back into the carriage and rolled away. Now that the sea had spoken to me, my heart would not be at peace until I found the future it promised me.

Chapter Five

It rained for three days, a blessing to the struggling farmers but stifling confinement for me. Alice rarely spoke, and no one braved the drizzling gray to visit. By the third day, my fingers were raw from the wool twisting through them. I felt as if I'd spun enough thread to clothe all of Wales. I stretched and stood from my spinning wheel to wander the rooms like a soul trapped in purgatory. With the shutters closed, the *plasty* stank of stale smoke and wet dog.

On the far end of the great hall, past the main stairs, was a door I'd never seen used. I pushed it open and stepped into a chapel. I drew a deep breath of dusty air. A simple, dark wood rood screen separated the altar from the pews, and the walls of the room were plastered white. It was chilly and smelled a bit musty, but still I could imagine it blazing with the warmth of candles as a priest said Mass, and in my mind's eye, my father, mother, and brother were there with me.

"Joan?"

Alice stood outside the open door, her arms wrapped tightly around herself.

"I was just going to sit," I said.

"We do not go in there anymore."

I glanced back at the little sanctuary, and the light and warmth I had imagined faded. "Do you not miss it?" I whispered as I stepped out.

Alice stared into the dim room, her eyes sad. "'Tis cold and empty. There's nothing there for us anymore."

She shut the door and returned to her sewing. I crossed the great hall for the little passage that led to the kitchen and back staircase. Mistress Lloyd and a few servants were busy in the stillroom down the corridor, making vinegar by the smell of it. I peeked in, comforted by the sharp scent and the familiar routine of the work that had been mine in my father's home.

"Can I help?" I stepped inside.

"Nay, dear. I'm fine." Mistress Lloyd turned back to her work.

One of the serving girls nudged me out of the way. A polite dismissal. I was not wanted anywhere in this house. A deep, painful yearning ached through me. What was I to do with myself? There was only so much time I could spend staring at my needlework before I saw it when I closed my eyes and dreamed of it at night.

Weak slivers of sunlight slanted through the windows in the hall for the first time in days, and I rushed out for the gardens. My father's had been mainly practical, squares full of tangled herbs and flowers for flavoring food and making medicines. The same plants filled the gardens of Plas Lloyd, but they were laid out in patterns: geometric shapes, interlacing knotwork, even a coat of arms delineated by the different colored leaves and flowers. Low, dark green boxwood hedges enclosed them all. The rain brought the scents of the herbs to life, thick and savory like a good stew. I closed my eyes and breathed in the memories of home.

A labyrinthine path lined with flowers curved around to a turf bench. Next to it was a small carving of Christ carrying His cross. What an odd garden decoration. I moved on to the next bench, where a second carving showed Christ falling under His burden. A chill sent goose bumps over my skin. The Stations of the Cross! My father had told me of this pilgrimage in miniature, and an early tutor encouraged my brother and me to picture the story of the crucifixion as we prayed, but the images were outlawed. I smoothed down a flake of weather-worn paint. How much trouble could the Lloyds be in for having these so easy for a stranger to find?

I walked the route, stopping at each image to pray. The rebellious act warmed me, telling the far-off queen that my mind and spirit were still free.

The next morning dawned bright, and I hurried outside again after breaking my nightly fast. Hugh sat on one of the turf benches, deep in thought. My heart fluttered at his handsome face, though I felt a flicker of annoyance at his invasion of my newfound refuge. I almost withdrew, but he looked up and smiled.

"Mistress Pryce! I see you found your way to the garden." There was a sparkle of amusement in his eyes.

"As have you."

"Aye." He stood and put on an expression of mock seriousness. "Now, then, are we going to speak in half-truths and veiled meanings, or shall we be friends?"

I thought of the mysterious person who had searched my old room and the man with the red plume following us in Conwy. "One must be cautious in one's choice of friends."

"Indeed, one must. Then I'll make the first leap of faith, so to speak. As a man, I'm more likely to be punished, so I am putting my life in your lovely hands." He met my gaze. "I am Catholic. I refuse to attend so-called divine services, and I confess my sins and take the Mass from priests. I have even given them shelter." He smiled. "Now you have enough to set the queen's agents on me. Shall I go on?"

My skin went cold at such a blunt confession. "Nay, Master Richards, you had better not."

"Are you saying your sympathies are not in line with my own?"

I began to feel confident Hugh meant me no harm, and I liked the teasing gleam in his eye, so I shrugged. "I'm saying that you should be cautious when you speak. I may be just a woman, but I could still be dangerous."

"And you do not like to see me in danger?" He stepped closer, his voice dark and rich.

"I do not like to see anyone in danger."

"So clever, Mistress Pryce! You'll not put yourself in peril that way either. I can see Father Davies was wise to trust you."

"You have seen Father Davies?"

He laughed. "You forgot your pretense of innocence at the name of a friend. You're more easily broken than I expected."

I smirked in return. "But I have confessed nothing, yet I might have extracted from you the location of a priest."

"Well done." He winked. "But I confess to more than knowing him. I come bearing illegal messages." He pulled a folded letter from his doublet. "I could hang for this."

I paled at his easy talk of hanging. "Then you should not have it!"

"Sometimes a man must take risks for things he loves. You should not complain, because the letter is for you."

I stared at him for a moment. "Will you be kind enough to give me the message, then?"

"Of course." He passed it over.

I quickly unfolded it and wrinkled my nose. It was just some doggerel verse mocking an English lord. "Is this some sort of game?" There was also the possibility that he had tricked me into saying something I should not have.

"Not a game, but a risky sport. Read it by your fireplace tonight and you may see it in a different light." He stood and bowed. Before he walked away, he looked back and smiled. "I hope we'll be speaking again soon."

I was hardly going to wait for night to decipher Hugh's enigmatic words. His risky sport might be part of the plan to free Wales he had hinted at. As soon as he was out of sight, I raced upstairs and huddled by the fireplace in my room, opening the letter again. Still nothing. Was there such thing as a letter that could only be read at night? That sounded like the magic of hedge witches and charlatans. Hugh had said I would see it in a different light. I held it at an angle, tilting it close to the fire. The blaze's heat seeped over my fingers, and brown words appeared on the warmest parts of the paper.

Grinning in delight, I held the whole paper close to the flames. The words appeared as though written by a ghostly pen.

Greetings, Child,

I hope this letter finds you well and that you are able to discover its secrets. Should you need to respond, you can create the same effect by writing in lemon juice or strong vinegar. Write a mundane message along the top to diffuse suspicion. I ask you to burn this when you have memorized what I have to say. I am engaged in an important work, and hope to solicit your help. I will not write the details, but the friend who delivered this can tell you if you choose to participate. I will warn you that it is dangerous, and I only ask because I believe God has a reason for bringing you to this place at this time.

In service to God,
W. D.

I reread the words. A purpose for being here, perhaps a reason for everything I had been through. But how dangerous would it be? Treasonous, no doubt. I was not bored enough to welcome death, but I did want my life to have some meaning. Hugh could tell me more. He might offer some advice or reassurance. I had no one else to ask. On horseback, I could catch up with him.

I found Master Lloyd meeting with some tenants in the great hall. As soon as he had a moment, I swooped in to speak with him.

"May I go riding, Master Lloyd?"

"Riding? Of course, if you stay near the *plasty*. If you want to wander farther afield, ask someone to accompany you."

"Thank you." I hesitated, remembered a question that had bothered me since my first day at Plas Lloyd. "What if I wished to go to my property? Could I ride there?" That might be a place I could create my own refuge.

He gave me an odd look. "Your lands are to the south, perhaps a day's ride."

"But they border Master Bowen's lands, do they not? I thought he lived nearby."

"Aye, his other lands. They used to belong to an abbey, and both of your parents bought a piece to protect them when Henry VIII seized the church's assets. Nicholas Bowen is a wealthy young man, Joan, and would be wealthier still if you married him and joined your lands to his."

When he turned to speak with another tenant, I rolled my eyes and hurried to the stable. Hopefully Hugh was on foot. I asked one of the stable boys to put a sidesaddle on a mare, and I was off, riding a wide circle around the *plasty*. Hugh must have ridden too, though, because there was no sign of him. I almost turned back, but the freedom of cantering across the open fields called to me.

So I added riding to my daily activities, and my world felt a little broader. Still, there was nothing I could do about Hugh but wait for his return and wonder about his message.

He finally reappeared a few mornings later as I sat at my usual needlework in the great hall. I jabbed the needle through the linen and set it aside, my feet fidgeting beneath my skirts.

Hugh paid his respects to the Lloyds, then asked if I might accompany him around the gardens.

"Ah, I hope you're not courting the girl," Master Lloyd said. "I feel the issue with Nicholas Bowen is not rightly settled."

I flushed, but Hugh chuckled. "Never fear, Master Lloyd, I'll not court her without your permission."

Master Lloyd grunted and gave us a nod. Hugh escorted me to the garden.

"I'll not insult your intelligence by asking if you deciphered the note. What did you think of its message?"

"I was intrigued." I met his gaze. "I want to know more."

"How much did Father Davies tell you?"

"Only that he may have found the reason that God brought me to this place—something I could do to help." I leaned forward. "He said you would tell me more."

"Did he tell you that it will be dangerous?" Hugh's gaze searched mine. All his humor was gone, but he radiated excitement.

"He did."

"This knowledge could condemn you, Mistress Pryce—could condemn a great number of brave men. Women too. You're not the only one to have joined our cause."

My heart beat faster. Which cause? Freedom for Wales? For Catholics? Perhaps they were the same. "I understand. We must be discreet."

"Even your godparents cannot know what you're involved in. The knowledge would endanger them as well. I'll only tell you as much as you need to know."

More secrets I was to be shut out of. I almost insisted that he tell me everything, but then I realized the danger. If I were caught, taken to prison and threatened with death, could I trust myself not to buy relief from torture, maybe even save my life, for the price of a few words? I was my father's daughter, heir to his legacy of betrayal.

"I understand. Tell me what you can."

Hugh's eyes brightened, and he led me deeper into to the garden with the enthusiasm of a schoolboy freed from his studies. He pulled some papers from his pocket. I expected another secret letter but instead saw a page covered in Welsh print. That was unusual enough; most books were in English. The title was *Y Drych Cristianogawl*— *The Christian Mirror*—and it spoke of the love of God and the path to finding Him. It filled a hungry ache in my soul I had not been aware of, as if my spirit had been starving for words of faith, words that told me I was not alone.

"This is a Catholic book?"

"Written by a Welsh priest in exile in Italy." A secretive smile curled the corners of Hugh's lips.

I touched the paper with renewed reverence. Even possessing such an item was treason, but how precious it was! A Welshman in Italy. Did he long for home as he wrote tracts in his native language? I understood a little the sting of being banished from family, friends, and home, but it was hard to imagine knowing you would never again see Wales's green groves or be surrounded by the babble of your native tongue.

"'Tis wonderful," I said. "But what does it have to do with me?"

"We want to smuggle it to other Catholics in Wales."

My skin tingled with dread and excitement. "You want me to help smuggle?"

"Aye, women are less suspect than men, and less likely to be punished severely. In your case . . . I'm sorry to bring up a painful topic, but your father is deceased, and your guardians could argue that they know nothing of your activities and had not the means to stop them. You're a *feme sole*—a free woman without attachments, and able to move about more easily than most."

I hardly felt free, yet it was true that I might slip between the fingers of the law.

"Could the Lloyds be punished for it, though?"

"Not unless they knew about it. Were any consequences meted out, they would fall mainly on you."

I nodded. Smuggling was not exactly the revolution I hoped for, but it was still an act of defiance against the queen, a step toward freedom, and I wanted every crumb of liberty I could snatch from that pox-marked bloodsucker. It was more than that, though. I traced my finger over the paper. I could not be the only Catholic who felt helpless and alone. How many others hungered for the comfort of a priest's words, a boost to their faith in troubled times? "There are those who want these writings?"

"You would only be taking them to places where they were expected—those we believe we can trust—and all in Conwy, where there's too much danger that I or the other men would be recognized." Hugh leaned forward. "I am going to break my promise to you, a little. I am going to tell you something that you do not absolutely need to know, but that I think you should."

"Oh?" I clutched the paper.

"This book is being printed in Wales."

"In Wales!" I stared again at the unassuming page in my hands. "There's a printing press here?"

"Not a licensed one, of course. They are putting a false imprint in the cover, saying it was printed in France, but the work is being done right here—the first book printed in Wales—a Welsh book, a Catholic book. This is a step in winning our freedom from England. We will show them that we have our own minds and hearts. We'll win the country back to Rome and throw off the yoke of London. After over a hundred years of waiting, our time has finally come!"

I thrilled at his words. We would be our own people, no longer imprisoned and persecuted for our beliefs. We did not have to wait for someone else's permission to be free. We could seize the moment ourselves.

"I'll do it," I said.

The next week, Hugh sent me a gift of music written for the harp. Master Lloyd raised an eyebrow and turned the package over to me. I feigned a lack of interest until I got it to my room. Stashed between the sheets of music were the first pages of the Welsh book. I read the beautiful, neatly printed pages in my own language, my fingers trembling. I was holding a piece of the future, maybe the keys to my own shackles. The words were lovely too, speaking of hope and courage. They sank into my lonely heart and reminded me that there were things bigger than just one person, that mattered more than food and clothing and comfort. Things worth sharing, worth fighting for, maybe worth dying for.

And that was good, because I could die for what I was going to do.

Saint David preserve me. This is for Wales.

Hugh had included no instructions. Was I supposed to just give the pages to anyone willing to listen? That was extremely risky. Nay, he had said there were people who wanted them. I smiled. The invisible ink!

I held the music sheets up to the fire, and in its warmth, new words appeared on one of the pages.

Greetings,

We owe you much for your willingness to spread the work we're doing. These papers are expected in Conwy by a bookbinder. I have drawn a map below. Wrap them up as we did and leave them. He'll take them to their next destination from there.

Your faithful servant,
H. R.

I memorized the sketch of Conwy, tracing the route to the

bookbinder's shop in my mind to check it against what I remembered of the town. I just had to get the pages there. That did not seem so dangerous. The image of the ravens picking at the dead men's hair returned to me, and I shuddered. Nay, I could not afford to forget the risks.

I burned Hugh's note—a little sorry to watch his flowing script curl into ash—and rolled up the precious papers. My first idea was to cut a hole in my mattress and hide them there, but a servant might stumble across them while cleaning. Someone had searched my room in my father's home, and the same could happen here. I needed some place less likely to be disturbed.

A tapestry on the wall depicted a pelican cutting her own breast to nourish her young with her blood. I grimaced at the thought and searched behind the tapestry to find a loose board. I slipped the papers under it, making certain they did not show, and pulled the tapestry back into place. It would do for now, but I had to find a better hiding place, somewhere where the blame for them could fall on no one but myself.

Chapter Six

I expanded my riding circuit of Master Lloyd's property, searching for a place to hide the papers. I moved beyond the view of the *plasty* but always stayed in areas that were open and populated. Of course, these would make poor hiding places. The tenants might report me to Master Lloyd—or worse, to one of the queen's agents—if they saw me sneaking about. If only my own property were closer. There could be no better place to store a sacred text than on the lands of an abbey rescued from that old sack of guts, King Henry.

One day, I came upon a dirt track cutting through tall grass. Oaks and neglected copses of hazel stretched to form a lacy arch overhead. Sunlight dappled the ground, and the rich smell of earth and sun-warmed grass wrapped around me. My mare flicked her ears at the birds singing in the brush and stretched out her neck to snatch a mouthful of leaves. The curving path looked wild but inviting, as if it led to the secrets of some forgotten past. I followed, half expecting to find fairies dancing in a circle on the other side.

The trees opened to neglected fields tangled with wild grain and presided over by a cottage. Its thatched roof jutted out over two shuttered windows like quizzical eyebrows on a friendly face. I patted my mare and urged her forward.

The cottage had an empty look—the shutters closed, no smoke rising from the hole in the center of the roof—but otherwise seemed snug and safe. It might make a good place to hide the papers, but its cozy appearance could also invite thieves or gypsies. They would not know whom the papers belonged to, but those beautiful words might be lost, and all of Hugh and Father Davies's work along with them.

I shook my head and turned back, a little sorry to follow the trail away from that quiet place to the world I knew. The thud of hooves echoed across the fields. My hands froze on the reins. A rider broke through the trees just as my mare reached the main path. His sleek stallion and tailored doublet denoted him as a gentleman, even from a distance, but that did not mean he could be trusted. My mare snorted and tossed her head, sensing my tension, but I could not outrace such a confident horseman.

"Easy, girl," I whispered, patting her neck.

When the rider got close enough to identify, my heart sank. It was Nicholas.

He reined in beside me, studying me with surprise equal to my own. My gaze caught on the disfigured side of his face. I did not mean to stare, but it took me a moment to look away. He scowled and glanced down, turning his scars from view.

"Mistress Pryce. What are you doing here?" His voice was cold.

I straightened my riding skirts. "Master Lloyd allows me to ride on his land. I ventured a little too far and lost my way."

"Indeed you did. This is not Master Lloyd's land, but mine."

"Oh!" What a disaster that could have been! Nicholas might have found the papers, and he was not some illiterate thief. He likely would have reported them, and I could not be certain they would not have been connected back to me, or to Hugh. Truly, the dangers were more numerous than I had expected. I could not let Nicholas guess that I was anything but lost. "I apologize for trespassing. I did not think I had gone all that far, just a little distance from the *plasty*."

"Aye, Master Lloyd's property is oddly shaped. Nant Bach's lands come quite nearly within sight of the *plasty* at Plas Lloyd, though I rarely visit this part. The soil's so boggy in places, 'tis not worth the effort to plant."

That explained the empty cottage; no one would wish to lease marshy ground. "I suppose I thought of Nant Bach as being farther away, like the woods where we used to—" I flushed. Remembering the past sent new waves of loneliness washing around me. Nant Bach was supposed to have been his brother's, but Nicholas referred to it as his own. There was no tactful way to ask what had happened. If only Nicholas were not such a churlish fool. We might have been friends.

He looked down, toying with his reins, and said nothing. Pain creased the corner of his good eye. I lifted my hand to him, wanting to apologize, but he turned his stallion toward Master Lloyd's estate. "I was riding to Plas Lloyd. May I accompany you back? I would not want you to come to some harm and have it on my conscience."

"Of course." I had little choice. "What brings you to visit Master Lloyd?"

His mouth twitched. "I am actually coming to see Mistress Alice."

He clutched a little nosegay in his hand, made of bright, sweet-smelling flowers. I smiled. He would see now that I was not going to interfere, and perhaps there could be peace between us. "I'm certain she'll be delighted to see you."

"You think so?" he mumbled.

"Oh, aye. She's seemed sad these past few days." More so than usual, but it would be unkind to remind him.

Nicholas sighed and said nothing else. Were they both so love-sick? Only Master Lloyd and his concerns about adjoining land kept them apart. What a foolish reason to deny two people happiness. The Lloyds' lands were next to Nicholas's as well, after all.

We dismounted at the stables and made our way to the front door in silence. I preceded Nicholas into the great hall, where Alice sat staring absently at her needlework. She gave a start when she saw him, but instead of the smile I expected, her lip quivered and she looked away. Nicholas slowly crossed the hall to present her with the flowers. I sat at an unoccupied spinning wheel and starting it whir-ring to cover their private conversation as servants came and went. In spite of my good intentions, I could not help glancing up from time to time.

Alice kept her head bowed, though she spoke and once wiped a tear from her cheek. Nicholas sat rapier-straight, not close enough to touch her, but near enough to offer quiet words when she stopped talking. The whole visit lasted only a quarter of an hour; then Nicholas left her with a formal bow. She did not watch him leave.

I turned back to my work. The hypnotizing twist of the wool slipped through my fingers to wrap into thread. Nicholas and Alice's obvious pain pierced me. I had to find a way to convince Master Lloyd to allow them to court freely.

I thought of Hugh's bright, amber-colored eyes. If he were to show serious interest in me, and I in him, Master Lloyd would not be cruel enough to forbid us from seeing each other, and that would clear Nicholas of any imagined obligations to me or our fathers. For my own part, I would not mind capturing the fancy of brave, handsome Hugh Richards. My success in his scheme would show him I was clever and brave too and encourage him to trust me with more, let me into his secret world.

The next week, Mistress Lloyd finally invited Alice and me on another trip to Conwy. I had not yet found a better hiding place for the papers, but I had given thought to how I could transport them. It would look odd if I carried around a stack of music sheets, or even a book, while shopping. Instead, I turned to my needle for help.

I had a tall, brimmed hat I was fond of for traveling. I carefully picked out the silk lining and laid the papers around the inside of the crown. I sewed the lining back over the papers to secure them. It did not quite fit back into place, but I did my best, leaving only a small gap where the papers showed through. They stayed secure, even when I gave the hat a vigorous shake. It would be enough, I hoped. I could pull them out unobserved or, failing that, leave the entire hat where the bookbinder would find it and see what lay inside.

With my treasonous hat secured over my looped braids, I rode out with Mistress Lloyd, Alice, and the small army of servants necessary to carry bags, watch over horses, and protect us from thieves. I carried my feathered fan the whole way to keep my hands from shaking.

We left the carriage at the ferry and passed the gates of the town. I felt like a rabbit stepping into a snare. I kept my gaze down, avoiding a glance in the direction of the gallows.

My palms sweated and stuck to the feathers in my fan. I took deep breaths as I walked past shops and market stalls with Mistress Lloyd and Alice.

"Mistress Pryce!"

I jumped and grabbed the brim of my hat. Mistress Meredith only waved and passed by with her family, but my heart lodged in my throat. She stopped to greet Alice, and Mistress Rhys joined them. Everyone was in Conwy for market day. If I made a mistake, I had an audience for my downfall.

A gust of wind tore at my hat and brought me the stench of the jail. I gagged and turned away, glancing over my shoulder for the red plume I had seen following us before.

"Hot mutton pasties!" a woman shouted in my ear.

When I flinched away from her, she turned to the next potential customer.

"Rosemary and sage! Fresh bays and rosemary!"

I sidestepped the girl draped with bundles of pungent herbs. No sign of the feathered hat. Except for the merchants appraising my fine clothing, no one paid me any heed. I grimaced and wiped my hands on my skirts as unobtrusively as possible. This was my chance to prove myself. I could not let anything give me away.

Mistress Lloyd and Alice were too busy deciding which color of velvet would be best for Alice's new gown to pay me much attention as I drifted farther from them and the servants. I hurried around a corner to the steep street where I was supposed to find the bookbinder's shop and leave the papers. Of course it was at the very top. I spotted Nicholas in the crowd of shoppers, but he ducked into a pewter smith's stall. I exhaled and trudged up the street, my legs burning from the climb.

I paused at the entrance to the shop, breathing in the rich scent of leather and glue and watching the street for anyone who seemed too interested. Without glancing at the bookbinder, I pulled off my hat to straighten my smothered braids.

A salt-scented wind gusted past, catching the hat from my shaking fingers. My stomach lurched, and I gasped.

"My hat!"

I clenched my teeth, but it was too late. Several gentlemen scurried after it. I tried to outrace them in my swaying skirts. They took my urgency as a sign of a particular love of the hat and scrambled all the more to recapture it. The sea wind frolicked down the steep street with it, dodging between people and under horses' hooves. I almost could have laughed if the contents of that hat were not a death warrant.

I darted in front of a cart full of sheep. The startled pony tossed its head, and I barely avoided its trampling hooves, but I left my gentlemanly helpers behind and closed in on the hat. It bounced toward the bottom of the street, where Master and Mistress Rhys visited with their friends from the parish. I clenched my teeth and ran harder.

Nicholas jogged from the shelter of a shop's overhang to snatch the hat before it reached the Rhyses.

Saint David, preserve me!

The breeze whipped back in my face as if taunting me with its triumph.

I clasped my hands, trying to catch my breath. "Sir?"

Nicholas raised an eyebrow at the torn lining and met my eyes. I did not flinch from his gaze or stare at his scars. I buried my trembling hands in the folds of my skirt and focused on trying to read his expression.

"I saw you chasing this hat as though your life depended on it," Nicholas said. "I suppose it must be a favorite of yours?" His voice was as cold as ever, but there was something in his eyes, a spark of interest. He was too good at hiding his thoughts for me to know what direction they ran. I could try lying, but I sensed he would not take that well.

"'Tis very important to me," I said, the closest I would get to pleading.

"So you claim it? You have put your own handiwork into it?"

He was playing a game with me, as Hugh had. Hugh's questions had carried an undercurrent of flirtation, though. Nicholas's were deadly serious.

I straightened my shoulders. "It has always been one of my

favorites, but I made several improvements, which make it all the more precious to me."

Nicholas glanced again inside the hat, and I forced myself to breathe. If only I could read some trace of emotion beneath his perpetual, disfigured smirk. My future sat in his hands in the truest meaning of the words. The Rhyses watched our exchange with curious looks.

Nicholas smiled: a strange expression that twisted his scarred cheek. "Women do get worked up about the silliest things."

Master Rhys and his friends chuckled as Nicholas returned the hat to me, covering his low parting words. "Take care, Mistress Pryce. Hats are an easy thing to lose, like the heads they sit on."

"Joan!" Mistress Lloyd and Alice huffed over to me. Nicholas gave me a quick bow and retreated. My heart was pounding so hard, I barely registered Mistress Lloyd's scolding.

"I lost my hat," I replied in a daze. "Master Bowen was kind enough to retrieve it for me."

"You were with Master Bowen?" Mistress Lloyd's expression drained of anger. "Well, that's perfectly appropriate, then."

I winced and glanced at Alice, but she gave me a look devoid of concern and slipped past me to greet Mistress Rhys and her brother. How odd. Almost as strange as Nicholas hurrying off without even a glance at her. Perhaps they had quarreled.

"Oh!" I clutched the hat stuffed with precious papers and looked back at the bookbinder's shop. I still had my delivery to make. "I dropped my fan."

Mistress Lloyd glanced up the hill in dismay. "I should just make you buy a new one."

I could not help smiling. "The shop where I lost it is closer than the shop that sells fans."

"Very well, hurry along."

I did, scurrying back up the street. The bookbinder continued stitching pages together without even a glance at me. I wanted to just leave the hat behind, but that would look very strange after my performance. I knelt down carefully, slipped the stitches in the lining, and slid out the papers. What was I supposed to do with them? I tore the lining all the way out, wrapped it around the papers, and shoved them behind the counter. The bookbinder gave me a withering look. My face burned, but I walked out of the shop with my head held high. Hopefully, the bookbinder would not complain to Hugh about my incompetence.

As I strolled from the shop, clutching my fan and my hat, my dread seeped away and I felt like I could fly back down the street. I had done it! I helped Hugh, defied the queen, and spread those beautiful Welsh words heralding the future. Heat tingled through me, and I shoved my hat back on with a smile. Hugh would come to see me soon. I itched for another stack of smuggled papers.

Chapter Seven

Clear autumn weather brought daily visitors to Plas Lloyd. I was restless with their presence, afraid they would keep Hugh away. One bright, chilly morning, Alice sat talking with Mistress and Master Rhys. I focused on my stitching, making curling green leaves along the edge of a pillow cover. The word *treason* caught my ears.

"Aye, 'tis a pity there were Welshmen involved in the scandal with the Queen of Scots," Master Rhys said. "'Tis one thing to tolerate Catholics—their old-fashioned beliefs will die off soon enough—but there's no excuse for turning against our own queen. There's no treachery more vile."

"Betraying the queen is betraying Wales," Mistress Rhys added softly.

I bit down on my tongue. If I let it loose, I could not trust myself not to say too much. I gripped my brass needle until my fingers ached, longing to jab it into Master Rhys's fine silk hose and wipe the self-satisfied smirk from his face. No treachery more vile? As if the queen was to be our all—more than home or family, heart or God. It might be treasonous to turn against her, but what option did she give us, outlawing our beliefs, forcing us to choose between faith and country? We had no alternative but to fight her.

I put my needlework aside and slipped out the front door. The crisp air stung my face. I leaned against the house, taking deep breaths. When would the time come that I did not have to stand silent, helpless, alone?

Mother Mary, help me be patient. Help me hold my tongue.

A ride. That would ease the sting of their words and calm my roiling temper. I called for my horse, pacing until the stable boy helped me into the saddle. My mare fidgeted under me, her restlessness as keen as mine. I spurred her on and gave her free rein. We galloped past woods sharp with autumn golds and reds, jumping fences and skirting fields where farmers stooped over their harvests. The furious wind tore strands loose from my braids and raised tears in my eyes only to whisk them away. We reached the edge of Master Lloyd's lands. I slowed our pace, my heart lulled back into an uneasy peace.

"Good girl. Thank you." I patted the blowing horse and turned her toward the *plasty*. The main road opened before us, and I followed, enjoying the crisp day. Racing hoofbeats rang on the packed dirt. I jumped and looked back. Hugh galloped toward me, his dark brown horse lathered with sweat.

"Mistress Pryce! Come, make haste!"

I tightened my grip on the reins. Were we detected? Did we have to flee?

Saint Winifred, protector of maidens, help me. I have nowhere to go.

I urged my mare to race alongside him until we reached a secluded spot off the road. Hugh reined in, panting for breath. "Here is a place we can talk in private."

"Are we in danger?"

"No more so than usual." He gave me a brilliant grin. "You did splendidly, Mistress Pryce. I heard about you chasing your hat down the street."

I laughed in relief. "I'm afraid I made quite a spectacle of myself."

"It all ended well."

"Thanks to Master Bowen," I mumbled.

"Really?" Hugh's eyebrows arched.

I quickly told him of Nicholas finding the hat.

"That was a lucky stroke," Hugh said. "The hat was a clever idea, but he's right—next time you should use something less apt to fly away."

"You're not upset that Master Bowen knows?"

Hugh shrugged. "It could have been very dangerous for you, but Nicholas Bowen was not likely to turn you in."

"He seems very law-abiding."

"Oh, he is, but he's not heartless."

"Is he not?" I said, then bit the inside of my cheek. My tongue was too quick against someone who had spared me from prison or worse.

"Now, Mistress Pryce, do not be hard on the man. He'll never see things quite as you or I do, but he bends over backwards to avoid trouble if he can. He's always had Catholic sympathies, even if he refuses to act on them, and I doubt he wants to see a woman in jail. That's one of the reasons we chose you, remember."

Aye, because I was a woman. Less suspect since everyone saw me as helpless. I frowned. And how had I accomplished my task? Foolishly, dangerously. "I'll do better next time."

"I have no doubt you will. That's why I brought you more papers."

I grinned when he showed me the freshly printed pages. "I need a safer place to keep them, though. I do not want Master Lloyd to be endangered if I'm found with them."

"That's wise. Do you think your guardian would let you ride out with me?"

"Perhaps." I hesitated. "But he does not approve—"

"I know." Hugh scratched his beard, and then a smile spread over his face. "He could not complain if I was taking you to visit Master Nicholas."

"To visit him? I do not think he would welcome me."

Hugh laughed. "He does not seem to welcome me either, but he never forbids me from coming. I think he secretly likes the company. 'Tis dreary up there, all alone at that big house."

"All alone?" I asked.

"Did you not hear?"

"Our fathers had a falling out. I heard nothing of him for years."

"Hmm." Hugh looked down and patted his horse's neck. "'Twas the plague. The local magistrates locked up the house when it struck—boarded over the doors and windows and set guards so none could enter or leave." His voice dropped. "You could hear the women and children crying inside. When the sickness had run its course, only a couple of kitchen maids walked out. Everyone else was dead. Nicholas only survived because he was away, helping to put down the rebellion in Ireland."

"Oh!" I shivered. Poor Nicholas! Now I had no desire to return to Nant Bach. Of course, the plague would not be lingering there still or none would go near, but the thought of death claiming all those people I had played among as a child made my stomach sour.

"Come," Hugh said. "That place could use some brightening up, and it will give us an excuse to be together." He looked down with a sly smile. "A chance to plan, I should say."

My heart skipped. Were our secret meetings more to Hugh than just a part of his smuggling operation? I did not like the idea of using neighborly visits as an excuse for plotting, but I longed for some friendly company. "Very well. I'll ask Master Lloyd. I'm certain he'll have no objections."

Master Lloyd seemed pleased with the idea, though he still eyed Hugh suspiciously. Hugh and I rode up the lane to Nant Bach and arrived unannounced at Nicholas's front door. I was uncertain what to expect, but the *plasty* was not much different than I remembered it: three stories high, made of wood and stone. A new wing added a few rooms on one side, but otherwise it was the place where Nicholas and I had played as children. I recognized the grove of trees we had explored and the orchard where he taught me to shoot a bow.

Hugh knocked, and I stood beside him, clasping my hands to avoid fidgeting. A steward answered and announced our presence. Nicholas came to the door. His gaze darted between us, and he set his jaw.

"Master Richards, Mistress Pryce, what brings you here today?" he asked coldly.

"A friendly visit, Master Nicholas. Where's your Welsh hospitality? Are you going to leave us standing here to catch a chill?"

"Very well, you may come in." As usual, he kept his face slightly turned from us. Would a person ever get used to being stared at, to having people wonder, whisper, fear? And he had been handsome before—half his face still was. To go from being admired to shunned would be painful. I looked at him with pity, and he caught my gaze. His mouth hardened into a thin line.

Perhaps being pitied would be the worst of all. Pity was not the feeling of equals for one another, as sympathy might be. Pity was what one felt for someone lower. Someone less. Once, Nicholas had been my friend. I had felt neither fear nor pity toward him. Nothing had changed, really, except that terrible scar.

Of course, that was not true. Whether it was the scar, or the accident that caused it, or something else entirely, he had changed—cold and withdrawn and nothing like my old companion.

I stepped into the warmth of Nant Bach's great hall. High overhead, the ceiling showed off its golden oak beams. The walls were plastered white, with coats of arms and the red dragon of Wales painted over the huge fireplace. A crackling blaze drove out the autumn chill. Red and white patterned fabric covered the lower part of the wall, just above the benches lining the room. Swords and armor hung at the far end, a common enough display for gentlemen. They were polished to a silver gleam, but the breastplate had several noticeable dents on the left side.

The hall seemed strangely bare, despite its decorations. Beautiful tapestries had once decorated it—not painted cloth, but carefully stitched scenes created by generations of Nicholas's family.

"Oh," I whispered.

"What's wrong?" Hugh asked.

"I—" I faltered, and they stared at me. I could think of no lie to cover my exclamation. "There used to be such beautiful tapestries."

Nicholas threw another stick into the fireplace. "They had to be burned."

I winced. Of course, destroyed in the purging after the plague. Nicholas rested his hand on the stone mantle, and his heavy gold ring glinted in the red light of the fire. A single band for all he mourned, all he had lost in one blow.

"I'm sorry, Master Nicholas," I said softly.

He gave a start and glanced at me, revealing the disfigured side of his face, eerie and impish in the dappled light of the fire. I was careful to meet his eyes without staring or turning my gaze down. It was too familiar of me, perhaps, to use his Christian name, but seeing him in his home, where we had once played with his sisters and brother—it was confusing, my old and new lives colliding. I hoped my expression was one of sympathy and not pity. Whatever he saw in my face, he only nodded and went back to staring into the fire.

Hugh strolled over to the table, shooing aside some dogs resting on the floor, and sat with comfortable familiarity. I found a seat on one of the benches, my hands resting awkwardly in my lap with nothing to do. The lack of female presence showed everywhere. The spinning wheels sat dusty in the corners, and there was no evidence of needlework or sewing, not even flowers to decorate the table or sweeten the rushes on the floor.

"What is this?" Hugh exclaimed, looking at a document on the table. His voice was hushed and urgent.

Nicholas strode up to peer over his shoulder, and I moved behind them, not certain my curiosity was welcome.

" 'Tis scripture," Nicholas said. His voice was level, but the good side of his mouth curled in a faint smile.

Hugh stared at him. "In Welsh! This is not the New Testament."

"Nay, 'tis few snippets from Isaiah and some of the psalms."

Hugh flipped through the handwritten pages, his eyes fixed on the page. "Is this your work?"

"I wish I could claim credit for it. 'Tis the work of William Morgan."

"Morgan." Hugh's elation faded. "A Protestant bishop."

"Is it not still the Bible, regardless of who translates it?" Nicholas asked.

"He may have corrupted its meaning." Hugh pushed the pages away.

" 'Tis his life's work. I doubt he let politics interfere with his calling. He has corrected the old translation of the New Testament too. He thinks by next year it will be ready to send to London for publishing."

Some of the fever returned to Hugh's eyes. "The entire Bible in Welsh?"

"Aye. Think of it. The Irish and Cornish—all our ancient British cousins—none of them have the Bible in their own language. 'Tis a peace offering for our loyalty. If we continue to show Her Majesty we are faithful subjects, she'll grant us more."

I shook my head. Elizabeth might make peace with Wales for the sake of her Tudor blood, but she would never make peace with Catholics. There could be no compromise.

Hugh pounded his fist on the table. "She's trying to buy our complacency. If she truly wishes to grant favors to Wales, the Welsh Bible ought to be printed here, without her agents leaning over our shoulders."

Nicholas shrugged.

"And why should we need her approval to read God's word?" Hugh asked. "That mewling worm Cecil will probably censor it. He knows just enough Welsh to butcher Holy Writ. 'Tis time we ended this tyranny!"

Nicholas's eyes flashed anger. His voice dropped to a whisper. "You're welcome to your opinions on religion, but you'll not speak treason in my home."

Hugh straightened with a glare, and they stood face to face. It suddenly occurred to me how equally matched they would be, nearly the same height and build, the similarity emphasizing the contrast between Hugh's dark, handsome features and Nicholas's fair, mottled ones. I wondered for a moment if Hugh would draw his sword, but his hands relaxed, and he gave a quick bow.

"I apologize, Master Bowen. This is your home, and I respect that."

I exhaled. There was something in their odd friendship that appealed to me, seeing that two men so different could learn to get along.

Nicholas nodded curtly and turned back to the papers. "London is the only place to have it published, unless Morgan wishes to take it to Oxford or Cambridge." His voice softened. "'Twould be a miracle, though, to see books printed in Wales."

He brushed his fingers over the paper, longing and sadness in his eyes. Hugh's gaze met mine, and he winked. I looked away quickly. Our little secret. If only we could tell everyone, shout it in the streets of Conwy. Wales could publish its own books. Wales could think for itself.

I glanced at the handwritten pages on the table, the work of one man's life. The words of Isaiah leapt out at me: *He giveth power to the faint; and to them that have no might, he increaseth strength.*

"Think what this will show people, though," I said, hardly aware that I spoke aloud. "Wales has little might compared to our conquerors and the other powerful nations of the earth, but its language is as worthy of God's word as English or German or Latin." I thought of the servants who only knew Welsh, and my aunt and cousin who scorned to speak it. "It will give them a reason to learn to read the language, not to throw it off in favor of English. In the end, maybe it does not matter where 'tis printed, as long as it is done."

I ran my fingers over the Welsh words, caressing the faintly raised lines of ink. I felt the men watching me, and my skin flushed as I pulled my hand away. I met Nicholas's eyes and saw, for the first time since I arrived, some of the friendliness we had shared as children.

"Of course that is true," Hugh said, "but we still should have the right to determine our own destiny. This great accomplishment comes only because the queen allows it."

"Or because God does." Nicholas raised an eyebrow. "Where is your faith?"

"In my actions, Master Nicholas. In my works. 'Tis all well and good to trust in God's good will, but I do not believe He means for us to sit back and wait for Him to do everything for us."

"No doubt," Nicholas said, a quiet sadness in his words. "Yet how can one know the work they are doing is God's and not their own? Sometimes a moment of bold action leads to a lifetime of regret."

The sorrow in Nicholas's face was so heavy, I had to look away.

Hugh shook his head. "The longer we wait, the more powerful our enemies become."

"*Our* enemies, Master Hugh? Are you so certain of who Wales's true enemies are?"

Hugh drew a deep breath, his face bright with the heat of his argument, but he just exhaled and shook his head. "It has been an enlightening visit, Master Bowen. Unless we are to impose on you for supper, though, I had best get Mistress Pryce home."

"Of course," Nicholas said, turning away. "I would not want Master Lloyd to worry."

Hugh and I left Nicholas with awkward farewells and rode off, but Hugh took me on a different route to Plas Lloyd that avoided the main road.

"We need a good place to keep the papers." Hugh sounded upbeat, but lingering annoyance from his conversation with Nicholas still flickered in his tight expression. "Also, 'twould be convenient to be able to leave messages somewhere without anyone watching."

Exciting too. The discussion with Nicholas had reminded me that I was involved in something important, something bigger than spinning and embroidery.

"There's a place I remember seeing," Hugh said. "It might be perfect, if I can find it again." He guided us between sloping hills to a rocky rise. "There!"

An outcrop of rocks sheltered a small cave. We guided our horses up a narrow trail. The cave was so shallow we could barely fit our mounts inside.

"Would bandits come here?" I asked.

"'Twould not be sheltered enough for them. I'll dig out a hiding place and cover it with a rock. We can store papers in here with little chance of anyone finding them. 'Tis on Master Lloyd's land, but not so close to the *plasty* that anyone could prove you—or he—had anything to do with it. We can choose a tree near Plas Lloyd, and I'll tie a token on it to let you know if there's anything new here for you to retrieve."

I nodded. "I think it will work."

"I'm glad we are in agreement." Hugh smiled and pulled out another stack of papers. "Shall we keep these here, or will you be able to deliver them soon?"

"Do they go to the same place?"

"Someone different this time. The queen's agents watch the

bookbinders and sellers carefully. The directions are on the top sheet."

"I doubt we'll go to Conwy before next week. They'll be safer here. Only, I would like to take a copy for myself. I gave all the others away without thinking of it."

Hugh held the papers back. "Do you have a safe place to keep it?"

I folded my arms. "Aye, with other things that would cause me trouble if they were found. This one paper will not be any worse than everything else I'm hiding."

He pulled out a sheet and passed it to me. Our fingers brushed as he did, sending a tingle racing up my arm.

"Be cautious," he said. "You cannot know how much depends on your secrecy."

"Then perhaps you should tell me," I said, only half teasing.

"Come now, Mistress Joan, you know there's no reason to burden you with more."

The airy dismissal in his voice brushed away some of my excitement.

The evening grew cold as I watched Hugh hollow out a spot in the ground and tear the lining from his cloak to wrap the papers. He pulled a rock over the hiding place.

"There. 'Tis done. We'd best be getting you home."

He helped me onto my horse, slipping a quick kiss on my cheek. For once, his flirtation did not warm me. Hugh had chosen a dangerous life, full of secrets—one I only glimpsed in pieces, like peeking through a door held ajar. Would he ever open it all the way to let me in?

Chapter Eight

When we reached Plas Lloyd, Hugh tore another strip from the lining of his cloak and tied it to a tree branch within sight of my window. It hung there like the rag offerings pilgrims secretly left at holy wells and shrines.

"So you'll think of me," he said with a grin. "I'll leave another when there are more papers at the cave." He bid me farewell and rode into the gathering dusk.

After supper, I snuck upstairs with my forbidden paper. The breeze moved through the trees outside, making Hugh's token flutter like a ghostly finger, beckoning me into an unknown future. I huddled in the candlelight to read the paper again, soaking in the words of comfort and faith—like having a priest with me always—and then opened my little leather trunk. If only I had a copy of William Morgan's Welsh Bible too. *That* I would not have to hide.

My hand rested on Nicholas's childhood letters. I flipped through them until one caught my attention.

Dear Joan,

Father and John have gone away, and I'm desperately lonely. I wish you would come back. I would take you exploring again, or perhaps we could run away and visit Italy. I miss having someone to talk to. Please write back soon.

Your faithful friend,
Nicholas

The words were written long ago by someone who, in many ways, no longer existed, but they reached across time to tug my heart. I wished I could write back to the Nicholas in the past and tell him I missed him too.

He was so much more alone now. His family was gone beyond reach. The parish treated him like some specter risen from Annwn's cauldron: a cursed creature not living or dead. He did not seem to welcome my friendship either.

I returned the leather trunk to its hiding place but kept Nicholas's letter. People changed, sometimes beyond recognition. We could not control their choices or force a fleeting friendship to stay. That was the most frightening thing about any kind of relationship: it relied on trusting your heart, your secrets and weaknesses, even your life to another person.

I could always go to Italy, hide behind the walls of an abbey to keep my heart to myself, and never fear it being hurt. I reread Nicholas's letter, tracing his boyish handwriting. What had happened to his heart? Had he walled it up so it would not feel the loneliness and pain? Perhaps we were not so very different. If one did not feel pain, though, did they also become callous to love or friendship or kindness?

I lay down, but my sleep was restless. The bright sunrise pierced the bed curtains and stung my heavy eyes. I pulled a blanket over my head and wished it away. There was nothing I could do about the morning noise: dogs, roosters, servants, all boisterous in greeting the new day.

Nicholas's letter lay beside my pillow.

I'm desperately lonely. I wish you would come back.

I could not shake the feeling I had wronged Nicholas. He might have become withdrawn, even cowardly in defending his honor, but after watching him debate Hugh, I did not believe his heart was beyond caring. If he could still feel, then he must be hurting.

I called a maid to help me dress. My page of *Y Drych Cristianogawl* sat on the table, forgotten the night before. I slipped it into my sleeve before the maid noticed. She arranged my hair, and then I hurried down the side stairs.

Before I could think about what I was doing, I called for my mare and took the winding road to Nant Bach.

The steward calmly announced my arrival, but Nicholas, who was reading by the fireplace, nearly dropped his book. Calm fell over his expression like a curtain, and he rose with a bow.

"Mistress Pryce," he said coolly. "To what do I owe the pleasure?"

My mouth went dry. This was a foolish idea. I could not just reclaim my childhood friend, no matter how lonely either of us was. Hugh said Nicholas had Catholic sympathies, but that did not mean he would not decide to turn me in if I said the wrong thing. I swallowed and shook my head.

"Mistress Pryce, are you unwell?" His voice betrayed real concern. "Jenkins, fetch wine."

I wet my lips. "Nay, thank you. I'm fine. I . . ." I glanced at the steward and the servant sitting in the corner repairing a bridle. Even if I decided to trust Nicholas, what about the rest of his household? Some of the servants could be spies in the pay of the queen's agents.

"Would you like to walk in the gardens?" Nicholas asked after a long pause.

I let out my breath. "That would be excellent."

He showed me the way out, though I remembered it well enough. The gardens were more glorious than Master Lloyd's in their array of colors and patterns laid out around neat, straight paths. Vines laden with clusters of grapes climbed the walls, and trees trained in intricate shapes fenced us in.

"You've changed it so much," I said, then winced at the reminder of the past.

Nicholas's eyes brightened as he looked over the gardens. "Aye, my father and John made some of the improvements, but I wanted to try growing grapes and fruit. Planting them along the walls keeps them warm enough to protect them from frosts. I think, with ingenuity, we can do most anything for ourselves here in Wales."

"Indeed."

"You did not come here to see my gardens." He watched me from the corner of his good eye. Curious, perhaps?

Why *had* I come? Atoning for my unfairness toward Nicholas?

I was not certain my motivations were so selfless. I fidgeted with my sleeve, and my fingers brushed the crisp paper hidden there. Nicholas had not betrayed me when he saw the papers in my hat, and the longing in his eyes when he spoke of books printed in Wales had been the most intense emotion I had seen from him since my return. Hugh had forbidden me from sharing it with anyone, but I would not let him dictate my actions. I cleared my throat.

"I wanted to show you something. I thought, well . . ." I fumbled with my sleeve and drew out the folded piece of paper, trying to keep my hand from trembling as I handed it to him.

He skimmed the paper with a frown. "Are you trying to catechize me? I assure you I'm firm in my religious convictions."

I bit the inside of my cheek. Firm in his convictions? Once he had been a devout Catholic. Now he went to Protestant services, though he had not scolded Hugh for his religious beliefs, only for his talk against the queen. Nicholas's views seemed anything but resolute. "Not that. You looked so . . ." How did I explain it without sounding ridiculous?

He frowned, the veil covering his emotions again. Maybe I should not have mentioned looks. He handed the paper back. "'Tis illegal to own any documents from Rome."

"'Twas printed in Wales," I blurted and then covered my mouth. *Lackwit girl!* What was I thinking? There was no bringing back the past. My attempt to reach out to the Nicholas of my childhood put myself—and possibly Hugh—in danger.

Nicholas's good eye widened. He stared at the words again, like the thing in his hand had sprung up there by magic. "Printed in Wales, but . . ."

"I'm sorry! 'Twas wrong of me to say anything. I have put you in a difficult situation."

He rubbed his eyes and chuckled. "Aye, you have no idea. I want to ask a hundred questions, but I do not want to know the answers, and I rather hope you do not know either." He shook his head and sat on a bench so blindly, it may have been only luck that it caught his fall. I edged over to sit next to him as he read the paper again. A genuine grin spread over his face and, for a moment, he was like my old friend. I basked in the warm glow of memory. When he looked up, we found ourselves smiling at each other. Nicholas quickly looked away.

"I never thought I would hold something in my hand that was printed right here in Wales." His smile faded and he sighed. "Thank you for showing me." He held it out.

"You can keep it," I said.

He shook his head. "I cannot. Its very existence, miracle though it is, is illegal."

"Oh." I folded the paper and twisted it around in my hands. "Why did you not turn me in?"

"What?"

"When you saw what was in my hat, why did you let me go?"

He gave me a sidelong glance, and once again I saw a glimpse of my childhood friend in his quizzical look. "You thought I would turn you in?"

I stowed the paper back in my sleeve. "Well, you seem very concerned with the law."

"I am, but that does not mean I always like its consequences. I saw enough of the papers to believe they were matters of faith, not designed to stir trouble."

He left the words hanging, but I felt emboldened, as if, for this quiet moment in his garden, the rules did not apply anymore and I could speak freely.

"If they had been inflammatory, you would have turned me in?"

He sighed. "I would ask you not to force me to find an answer to that question."

"Why do you get to decide what constitutes trouble?"

He looked up, his expression perplexed. His scar pulled at his mottled skin. "Why do you have to question everything? Can you not just leave things as they are?"

"Do you *like* things as they are?"

"I cannot understand what you're hoping to accomplish. Do you want to be a martyr?" His voice dropped. "Have you not heard of Richard Gwyn?"

"I think I heard my father speak the name."

"As well he should have. Gwyn was a Catholic—not even a priest—but a Welsh schoolmaster. Two years ago they executed him for treason for teaching children Catholic doctrines. He was hanged, drawn, and quartered." Nicholas took a long breath. "Do you know—?"

"Aye," I said quickly. I had heard it described: the traitors strung up on the gallows until nearly dead, then cut down, their bellies sliced open to remove their guts and their bodies torn into four pieces, all while still alive. I did not think they did it to women, though. Women only hanged. Still, if the queen's lackeys killed a schoolmaster for teaching Catholicism, they could kill me for smuggling books and befriending priests. I was a traitor a dozen times over, perhaps more. My father had tried to buy his life by turning his back on his beliefs, though, and he had died anyway.

"I do not wish to die," I said softly, "but someday I will, and I want to know I lived following my conscience and left Wales a little better for it."

"You think one person can actually change anything?" he mumbled.

"Maybe there's not much I can do, but when I see injustices all around me, it . . . it burns me. I cannot sit still, I cannot stay quiet. I do not have your"—I almost said "cowardly complacency," but swallowed it back—"your calm certainty that all around me is as it should be."

"Do I seem certain?" He turned his disfigurement from me again, so I could see only the profile of his troubled face. It shook me, to see him so unsure. He seemed younger, almost vulnerable. I thought of him left to manage this huge estate alone. He would have to make decisions all the time and act certain of them, because he had no one else to turn to. I reached, thinking to touch his hand, but he stood.

As soon as he left the bench, it was as though a spell had broken. His expression was cool again as he helped me to my feet. He dropped my hand. "Thank you, Mistress Pryce. It was an interesting conversation."

"You ought to come to Plas Lloyd to visit. You know you would be welcome there."

"Would I?"

"Aye. I think Alice, especially, would appreciate the visits."

"You think that?" He scowled and turned away.

"We all would," I said quickly.

"I had best ride back with you, at least. 'Twas unwise of you to come this far alone."

I did not mind the company, but I was tired of being told that everything was too dangerous for me. "Are the roads really so wild between here and Plas Lloyd?"

"Perhaps not, but you ought to take care, Mistress Pryce. I do not think you consider your safety as you should."

With that statement, full of dangerous undercurrents, he ordered the horses brought around. We rode back within view of Plas Lloyd without a word other than farewell.

Chapter Nine

Mistress Lloyd proposed another trip to Conwy later that week. As soon as I could escape the house, I rode to the little cave. I settled on the hard ground and pored over the marvelous words again, forgetting the chill seeping into my fingers. How long until they had the rest printed? Then they would bind it, and we would have real books.

I slipped the papers into secret pockets I had sewn into my cloak's lining and remounted, cantering to Plas Lloyd, light and warm despite the autumn chill. I bounded into the great hall, stopping short at the sight of Nicholas. He sat stiffly next to Alice, whose gaze focused on her needlework.

"Oh, forgive me," I said. "I did not mean to intrude."

"You're not intruding," Alice said quickly. "Come, sit and visit Master Bowen with me."

The only stool available placed me between Nicholas and Alice. I should have stayed longer in my secret world at the cave. I pulled my cloak close to keep the papers hidden as I settled between them. Nicholas had seated himself so his scars were not visible. I thought I saw just a trace of the Nicholas I used to know in his expression, so I pressed the chance to draw him into conversation.

"Master Bowen, how is the harvest from your trees?"

Alice gave me a strange look, and Nicholas blinked. Had he thought I would not remember?

He cleared his throat. "'Tis good this year. I'm hoping to have enough cider for the winter, and I plan to make wine from the grapes, though it will only be enough for a small batch."

I smiled. "At least it will be Welsh."

He returned my grin. "Aye, that it will, though 'twill not be as good as the French or Spanish, so I'll not put the smugglers out of business."

"Just as well," I said. "Smuggling seems to be as much a part of the economy as sheep and oats."

He raised an eyebrow. "Indeed, 'tis a national sport, and it does as much as archery to keep us fit, would you not agree?"

My eyes widened. Was he actually teasing me about my hat chase? Not wanting to press my luck, I turned the conversation to safer topics. Alice contributed an occasional thought about the weather and neighborhood gossip. After half an hour, Nicholas rose and bid us farewell.

Once the echo of his horses' hooves died away, I turned to Alice. There seemed no better time to bring up the subject of her and Nicholas.

"I truly am sorry to have interrupted."

She looked up from her neat little stitches, blinking owlishly. "Interrupted? You mean Master Bowen's visit? Good heavens, I was grateful you showed up."

"You were?"

"The man hardly says a word. At least you know how to coax some conversation out of him."

What an alarmingly awkward love affair. "You enjoy his company, though?"

"I suppose. I could just as well do without it."

"Yet he brings you flowers. He comes to see you."

She looked at me as though seeing me for the first time. "Oh, that?" She laughed sadly. "Is that what you thought?"

The rare smile faded, and she lowered her needle. "He brings me flowers on the anniversary of . . . when the plague came. He seems to think it his duty. His sister, Margery, was my best friend. I still miss her every day, and I'm certain he misses all of them. And then there was John . . ."

Her eyes turned distant, illuminated by a memory of happiness. I'd guessed the wrong brother! Did Nicholas know?

Alice resumed her needlework. "Honestly, John and Master Nicholas looked enough alike, before . . . 'tis painful to see his face, like some grisly specter of John coming to haunt me. It must be hard for you too." She glanced at me. "I'm sorry. I should not say such things."

"'Tis no matter," I said and buried myself in my own needlework. Nicholas, a grisly specter? I had thought the same thing myself, but I was becoming used to his scars. "Does he visit often?"

"Not usually. He's too wrapped up in Nant Bach. Everyone knows Nicholas Bowen only cares for his own affairs."

Aye, that sounded like him, hiding from everything by getting lost in his work. He had enough to hide from, though; I could not blame him.

The Lloyd household prepared for our trip to Conwy. This time, I had to deliver my smuggled pages to a house on the outskirts of the town. When we entered the gates, my mind was lost in planning. There was no excuse that would let me wander so far by myself. I would simply have to pretend to be lost. The Lloyds would think me a goose-brained girl, but there was no help for it. I dropped back from Mistress Lloyd and ducked down a side street.

I moved through the narrow streets, lifting my skirts to avoid the refuse dumped in the gutters. Beggars huddled by the side of the road with flies buzzing around their hollow faces. Some were too starved to sit up, but lay by the road and waited to die. Nicholas's words haunted me. *You think one person can actually change anything?*

My steps faltered. It was possible these beggars would be heaped in a grisly death cart soon, but it would not happen while I had power to act. I hurried back to a woman with a basket of meat pasties rich with the scents of onion and sage and bought all I could afford, dividing them between the beggars and hurrying on my way.

As the shops gave way to houses, I heard less Welsh in the mix of voices. I paused amidst the bustle of people. This did not seem right. Why would an English merchant want Welsh writings? Of course, some Englishmen were Catholic too, and might know enough Welsh to read it. Smuggling made for strange bedfellows. Still, as I stood there in the English enclave, I felt a stranger in my own land. Someday, would there be nothing but English spoken here, so the Welsh were just ghosts of the glory days of ancient Britain? Nay, that was why the papers mattered. We were still here.

A stranger studied me from beneath a brimmed hat. I thought of Nicholas for a moment, forever hiding his face, but this man was shorter, and his hat had the remnants of a broken scarlet feather. My hands turned clammy. The red plume again. Was it a coincidence?

I forced myself to keep walking, trying to appear casual. That would not do, though. Shoppers did not wander aimlessly through these streets of homes. I needed a purpose, or to better feign being lost. I stopped to tighten my bootlaces and glanced back. The man in the hat strolled along the street, his eyes never resting on me. That in itself was odd. Other people glared at me for blocking their way.

My cloak was heavy with illegal documents, and I could not deliver them with him watching. I could see no easier way out of the problem than confronting it directly. I straightened and walked up to the stranger.

"Excuse me," I said in English. "Can you direct me to the home of Mistress Tucker?"

"*Dydw i ddim yn siarad Saesneg,*" he protested. He did not speak English, or so he claimed. Unlikely for someone dressed so well. Pigeon-brained liar.

He hustled around the corner, not looking back. I wandered on, pretending to look for the fictional Mistress Tucker. Finally, I came to my destination. No sign of Master Red-Plume, but I could not take any chances. I sat heavily on the stoop and rested my head in my hands. There was a basket for laundry where I was to leave my papers. I could stuff my whole cloak in, but then I would have to explain what became of it.

Instead, I pulled it closer around me and carefully slipped the pages out of their hiding places. I rolled them into a tube and clutched it under my cloak. Still no sign of the broken red plume.

Best to do it quickly. I pushed the papers under the woven lid, stuffing them into the jumble of dirty smocks and linens. Hopefully none of the pages were stained now.

With that, I stood and stretched, then ambled my way back down the street, still pretending to be lost. When I reached the market, I joined a crowd watching a puppet show. I laughed along as the puppet washerwoman beat a little English knight with her laundry paddle, but kept my eyes on the crowd. Still no Master Red-Plume, though the Lloyds marched up the street, obviously upset.

"Joan!" Mistress Lloyd pointed to the puppet show in exasperation. "Is this where you have been?"

"Of course." It was only a partial lie. "I was enjoying the show."

Mistress Lloyd shook her head, giving me an odd look. Alice scowled at me. The Lloyds were no fools. If they were suspicious, others might be as well. Yet how else was I to fight for Wales and my faith? I could not stop now.

As I followed the Lloyds toward the town gates, I once again spotted Master Red-Plume. I ducked my head, but he was busy in whispered conversation with a squint-eyed little man. They walked together down a lane toward the town churchyard. This was my chance to learn more about the man who hounded me. Mistress Lloyd had paused to buy candles. I slipped down the side lane after the two men, hanging far back in the shadows.

They stood together in the shelter of the church's arched doorway. I darted forward to huddle behind a large tombstone, hoping to catch some hint of their conversation, but their voices were too low. The squint-eyed man nodded, and Master Red-Plume handed him a heavy-looking coin pouch. They hurried their separate ways. Mulling over the meaning of what I'd seen, I rushed back up the lane to find Mistress Lloyd searching for me. She gave me a dangerous look and took my arm to guide me back to the ferry.

That night, I sat by the window and brushed out my long curls. I watched the dark sky and tried to guess where the papers were going now. Who else was part of this invisible chain, moving documents, dodging Master Red-Plume and his ilk? Who else was trying to break it? Somewhere in Wales was the heart of our network, the plates of the printing press beating together day after day to produce a flow of papers. It could not be terribly far away. I wondered if Hugh was working there now. There were so many secrets hidden in the darkness, I supposed only God and the stars above saw them all.

Chapter Ten

A rap sounded on the front door, and I straightened from my work with a sigh of relief. Alice and I were readying the loom in the great hall for Mistress Lloyd. With autumn fast wearing on, she kept us in a constant flurry of preparation for the long winter days ahead. My back ached from leaning over to pass the long warp yarns through their tiny slots, like threading a hundred needles. Our only respite came when a visitor interrupted—occasionally Nicholas but more often the Rhyses. The steward opened the door, and Mistress Rhys fluttered into the room, waving her feathered fan. Her brother trailed in with a polite nod. The smile froze on my face when Mistress Meredith appeared behind them.

"*Mais non!* You underestimate the risk, Master Rhys," Mistress Meredith said. "The Papists conspire with the Spanish. They will murder us all in our beds."

I dug my fingers into the soft ball of yarn in my hand. I had no intention of murdering the goose-brained girl, but I wanted to shove the yarn into her mouth.

"Your imagination runs wild, Mistress Meredith," Master Rhys said. "The worst we have to fear from them is their backwardness. They are ignorant, superstitious folk and deserve our pity."

Master Rhys droned on about the defense of the Welsh coast and the recent arrests of Catholics, while Mistress Meredith interrupted with bitter, mocking complaints against us: idolaters,

devil-worshippers, heretics, hypocrites, lazy, lying, deceitful, unfaithful, whore of Babylon. I flinched inwardly at each word striking,
striking, striking until I felt battered and raw, as faceless, helpless,
and inhuman as the broken statues of my saints.

My whole body trembled. I carefully set my yarn aside and
escaped to the sweet freedom of the garden. The breeze greeted me
with the musty scent of autumn leaves and fluttered through Hugh's
tokens in the tree, reminders of recent trips to deliver more papers,
though the victories felt hollow now. I closed my eyes, willing the
hurt to fade, but unable to stop the echoes of the others' crushing
words.

"Mistress Pryce!"

I gave a start, tensed to see another enemy striding toward me,
but it was Hugh waiting by one of the turf benches. His travel-
worn clothes hung loosely, and his unkempt hair and beard needed
trimming, but his eyes brightened when he stood to meet me. The
sight of a friendly face brought me to myself like a lure calling a lost
falcon. I was not what they said. I could stretch my wings again. I
could strike back.

"Good morrow, Master Richards." I managed a smile and hurried over to him. "What are you doing in the garden?"

"Praying you would come outside."

His kiss of greeting lingered a little longer than necessary. "I left
new pages for you in the cave, along with the directions for delivering them, and I have a surprise for you. Come!"

He led me past the gardens and into a grove of weather-weary
trees just beyond the rise of a hill. There, a short, thin gentleman
with a clean-shaven face sat staring at the ground as though deep in
thought. He had the sharp look of a winter-starved fox. When Hugh
and I rustled through the freshly fallen leaves, the stranger jumped
to his feet.

His eyes burned with an inner vivacity that reminded me of
Father Davies, yet where Father Davies's expression was usually
warm, this man's was shrewd.

"Mistress Pryce," Hugh said, "may I introduce Father Robert
Perkins."

Another priest. Where was Father Davies? I curtseyed. "Father Perkins, 'tis an honor."

"I understand you are helping in our holy cause."

I drew back at his abruptness and glanced at Hugh, who nodded his reassurance. I could only trust Hugh that we were safe.

"I am."

"That is good." Father Perkins nodded. "Too many people are sliding from the old faith. They are unfaithful, hypocritical. We need to bring them back, liberate their minds and hearts before we free them bodily from the grasp of that heretical so-called queen."

I glanced toward the house, where Alice still sat with our Protestant neighbors. "Perhaps it would be better to whisper, sir."

"I will not be silenced by the fear of man," Father Perkins said.

Hugh cleared his throat. "We were going to visit Nicholas Bowen for dinner, and we hoped you would accompany us, Mistress Pryce."

"I was not invited."

A grin cut across Father Perkins's thin face. "Neither were we, but when times are difficult, we cannot afford to be meek."

"Perhaps Master Nicholas will provide us shelter for the night," Hugh said softly, "or at the least a decent meal before we start on our way again." There was a lean urgency in his look as he glanced over his shoulder.

"You're always on the move?" I asked.

"Aye," Father Perkins cut in. "Busy about the Lord's work, so he provides for us."

"Sometimes I wish he provided a little better." Hugh chuckled.

"It is an honor to suffer for the Lord." Father Perkins shot Hugh a harsh look. He did not seem at all like Father Davies, who suffered without boasting of it, who would accept martyrdom but did not seek it.

Hugh sighed. "I know, but I lack your self-sacrificing nature. There's a reason I'm no priest." He glanced at me. "Maybe more than one reason."

I almost scolded him for talking so in front of a priest. Father Perkins frowned but said nothing else.

I turned back to Hugh. "Why not ask Master Lloyd? He's your friend."

Hugh's mouth twitched. "He's known to be such, and a Catholic sympathizer. Many unfriendly eyes are watching for a man matching Father Perkins's description. The more we can do to keep up appearances as gentlemen, the safer he'll be. If you accompany us, he'll seem less like a priest."

Safer for him, more dangerous to me. I did not mind. I could always feign ignorance. Nicholas, though, would be in peril if he were caught harboring guests such as these. I hesitated.

In a lower tone meant just for me, Hugh added, "The noose gets closer around us all the time, and things have not been easy. Apparently the Lord is granting Father Perkins his desire for suffering."

There was something pinched in Hugh's expression, a weariness beneath his smiles. All they wanted was a brief moment of shelter, a respite from the storm of hatred and persecution—nothing most Welsh gentlemen would deny any traveler, and Nant Bach was a place of peace. If Nicholas did not know Father Perkins was a priest, there could be no harm in him offering a meal. "Let's go, then. You must be hungry, and 'tis almost dinner time. Where do you travel from here?"

"I do not know." Hugh rubbed his forehead, and his shoulders slumped. "The Lord will provide, if Father Perkins is correct."

"Then listen. I own a piece of property to the south that once belonged to an abbey. I know little about it, except 'tis uninhabited. You might be safe there."

Hugh exchanged a look with Father Perkins. "Aye, that might suit us. Do you know how far?"

"A day's ride, I believe. Can you walk a little farther?"

"We must, so we can," Hugh said.

I squeezed Hugh's arm and rushed to tell Mistress Lloyd I was walking the grounds and might miss dinner. She made no objections, so we made the journey past harvested fields to Nicholas's home.

Hugh walked beside me, swinging a stick at a few stray heads of overripe grain. "'Tis a hard time to be a Catholic, but there are great things afoot. Things I have long dreamed of . . ." He chewed his lip as if restraining the impulse to tell me more. I stepped closer, hoping to encourage him.

Father Perkins glared at Hugh and drew me aside. "I understand Father Davies has spoken to you about going abroad?"

"Oh, aye, he has."

"I think for a woman with your willingness to serve God, that would be a fine choice. Taking orders is the purest way to live one's life, in full devotion to God."

"I was intrigued by Father Davies's mention of going to Italy, but, as I told him, I'm not certain taking orders is my calling."

"Think, Mistress Pryce, of devoting your whole self to God. As a woman, especially, that is the best course open to you in life."

"Perhaps," I said slowly, "yet family life appeals to me. Having my own husband, children, household." I carefully avoided looking at Hugh, though I could feel his gaze on me.

"Too many things to distract you from your higher purpose."

"At my father's *plasty*, I was always busy helping others, tending to the sick and the poor."

"Things you can do just as well in God's service. As a wife, you would always be under your husband's rule as well as God's. As a nun, you would be under God's alone. Your desires for a household—for worldly possessions and pleasures—are distracting your heart. You must learn to govern it."

I said nothing more, troubled by his words. Were my desires self-ish? I had seen enough people unhappy in marriage to understand the appeal of having no husband to answer to, but I had also known my parents to be happier, more patient and thoughtful, when they were with each other. Was it weakness to long for someone to share your life with, or was it strength to love enough to do so? I had no answers by the time we reached Nicholas's home.

"Master Bowen!" Hugh called as he crossed the threshold. "We've come to test your *bonheddwr* hospitality and see if you'll provide dinner for a group of vagabonds."

Nicholas did not glance up from his papers. "Vagabonds, nay, though worthy beggars may ask for scraps at the back door."

"Hah! But you'll not ask Mistress Pryce to go begging."

Nicholas's gaze fixed on me. "That would not do. Of course you're welcome."

Hugh introduced Father Perkins simply as Robert Perkins, but Nicholas studied him suspiciously. We settled down to a meager dinner of smoked venison, eel, and bread. I pitied Nicholas's servants and poorer tenants with only the remnants of a solitary bachelor's meals to look forward to. My father had made every meal generous, knowing the extras would never go to waste.

Hugh ate with relish. Even Father Perkins smiled, apparently finding some happiness in the worldly pleasure of a warm meal. I hid my smirk behind my goblet.

"There is nothing like Welsh hospitality," Father Perkins said. "You manage all this without a wife?"

I stared at the slice of eel on my plate, willing myself not to blush. Nicholas's knife paused. "As you see."

"That is the best state for a man or woman." Father Perkins gave me a sidelong glance. "Especially for a woman. It is only through strict obedience to God that they can be saved."

I poked at the eel. Perhaps I was obstinate, but I could not endure being lectured in this roundabout way. If God wanted me for a cloistered life, He would have to find a less obnoxious way to tell me.

Nicholas raised an eyebrow. "Could not the same be said of men? We also must be obedient."

"Of course, but women, if you recall, were the downfall of every great man in the Bible: Adam, Samson, David."

Nicholas placed his knife and spoon on the table and leaned back. "I would say those men were their own downfall. If David had gone where his duty called, he would never have sinned. Bathsheba's only crime was taking a bath."

"That's right!" Hugh banged the table with the handle of his knife. "Men ought to take control of their own destinies and stop blaming their mistakes on others. I would say Bathsheba's only crime was not knowing when to say nay to her king. Maybe we ought to encourage women to speak their minds more."

I gave him a startled look and smiled.

"Chaos and confusion," Father Perkins muttered. "The only way for there to be peace is for everyone to know his or her place. When the natural order is out of alignment, nothing else will be right in the world. Look at the poor harvests the past few years."

Nicholas studied him thoughtfully. "That may be true, but I'm not certain 'tis my place to declare the natural order of things. It seems like pride for a man to decide he knows the mind of God, and fighting for false causes only adds more wrongs to the world. It never rights anything."

"You once thought there were some things worth fighting for." Hugh leaned forward, tightening his grip on his knife. "Do you not still?"

Nicholas shrugged. "I would fight to protect my home, were it in danger."

As Alice said, his only concern was for Nant Bach. I wondered, though, what he had once thought a worthy cause.

"So you would pick up your sword against an army of bandits come to despoil your lands?" Hugh pressed on.

"Of course. 'Twould be my responsibility."

"What of the threats that may not be so obvious? If you let wrongs exist in the world, 'tis not only cowardly, it also invites them to your doorstep."

I blanched at his indirect accusation of cowardice, but Hugh was right; there were things we had to fight for.

"A man could go mad, trying to fight every wrong he sees in the world." Nicholas passed his hand over his eyes and shook his head. "The best we can do is manage our own affairs uprightly and hope others will do the same."

"You know that is foolishness," Hugh whispered fiercely.

Nicholas pressed his lips together and stared down at his plate. I wished they would leave him in peace. He might be afraid to fight, but he was not a bad person.

Father Perkins pressed his advantage. "I understand you have no family, Master Bowen."

Nicholas's hands froze in the process of tearing off a chunk of bread. I looked away from the pain on his face. Even Hugh scowled at Father Perkins.

"My immediate family is deceased. I do have some more distant relatives. My father's younger brother is my heir."

"Why do you think God spared you alone of everyone in your family?"

Nicholas speared a piece of venison with his dagger. "I have my own guesses about that, but I imagine you'll suggest something different."

"God has given you this opportunity to serve Him."

"We agree thus far, and I do that in the best way I know."

"I can show you a better way. God needs those who would serve Him to give their full devotion now. The Queen is in a precarious position, and if we push our advantage—"

"Stop," Nicholas said, his face as still and hard as a mask. "The kind of help you're asking I cannot—I will not—offer. You may eat my food, enjoy the warmth of my hearth, but my hospitality does not extend to allowing treason to be spoken under my roof."

"A man in your situation, with nothing to lose—"

"That's enough," Nicholas said, and the deep, cold anger in his eyes chilled me. It knocked Father Perkins into stony silence, and we finished our meal without another word. When Hugh finished eating, he stood. Father Perkins and I followed his lead.

"Master Bowen, thank you for your hospitality." Hugh's voice was sincere. "We'll not intrude any longer. I apologize for . . . any inconvenience."

Nicholas met his gaze, and something seemed to pass between them. Nicholas gave a quick nod, and his shoulders relaxed. He gave no word of farewell to Father Perkins, but leaned back in his chair with his arms folded as the two men shuffled through the rushes toward the door.

I hesitated. What must Nicholas think of me for being involved in such a spectacle? I paused by his side, and he acknowledged me with a flick of his gaze.

"I'm sorry," I whispered. "When they invited me to come, I did not know that they . . ." What could I say? I did not know they planned to insult him, bully him, make him look a coward? If I was a falcon, I was one kept hooded, perhaps a little blind after all. Unable to find words for an apology, I touched Nicholas's arm briefly. He tensed and glanced at my fingers, his expression unreadable. I pulled my hand back and hurried after the others.

Chapter Eleven

A bang jolted me from a deep sleep. I peeked through the bed curtains. The embers in the fireplace cast a flickering red glow over the tapestry of the bleeding pelican. Male voices shouted downstairs, and footsteps pounded in the hallway. I scrambled for my dressing gown and dagger.

Master Lloyd's voice rose above the clamor below, summoning Alice and me. I swallowed and set the dagger aside. He would not call us into danger. I hurried into the hall, nearly colliding with Alice. Grasping hands, we crossed the dark gallery and huddled at the top of the stairs. Master Lloyd's indistinct shouts filled the rafters, echoing over the sounds of smashing wood. Alice's face was pale and her eyes wide.

A man with a rapier appeared at the bottom of the stairs. We screamed and clutched each other. Alice half-swooned in my arms.

"What do you want?" I demanded, pulling myself up as straight as possible with Alice hanging on my shoulder.

"We're searching this house," the man said. "Everyone down to the great hall."

"In naught but our dressing gowns?"

"If you try to go back to your rooms, we'll arrest you for treason."

The blood drained from my face. Had I misstepped? Had someone betrayed me? Hugh and Father Perkins might have been captured and broken under torture. I could be next. I rubbed my throat.

Holy Mary, David, and Winifred, thank you that the documents are safe in the cave!

All except the one hidden in my trunk.

There was no going back. I lifted my head and half-dragged Alice down the stairs, where Master and Mistress Lloyd stood. His face was as red as the coals glowing in the hearth, hers bleached pale as she clung to his arm. The servants huddled on the benches, whispering to each other and watching their master with various degrees of fear, concern, and curiosity.

The invaders ripped down tapestries and overturned benches, examining the walls and thumping the floor for hollow spots. Mistress Lloyd covered her face, and I squeezed my eyes shut, jumping at each new crash. The men tromped upstairs, rapiers drawn. Shouts and smashing echoed from above. I clenched my fists to keep from crossing myself.

Mary, David, and Winifred, please do not let them find the hidden compartment.

"Why is this happening?" Alice whispered to her father.

Master Lloyd's eyes narrowed. "Perhaps I was too lax in attending services, or they found out about my . . . investments." His glance darted to me for a moment. "Ah, it may also be that we have been too friendly with the wrong people."

My stomach turned. Did he know what I was doing? What Hugh was doing? Exhaustion and fear throbbed behind my eyes. I swallowed and straightened my shoulders. If this was my moment of reckoning, I would face it bravely. No one would pay for it but myself. I could not deny my involvement if they found the false bottom in my trunk, but I would make certain the Lloyds stayed untainted, and Hugh too, if he was not already captured.

Finally, the queen's priest hunters paraded back down the stairs.

"You're fortunate, Master Lloyd," said the man in charge. "You never can tell whom to trust, though. There are dangerous outlaws at large. To be certain that you stay safe, we are going to leave one of our men with your servants."

I exhaled quietly and wrapped my arms around myself.

Master Lloyd's face reddened again, but he gave a curt nod. "I'll put the extra pair of hands to work repairing the damage you have done."

The man laughed humorlessly and motioned the others out.

As they passed, one man mumbled, "You know what Master Bowen said."

"Aye, this is not over," another whispered.

Nicholas! My stomach clenched as though I had been struck. Could he be so cruel? It would be the blackest betrayal to turn a friend over to the queen's agents, but Nicholas hid behind the cloak of the law, and Father Perkins had upset him. My heart wrenched. Were I a man, I would have ridden to his estate immediately to challenge him.

The men rode off by torchlight, leaving one of their number behind. Had he any sense, he might have feared that Master Lloyd would tear a sword from the wall and murder him on the spot, but the simpering clotpole just smirked, secure in his knowledge of the queen's protection. Master Lloyd had no desire to join Hugh and Father Perkins as an outlaw.

Master Lloyd ordered us back to bed. I lit a candle in my room and trembled when I saw my precious trunk on the floor with the lid smashed off. I choked back a sob. The secret bottom held. My mother's jewelry, though, had been scattered among the sweet herbs on the floor by the queen's men. *Putrid knaves. Goat-faced blackguards.*

With my eyes stinging, I knelt to gather the necklaces and rings, counting each one until I had them safe again. Warm tears dripped on my hands. I had come so close to losing my precious connection to my mother. At least the men had been honest, in a terrible way. I placed the jewelry back in the broken box.

The chests holding my clothing sat open, bodices and skirts strewn about, and the pelican tapestry lay on the floor, a rend severing the image of the wounded bird. Then there were Nicholas's letters. I snatched them off the floor, tore a few in half, and balled one to toss into the flickering blaze. A glance at the childish handwriting stilled my throw. There was no point, really, in clinging to the notes, but I could not quite bring myself to destroy them, not until I knew for certain Nicholas was guilty.

The soldiers had slit my mattress—*thank you David and Winifred for the cave!*—but I sat heavily on my bed. Feathers drifted around me. I had no way of knowing if Hugh and Father Perkins were safe, but Nicholas did not know where they were going, so they might have escaped. Fresh tears rolled down my cheeks. How could he be so wicked? If Hugh were captured, tortured to death, I could not let such treachery stand. I could not trust that Nicholas would not hurt us again.

A shiver raised the hairs on my neck. I had the ability to stop him.

I might not be able to fight him with a sword, but if I hid some of Hugh's documents at Nant Bach and warned the priest hunters about them, Nicholas would look like the traitor. It might even clear Hugh of suspicion. I was just a woman, but I was steeped in danger now, and I could find my revenge as well as any man. Perhaps better, because dishonor hurt a gentleman more than a thrust with dagger or rapier, and it was a weapon a woman could wield as well as a man.

I glanced at the balled up letter in my hand, the scrawled words *Your friend, Nicholas* black against the yellowed paper. My fingers relaxed. I would not act until I knew for certain.

Sleep eluded me, with anger burning hot in my heart. I tossed and turned, and morning found me with puffy eyes, a headache, and many unanswered questions.

I had to make sure the papers stayed safe. With the queen's guard watching our every movement, though, I hardly dared even look in the direction of the cave. I tried to repair the torn pelican tapestry, but my needlework was full of uneven stitches, and the image would not line up correctly. The thread I spun came out too lumpy to be good for anything but teasing the cats. I kept up pretenses enough to avoid suspicion—in fact, the guard hardly even glanced at me—but as often as I could, I wandered to the garden.

Hugh's cloth strips still waved from the tree. Thankfully, the guard thought nothing of it. I could always explain it as a message from a suitor, and it would not be entirely false, but Master Lloyd would be furious, and I did not want to draw attention to Hugh if they were still searching for him.

The only visitors who dared brave our company those first couple of days were the Rhyses. No sign of Mistress Meredith—proof some good could come even from a dreadful event—but also none of Hugh. The wind blew, whispering of winter's approach, and I hoped, wherever he was, he was safe and warm.

Chapter Twelve

The queen's agent left Plas Lloyd after a few days, though everyone still spoke in whispers and checked over their shoulders. I slipped out to the stables to find my mare, wrapping my arms around her warm neck and burying my face in her hay-scented mane. My back prickled as though we were being watched.

"I'm sorry it's been so long, girl," I whispered. "I need you to fly for me today. Make certain we are not followed."

The stable boy saddled her and helped me up, and I gave her free rein. She tossed her head and ran, her breath trailing in white streams behind us. I ducked my head into the crisp wind. Even through my soft leather gloves, my fingers stiffened with cold. I glanced back often but saw no one.

When we neared the edge of Master Lloyd's property, I reined in and guided my mare toward the cave. I slipped out of the saddle and tied her near some fresh grass and then wandered casually in the direction of the rocks. The woods were quiet except for the calls of sparrows, and nothing moved as I watched the trees. I hiked amidst the rocks, stopping from time to time to check for pursuit.

The documents were not safe with the queen's men crawling over the countryside like lice. The thought of burning the papers made me ill, but at least I could bury them better, make certain no one would find them until Hugh returned. I could not deliver them safely with unknown enemies lurking in the shadows. Had

I lost all my value to the cause? My chest tightened, and I walked faster.

The cave came into view ahead. Ashes blackened the ground near the entrance. Bandits! Or the queen's men. Perhaps Hugh had come back to destroy the evidence himself.

I turned to sneak away, and my boots crunched on the rocky ground.

A girl's voice called, "Gwilliam?"

Chills raced up my spine. Bandits sometimes kept girls, forcing them to beg and worse. I could not leave her at their mercy.

"Hello?" I called.

No response. Did she not want to be found, or was she too frightened to call for help? I crept up to the cave entrance and peered inside.

The girl huddled against the cold stone wall, eyes wide in her skeletal face. Her wrists and arms, hardly more than pale skin over bones, stuck out from her tattered, too-short chemise. She could not have been older than eleven or twelve, barely more than a child. I choked back a gag.

Please, Mary and Winifred, do not let her belong to the bandits.

Next to her sat a younger child, perhaps seven or eight, as emaciated as herself. I could not tell if the child was male or female, with its hair cut raggedly and its figure buried beneath a threadbare cloak. The small child rocked back and forth, staring at nothing.

"Hello?" I asked softly, not wanting to startle them.

The rocking child did not acknowledge me, but the older girl shrank back, her gaze darting to the ground.

"Do you need help?" The girl would not look at me. I lowered my voice. "Are you hungry?"

She glanced at me with her wide, pale eyes. "Gwilliam will be back soon."

I clenched my fists. I would not let some bandit harm innocent children. I might kill him myself. "We can get away before he comes back."

She shook her head violently. "I cannot leave without him."

"What's this?" A voice echoed off the rocks, but it did not belong to a grown man.

I spun and found myself face to face with a boy holding a dagger at my chest. He was older than the girl by a couple of years, perhaps—almost as tall as me. His limbs were awkwardly proportioned to his thin body, and no hint of a beard stubbled his chin. He looked more beggar than bandit, though his clothes had once been fine. Still, he had a dagger and a wild gleam in his bright brown eyes.

"Are you Gwilliam?" I asked, my voice shaking a little.

"What is it to you?"

"You look hungry. I want to help."

His jaw tightened. "We need no help from you."

The wind moaned through the cave, a bitter chill in its touch.

"Winter will be here soon. 'Twill be cold, and the harvest has been bad. What will you do?"

His desperate gaze flicked to the other children. He cared about them. Good. I could use that to help. There might be little I could do for my faith or my country with the queen's men on my trail, but I would not let children starve.

"We'll take care of ourselves, and that's it," he said.

"Are you their brother?"

His eyes narrowed, but he shook his head.

"How long have you been watching out for them?"

"Since the summer."

"You have done well, then," I said, pressing my hands against the cold rocks at my back. He still held the dagger poised at my chest. "But what will happen when winter comes? They look so thin."

He pressed his lips together. "We'll just keep moving."

"Where are you trying to go?"

"That's not for you to mind!"

"Can you get there before snow sets in? The mountains are monstrously cold in the winter."

The point of his dagger wavered, and he shook his head.

"Let me help you." An idea blossomed through my fear. "I know a place you can stay."

"What do you mean?"

I hesitated. The deserted cottage sat on Nicholas's estate, and if he was heartless enough to betray his friends, he might also turn ragged children out into the cold. Even if he was innocent of the incident with the queen's men, he was not known for his generosity. This would cost him nothing, though, and he said he rarely visited the outskirts of his property. He need not know about it, and perhaps his unwitting charity would benefit his sluggardly soul.

"There's a cottage near here, and 'tis empty this winter. If you maintain it, bandits will not trouble you, and the owner will pay it no heed until winter's over."

"Why would you help us?" Gwilliam asked.

I held out my hands. "I do not want to see anyone starve, and I know what could happen . . . " I glanced at the girl.

He sheathed his dagger, his shoulders slumping in defeat. "Very well."

I was taking on another secret. Would I ever untangle myself from them? I led the children to Nicholas's deserted cottage and pushed the door open. It was no more than one long room, probably scarcely warmed by the central hearth whose smoke would trickle out the hole in the roof. The walls were bare stone, and the floor covered with dirty boards. Gwilliam looked in with an approving nod.

He beckoned to the girl. "Have a look, Hannah. It seems cozy."

Hannah took the smaller child's hand. "Come along, Beth," she whispered. Beth followed mutely.

They wandered around their new refuge, their eyes brightening. My smile faded as I studied them. Their clothes were probably more vermin than threads. They itched and scratched, and my skin crawled in sympathy. There were wild oats in the field they could gather, but they would need more to eat, and clean clothes. A comb for the lice. The fleas, there was no helping. The smaller girl, Beth, shivered, her cheeks bitten red by the cold. For now, at least I could build them a fire. I would not see those little hands hanging over the edge of a death cart.

The next morning, I asked for a large breakfast brought to my room. I pulled some old skirts and bodices out of my trunks and spread them on my newly repaired mattress. The brown silk damask would look pretty on Hannah when cut down to fit her, but it was not very warm. I trailed my fingers over the green wool of the last gown given to me by my mother. A lump rose in my throat, but I shook my head. The gown no longer fit, and Mother was always giving; she would want me to share it.

I wrapped up my breakfast—bread, gooseberry preserves, and eggs cooked with sugar and butter—and placed it gently in a basket atop the old clothing. Gwilliam would be more difficult. There was simply no way I could ask for boy's clothes. Master Lloyd would not invite beggars on his lands, and Nicholas might be my enemy. Gwilliam was in the most danger, too, for he was nearly of an age where vagabonds were whipped and had their ears slit in punishment for their poverty and homelessness.

I took a deep breath. One problem at a time. I hung the basket over my arm and trotted downstairs. A few servants gave me odd looks.

"I wanted to eat in the gardens," I explained as I hurried outside.

They watched me as though I had announced I wanted to fly to Ireland. I would need to find better excuses, or at least be more subtle. Something rustled in the garden hedge. I paused to watch, then strolled on, taking a circuitous route to the cottage. The path dipped under the canopy of trees, their branches blocking the weak warmth of the sun. I pulled my cloak closer. Leaves crunched behind me. My hair rose on end, and I turned.

A shadowed figure stood on the trail, watching me from beneath a hood. I gasped and stumbled back. He took a step forward, and I fumbled for my little knife. This could not be real. My hand, the man's footsteps—everything moved so slowly.

"Ho there, sister!" Gwilliam burst out of the trees beside me, panting. "Father is looking for you!"

I stared at him. His smile was tight, and his hand rested on his dagger. I glanced back. The cloaked figure was gone.

I sagged against a tree trunk. My whole body shook.

"Are you unharmed?" Gwilliam asked, his voice cracking.

I nodded. "Thanks to you. What were you doing out here?"

With a guilty look, he pulled a skinned rabbit from the bushes.

"Poaching!" I hissed. "They'll throw you in prison, maybe even hang you! You're in enough danger as it is."

"Only if I get caught. We have to eat."

The basket hung heavily on my arm. Giving up my breakfast would not be enough to feed three hungry children. "We'll find another way." I glanced back where the figure had disappeared. "We need to be careful, though."

Gwilliam scuffed his worn boot through the leaves. "Was that man looking for me?"

I blinked in surprise. Bandit or queen's agent, it was me the man had followed. "I do not think so. Why would he?"

He sighed. "After my mother died, I went to live at the estate of . . . our friends. One morning several months ago, I woke to find that everyone from the main house had vanished in the night. Men with swords came after me, shouting in English—something about Catholic fugitives—so I ran, along with Hannah and Beth. We've been hiding ever since."

A chill raced down my arms. I looked around and dropped my voice, beckoning Gwilliam to walk with me. "You mean you were at a *plasty,* like Plas Lloyd up on the hill?"

"Bigger. They were going to help me find my father and brothers."

"Were these people perhaps the Pughs of Plas Penrhyn?"

He looked at me sharply. "Do you know them?"

"I know some of their friends." I could well imagine Father Davies helping these children. It must have broken his heart to flee. How many other people had been depending on the Pughs and their household, now fending for themselves in whatever way they could? They were like me: orphans, cast aside, refugees in their own country. Perhaps I could finish Father Davies's work.

"Where is your family? I might be able to help you find them."

Gwilliam pushed his unkempt hair out of his face and looked away.

"You can trust me, Gwilliam." I remembered what Hugh said, about putting his life in my hands as an act of faith. The queen's agents might be cruel enough to use children like these as spies, but I believed Gwilliam. I had to take the risk. "I'm friends with Father Davies. If he's not in prison, I might be able to help you find him."

"'Tis Father Perkins we need," he said.

I kept my opinions of Father Perkins to myself. "I know him too."

He gave me a wary glance. "My father escaped to the Low Countries with my older brothers. One is training for the priesthood, and the other is a soldier. My mother and I were going to join them, but she was afraid I was too young to make the journey." His eyes teared, and he wiped them with his dirty sleeve. "After she died, Father Perkins offered to help me escape. Hannah and Beth's parents were the Pughs' tenants, but they died in jail. I'm sure my father would welcome the girls. If they stay here, there's not much for them. The bandits will find them, and—" He paled. "And sometimes being a servant is not much better."

I cringed, but it was true. I had seen girls thrown out of service, pregnant by their master and with no help or mercy from anyone.

Gwilliam went on, "I do not know what would become of Beth, especially, if we do not find somewhere safe for her. 'Tis illegal to leave the country, though. We need someone to sneak us out."

"I'll do what I can," I whispered as we reached the cottage. Our world was in commotion, but if there was a refuge for these children somewhere, I had to help them find it.

Inside, Hannah and Beth sat next to the fire, its orange flames casting a healthier glow on their faces. They had swept the floor and gathered enough straw for crude sleeping pallets near the central hearth, though Gwilliam's was a respectful distance from the girls'.

A smile flickered on Hannah's face when I presented the basket of food, but Beth took what was offered her without looking away from the fire. Her eyes remained vacant, and she never glanced at me. Gwilliam ate his bread and preserves with gusto but refused to take more, pushing Hannah to eat the eggs. He put the rabbit on a spit over the fire, filling the cottage with the smell of roasting meat.

"Hannah, do you know how to sew?" I asked.

"A little, mistress," she whispered.

"I'm going to help you make over these old clothes to fit you and Beth. They'll be much warmer than what you're wearing now, and if you look less like beggars, people will be kinder."

"Thank you," Hannah said in her airy voice.

Together, we laid out the clothes. I ran my fingers over the soft, green wool one more time, remembering my mother's smile as I modeled it for her. With my heart in my throat, I cut into the beloved gown. It would look pretty on Hannah, with the red highlights in her straw-colored hair.

Hannah handled the needle clumsily, but I guided her hand and soon she made neat stitches along the hem of her new skirt. She smiled unconsciously as she worked. Gwilliam went out and returned a short time later, carrying a handful of eggs and chasing a few clucking chickens into the house. He gave me a guilty glance. I pursed my lips but did not ask where he found them.

"Did Mistress Pryce tell you she's going to help us find Father Perkins?" Gwilliam asked as he rotated the meat.

"Really?" Hannah's eyes lit when she smiled at me. "Oh, thank you."

"We'll find a way to get you overseas—all of you. Things have been hard for the priests lately, but I'm sure they'll not forget you."

"I'm beginning to think everyone has forgotten us," Gwilliam muttered.

"I will not," I said. "I'll make certain you're safe."

Mary and Winifred, help me keep my promise.

Chapter Thirteen

The Lloyds' whole household marched to church on Sunday in somber silence, facing the parish for the first time since the raid like a group of prisoners headed for the gallows. Alice's pale cheeks bore pink spots of humiliation, and she fixed her gaze on the muddy road. I kept my head up, welcoming the gossip and the stares, though my stomach flopped and twisted like a fish on a line. Times of crisis opened a window into people's hearts, a moment of truth amidst all the deception. I watched each person we passed for signs of guilt, triumph, or sympathy, but all just looked curious. It was Nicholas I most needed to see.

He haunted the churchyard, pacing past the tombstones and the drooping old yews. As soon as we arrived, he swooped in on me. I stepped back, my hands clenched into fists. He gave me a short, cold kiss in greeting, and I nearly shoved him away, but he used the gesture to whisper in my ear.

"Are you well?"

I pulled back, studying his face. He flinched and looked away—an admission of guilt or just his normal shyness?

I pushed a stray curl back under my coif. "Is it any concern of yours?"

He turned his face to me, exasperation coloring his features. "Mistress Pryce," he whispered, "I am on friendly terms with the local Justice of the Peace, and he asked me about Master Lloyd. I assured him the queen's men would find nothing treasonous at Plas Lloyd, but after they searched there, they ransacked my home as well. They said they discovered . . . something that gave them reason to suspect I could not be trusted. I have nothing to hide, but you . . ."

My eyes widened. They had searched his *plasty* because of the letters. The notes connected Nicholas to me and—locked in a hidden trunk—painted him with the same suspicion that rested on me or the Lloyds. If he had kept the paper I offered him . . . My knees suddenly felt like they were made of water. An innocent person could have been arrested because of me.

Thank you, Mary and Winifred, that I did not seek revenge before learning the truth.

"Oh! We are fine," I managed to choke out. "One of the queen's agents stayed at Plas Lloyd for a few days, but they moved on."

Nicholas took my elbow. "Aye, the outlaws they were seeking slipped their trap. That ought to ease your mind."

I leaned on his support. Hugh and Father Perkins had escaped, then, and Nicholas had not betrayed us. Relief warmed me to the core like a sip of mulled wine.

"Please take care, Mistress Pryce."

"I will. I can see I've been incautious."

I expected to see some hint of smugness at my admission, but he looked at me sadly before squeezing my arm and releasing me.

I walked trance-like into church behind the Lloyds. The words of the sermon buzzed around my head, finding nowhere to land. If Nicholas had not turned the queen's men on me, then my enemy was still out there, unknown. Perhaps the stranger with the red plume? Or the man who had followed me in the woods? Indeed, anyone in the parish could be watching me.

The edge of the wooden pew dug into my legs. I shifted and clutched the prayer book on my lap, trying to look attentive. I could not let down my guard. Too many people depended on me now.

Even back at Plas Lloyd, I found no refuge. Alice cast suspicious glances at me, and everyone from Mistress Lloyd to the youngest servant moved about quietly, as if afraid too much noise would bring the queen's men swarming around us. Only Master Lloyd stomped through the house, grumbling under his breath. I paced the halls, checking Hugh's tree for a new token every few minutes. Was he safe? What was I to do now?

The savory scent of mutton pies baking for supper reminded me of my responsibilities. I gathered some leftover currant buns and pulled on my wool cloak to sneak out into the chilly evening gloom.

I was not safe on foot, so I asked for my mare. Long shadows reached across our path, and fallen leaves crackled under her hooves. The rocking of her strong, quick gait soothed away some of my tension, but I checked constantly over my shoulder as we rode. I did not want my help to endanger the children, especially if the queen's men sought them. They were a link to Father Perkins, so they might be targets. We were all bound together, knotted up in cords of treason. I left my mare a short distance from the cottage and snuck to the front door.

"Gwilliam? Hannah? Will you let me in?" I called quietly, with a glance at the deep woodland shade behind me.

Gwilliam opened the door. The dim light deepened the dark circles under his eyes. His expression was too old and worried for someone hardly more than a child.

I hurried inside. "I brought you something to eat."

"Thank you, Mistress Pryce." Gwilliam and Hannah's gaunt expressions melted into smiles as they bit into the soft bread. Beth took hers without a glance at me, but she held it close before nibbling the edge.

Hannah licked the crumbs from her fingers. "I'm having trouble with the sleeves on my bodice."

I settled beside her and helped with the difficult stitches. She leaned lightly against my shoulder as she watched. It reminded me of the way I used to sit by my brother, Richard, while he read, wrapped in the comforting scent of paper and ink.

Gwilliam sat on my other side, sharpening his knife by the firelight. Beth rocked, her gaze following a brown hen scratching at the gaps in the floorboards. The quiet peace of the scene soothed the lonely ache in my chest.

The soft scrape of the whetstone stopped, and Gwilliam cleared his throat. "The man who owns this cottage, his name is Master Bowen?"

"Aye, how did you know?"

"I heard some men talking when I was out checking my traps."

"Gwilliam! No more poaching!"

"I was taking them down," he mumbled, "but the men sounded angry with Master Bowen. They said he's heartless. I'm worried about hiding on his land."

I stabbed at the fabric. "He acts cold, but I do not think he's cruel." He had not turned me in. He had even tried to protect me. It was easy to misjudge someone so reserved. I sighed. "If anything, we can be grateful that his own business distracts him, because he'll likely not give any thought to this cottage."

"I'm glad." Hannah huddled against me. "I want to stay here with you."

The tension at Plas Lloyd abated little over the following week, so I escaped to the cottage as often as I could. There, I was not a burden, traitor, or outcast.

Gwilliam knew how to read a little, so I taught him more in hopes that it would improve his chances overseas. Beth's eyes never lost their vague expression, but her hollow face filled out, and all of them regained some color in their cheeks. I brought a spindle and distaff for Hannah, along with wool to make yarn and help her pass the time, but Beth was fascinated by the spinning and refused to let Hannah touch it.

Hannah and Gwilliam smiled and even laughed sometimes, especially when Gwilliam told stories about his antics with his brothers. When the laughter faded, though, he would turn sad eyes toward the fire. My heart ached for him, for all of them, and I hurt each time I had to leave. The little cottage with its smoky fire in the center felt more like home than Plas Lloyd.

Each morning, frost painted lacy designs on the glass windows of Plas Lloyd, a herald of the cruel winter approaching. Gwilliam foraged for firewood, and I snuck out the ends of candles, sometimes even small sections of peat to burn, and whatever food I could manage. I gave up my own meals in exchange, since it did not feel right to steal from Master Lloyd. Hunger gnawed at my stomach and kept me awake at night. How the children must have suffered! We could not go on this way, especially with winter approaching. Finally, I decided to approach Master Lloyd—indirectly—about the problem.

I found him in the great hall, listening to the harper try out a new poem about the glory days of Owain Glyndŵr, last true prince of Wales.

"Master Lloyd?"

"Ah, Joan, what is it? You look troubled."

"I am, a little. The harvests have been poor again, have they not?"

"Aye, another famine year. People wonder if this is the judgment of God for forsaking the old faith. Or for supporting the priests, depending on which side they fall on. Tempers are flaring, and more Catholics have been arrested."

I sat heavily on a stool. How could Wales hold together with the sifter of religious belief dividing families, parishes, and the whole country?

"Is that what you think? That God is punishing us?" I kept my voice low enough to be masked by the notes of the harp, in case any of the servants had been bribed to spy on us.

He shook his head. "I'm an old man, Joan, perhaps not too far from meeting God myself. I can remember when it was illegal to read the Bible, and now I hear from Nicholas Bowen we're to have a complete one in Welsh. We were told to pray to saints, then to smash their images, then to rebuild them, then to burn them. Old age may not be an excuse for giving up, but I'm weary. I just live as best I can and hope to work it out with God when I meet him. While I'm in this world, I'll keep my mind on practical matters."

"Like the harvest."

"Like the harvest. Though I'll not pretend I do not pray for next year to be better."

"What will happen this winter?"

" 'Twill be leaner than usual, but we'll not starve, and I'll be able to help our tenants a little."

A little. If there was already not enough to go around, he was not likely to support a family of orphans. I rubbed my gold mourning rings. My father and mother would not have let anyone go hungry, and neither would I.

"What will happen to beggars and poor laborers?"

"The parish will put them to work. Otherwise, they'll be whipped, marked, and driven off." There was no pity in his voice.

I shivered. Gwilliam and Hannah might be strong enough to work, but what would become of Beth? And the older children would be bound to their servitude, practically slaves, unable to join Gwilliam's family overseas. I imagined my own family alive, waiting and worrying in some far off place. What would I give to rush into their arms again?

Master Lloyd leaned back. "The only one who'll not be complaining this winter is Master Nicholas. The improvements he made in his fields paid off. He's a smart man." He gave me a significant look, which I pretended not to notice.

Would Nicholas be willing to share his harvest, when next year might not be so fortunate? Men were wise to hoard their extra and sell it for a profit when everyone else was hungry. Nicholas might not care much for what went on around him, but he wanted Nant Bach to prosper, and I had money. I straightened. I did not have to beg anything. If he had enough to consider selling, I might be able to get a good price from him.

The next day I rode for Nant Bach.

Nicholas rose from his table to greet me with a questioning nod. "Mistress Pryce. Have you come alone?"

I'd planned to put on a formal front, but his almost-friendly surprise shook my resolve. Nay, the children were hungry. It was no time for a neighborly visit. "I wanted to discuss a matter of business with you."

Negotiating trade was hardly a role for a woman—at least, not a single young woman with no estate to manage—and I did not know what to expect from him. Most men would be amused or annoyed by my presumption. Nicholas's brow knit together, but he sat at the table and gestured for me to join him. "Very well. I have time to discuss whatever you would like."

I sat and mimicked his pose, folding my hands in front of me on the table so my fingers did not tremble. "I have heard you had a good harvest this year."

"A decent one. Nothing to complain about when everyone else's was worse."

"Will you be selling any of your surplus?"

"Possibly. I do not think it wise to empty my larders, but I would not want any of it to spoil."

"I would like to buy from you."

"You would?" His eyebrows drew together again, and his voice dropped. "Is Master Lloyd having difficulties? He could have come to me himself. I would make him a fair offer."

I flushed. "He has sufficient. I come on my own behalf."

Something dangerous crept into Nicholas's expression, a hint of the anger I had seen when he lost his temper with Father Perkins. "Is Master Lloyd not giving you enough? As your godfather, he should not force you to provide your own board."

"Nay, 'tis nothing like that. I need the food for someone else. There are many who will go hungry this winter."

His expression drew closed again. "You know 'tis treason to succor a priest."

"A priest?" Of course, wherever Father Perkins and Father Davies were, they were likely hungry. Hugh as well. I sighed. "'Tis not a priest. They are children. Orphans." I almost added "like us." After all, it was a very fine line dividing our fates from theirs.

"Why are they your responsibility?"

"Because they need help, and I am in a position to do something about it. It is our duty as *bonheddwyr* and as Christians."

"Well." He sat back and cleared his throat. "Tell me more."

I meant to keep up my impersonal façade, but I longed to tell someone about my new friends, even if only indirectly. "They are on the verge of starvation. I cannot scrounge enough food for them, and the little girl is unwell. I know we cannot help everyone—there are people hungry and suffering all over the country—but I cannot watch it happen in front of me."

Nicholas stared without responding and then looked down at his hands, his lips twisted in a scowl. Did he think me a foolish woman, trying to save everyone, meddling where I had no right? Finally, he spoke. "How much do you need?"

I sighed and pulled out the paper with my calculations: grain, smoked meat and fish, cider, some dried apples or plums. No luxuries, but enough to keep them alive through the winter. Hopefully, the summer would bring better times and a chance for them to flee the country. My heart twisted at the thought of them leaving, the little cottage quiet and cold. Perhaps I would not send them off alone.

Nicholas studied the paper, his head tilted. "This seems very little. You're certain 'tis what you need?"

"Of course. After my mother died, I helped my father manage everything."

"Oh." He toyed with the corner of the paper. "I'm sorry about your parents."

The sincerity in his voice brought a lump to my throat. "And I about yours. I liked them. I'm sorry our fathers quarreled. I never heard . . ." I swallowed. I was walking on a precarious ledge, but there was so much I wanted to understand. "Why did they fight?"

His gaze traveled my face like he hoped to find something there. Finally, he looked down. "I do not know the details, but I think it had to do with my father's cooling religious devotion."

"They fell out over religion?" An argument over beliefs was the reason, then, that Nicholas and I were strangers. Nay, that also had to do with whatever demons haunted him. We had grown apart. What would it have been like, though, if our fathers had remained friends? Would I understand his sadness, his fear? Would I wish to marry him, or would his inaction still seem like cowardice? It would be a slow, painful death of the heart to be married to someone you did not respect.

"You stopped writing to me." I could not quite keep the accusation out of my voice.

"I was busy," he said coolly. He met my eyes, and his expression softened. "You spoke too freely in your letters. Of Rome. Of . . . things religious."

"Your religious devotion cooled as well, then?"

He folded his arms. "I would not say that, but my spiritual convictions do not require me to go seeking martyrdom with every breath. There is wisdom, Mistress Pryce, in knowing when to be still."

"Also in knowing when to fight." I should not have said it. I needed his help for the children. He would sit still until he turned to stone, though, and it made me nearly mad to see it, when once he had been active and robust.

He shook his head and picked up the list. "I think I can spare the things you ask for."

I unclasped my hands. "How much do you ask?"

He glanced up at me, his scar twisting his mouth into a smirk that did not match the sad look in his eyes. "You expected me to charge you?" he asked quietly.

"I—"

"I will give them to you, Mistress Joan."

My heart flipped, hearing him speak my Christian name. Did this mean we were friends again? "I'm not sure I'm comfortable with that. 'Tis too generous a gift."

"You insist on paying me?"

" 'Tis only fair."

He gave me an appraising look. "Have you any experience in brewing?"

"I made small beer and cider for my father."

"My cider is not turning out well. I'm afraid my cook, talented as he is in other areas, is not a skilled brewer. 'Tis probably for the best I did not get enough grapes this year to try wine."

"I'm sorry you did not get the harvest you expected."

"For the best, as I said, but if you would help me set my stillroom in order, I would be deeply obliged."

"Not enough to equal the cost of this food."

"You undervalue your skills. I talked to the brewers' guild in Conwy. I may be getting the better end of this bargain."

I did not believe him, but I nodded and accompanied him across the yard to the stillroom. Barrels of ripe apples sat waiting to be made into cider. The rich smell made my mouth water, but when I sampled his efforts, I grimaced.

He laughed, the first real laugh I had heard from him since I returned. It was worth the terrible sickly-sweet taste of the cider.

"I hope your pigs will eat that," I said, emboldened by his humor, "because if they turn up their noses at it, I cannot imagine what you'll do with it."

"You'll take pity on me then?"

I winced inwardly at the word *pity*, but he was still smiling. For the moment, we were friends again. That might be dangerous, though. Treason clung to me, liable to poison anyone who got too close. Nicholas had already survived one brush with the queen's men unscathed, and he did not fear the association, but the risk was great. I had to keep him at arm's length, avoid saying or doing anything to taint his reputation while at Nant Bach.

I nodded. "'Twill take some work, but I'll help."

"Then I'll load up the first part of the food you asked for. Will you tell my steward where to have it delivered?"

"I think 'tis best if I take it myself. Just bring me as much as my horse can carry, and I'll lead her back."

His look turned speculative, and I bit the inside of my cheek. That told him the children were not far away. Perhaps it was good he have some idea they were near so he did not shoot Gwilliam for a poacher. By the saints, I needed to warn Gwilliam again not to poach. He owed much now to Nicholas's generosity. Of course, as I looked at the sticky disaster in his stillroom, I wondered if I would be earning the food after all.

Chapter Fourteen

The scents of foamy yeast starter and freshly pressed apples mingled in Nicholas's cramped stillroom. I measured the starter and poured it into a cask of juice, reaching back for the paddle to mix it. My hand brushed velvet. I gave a start and turned to find Nicholas looming beside me. I blushed at his nearness, at the awareness of his warmth and his masculine smell of leather and the outdoors. He mumbled an apology and backed away, bumping into the apple mill.

I sighed and brushed back a stray curl with sticky fingers. Many men left brewing to the women, but Nicholas hovered like an anxious parent. I'd spent every afternoon of the last week, save the Sabbath, at Nant Bach, and he'd come to check on me every day. After the first couple of times, I realized he was not judging, just curious.

He cleared his throat. "Do you need anything?"

"If you moved those nearer, 'twould make the work easier"—I pointed to a barrel brimming with yellow apples—"and some of the tart ones as well. I'm ready to mill and press another batch."

He nodded and slid the heavy barrels over.

"If you help, 'twill be easier to do it yourself the next time," I said when he straightened.

"Do it myself?"

"Well, of course. Next winter I may not be bartering for extra food. If you know the process, you'll not have to pay a brewer."

"You're right, of course. Please, show me." He smiled a little, but his eyes looked sad. He must have been lonelier than he let on.

By the end of the day, our sleeves were rolled up with our hands and arms sticky and smelling of ripe apples, and several batches of cider sat in their casks. We smiled and talked as if the years had never come between us. The warmth of the work seeped through me, making my heart light.

Nicholas wiped his face, but he missed a smudge of apple. I grabbed my handkerchief and dabbed his scarred cheek.

He recoiled, covering the side of his face.

I yanked my hand back. "Oh! I did not mean . . . did I hurt you?"

His shoulders relaxed, and he moved his hand. "Nay, 'tis not painful anymore."

I swallowed. "What happened? I mean, how did it happen?"

He was silent so long, I regretted asking. Another secret I was not to know. Finally, he ran his fingers over the scar and said quietly, "An arquebus—a long gun. The man next to me fired his, and it exploded in his hands."

"I'm sorry," I whispered.

"I was lucky, I suppose. The man with the arquebus . . . Well, I was lucky." He moved his hand from his cheek and turned away.

I caught his arm. He tensed at my touch, and I pulled my hand back, leaving sticky prints on his black doublet. "I'm glad you were not killed."

He shrugged and looked down. "I came back to find my whole family gone. I believed I was supposed to die too. The destroying angel missed his mark and just neglected to return for me. Maybe he thought I was as good as dead anyway."

"You should not think like that! Things happen for a reason." I caught myself. Was I telling him God wanted his family dead? His face deformed?

"I believed that too, before Ireland. I was so determined to be brave, to do my duty. I was always there, in the front, like on the day with the arquebus . . ." He touched his cheek. "The fighting was so senseless, though. It turned men brutal. I looked for God in it, but all I saw were demons."

"You're here, alive, and your experiments with Nant Bach are successful. Maybe God is telling you this is where you're supposed to be."

"Sometimes I wonder if God has grown so sick of our bickering that he drew away and left the heavens silent, deserted us to fumble through this dark life on our own."

I felt ill-placed to advise him when he had suffered so much, but his misery was so raw, I had to say something. "Do not give in to despair; you'll find your hope again."

Nicholas's gaze found mine, his emotions no longer hidden. His eyes looked tired and much too old for someone only a few years my senior. That, so much more than his scars, seemed the saddest thing about his face. I reached for his arm again, and this time he did not flinch away, but stepped closer. I was aware of his smell again: leather and something pleasant from childhood I could not place but wanted to breathe in more deeply. He opened his mouth as if to speak, then sighed and stepped back. Awkwardness fell between us.

"I have to check on the archery range this afternoon." He gave me a sidelong glance. "Do you want to come?"

"To the archery range?" Many gentlemen neglected the sport, but the law still required all able-bodied men to practice for the defense of the realm. The English army owed much to Welsh long-bows. Naturally, Nicholas would comply.

"I think we still have some children's bows lying around." His tone was casual, but humor sparkled in his eyes.

"Children's bows!"

"You think you can shoot a longbow?"

I had felt his muscles through his doublet, and I appraised his shoulders, almost twice the width of mine. Nay, I could never pull his bow. I lifted my chin. "I think no matter which bow I shoot, my aim will still be better than yours."

He laughed. "We shall see, then."

He lacked the bounce of his childhood self, but his satisfied smirk reminded me of simpler days as he led me out to the range and inspected the archery butts.

I stood aside and admired his form when he drew back his heavy longbow. His face lost all joking and his good eye narrowed as he took aim. The arrow whistled through the air, thunking deep into the target just a finger's breadth from the center.

"Your turn." He grinned and handed me the smaller bow.

The string bit into my fingers as I drew it. I aimed and let the arrow fly. It glanced off the top of the target and flipped into the field behind.

"I suppose it would be ungentlemanly of me to make you retrieve that," Nicholas said. He was not laughing, but I could hear his grin.

I straightened. "I'll fetch it myself."

"At least let me walk with you, then."

We strolled through the tall grass. I swatted the ends of it with my bow. "'Tis not my fault, you know. I was not required to practice archery. My father did not encourage it." I found the arrow. The feather fletching was torn. "I'm sorry. I ruined it."

He wrapped his hand around mine. His fingers were strong and callused, but gentle against my skin. A tingle raced up my arm to set my heart beating faster. Nicholas turned to block the chilly wind blowing from the hills. His warmth wrapped around me as he turned my hand to examine the arrow.

"Easily enough repaired," he said, his tone low.

I could not bring myself to look at him. A breach of many years was not repaired in an afternoon. Nicholas was handsome, and I ached for the comfort and reassurance of his friendship, but we saw so many things differently.

"I suppose 'tis good that I'll never have to ride off to defend my country," I said with forced cheer.

"Aye, it is." Nicholas released my hand, his expression pained.

"I'm sorry. That was thoughtless of me."

He stared across the fields, his eyes distant. "I just hope I never see that kind of destruction here. Homes and fields burned, women and children starving, black haze hanging over everything, the smell of blood and . . ." He squeezed his eyes shut and swallowed several times. "You can lose everything in an instant. You're thinking about home, about tomorrow, and there's a click, and 'tis all gone, drowned in fire and smoke and blood."

I looked over the fields as well, trying to imagine what he saw in his haunted vision. If it had been bad watching that in someone else's country, how much worse it would be to worry about it on your own lands? I could not think of any way to comfort him, so I just stood beside him. He shook off his haunted expression and looked down at me, his gaze vulnerable.

I could not reassure him Wales would not rebel like Ireland did. Part of me hoped for it. Or, I thought I did. When I looked at Nicholas and what the war had done to him, taken from him, I did not want it either. Was he trying to buy peace at any price with his loyalty to the queen and her laws, sacrificing what he had once believed in to stop war from coming? I did not want to ask him. My underlying accusations of cowardice or foolishness might come to the surface.

Were Wales free, the queen could not summon its young men to go fight for her causes. If they fought, it would be to defend their homes, not to force another country to submit to the will of a heretic monarch.

We walked back in silence. I pulled my cloak tighter to ward off the chill settling over the field.

Chapter Fifteen

The next morning, I stopped to visit Gwilliam, Hannah, and Beth on my way to Nant Bach. Hannah sat by the smoky fire, nearly in tears as she tried to sew a patch onto threadbare fabric.

"Mistress Joan, how do I fix this?" she asked, thrusting it into my hands.

I studied it, then shook my head. "There's not enough fabric here to sew a patch to."

"Gwilliam's clothes are falling apart."

I smiled. "I have an idea to fix that."

I drew Gwilliam aside before I left. "Have you seen anyone around the cottage?"

"Nay, we could be all alone in the world out here."

They were secure as long as they remained undiscovered, but if someone came for them, there was no one to turn to for help. No place was safe. Nicholas might be willing to take them in, but he would be obligated to report them to the parish as vagabonds. If the queen's agents were looking for them, I would be handing over their lives. Nicholas had warned me not to bring him any more trouble, and fugitive orphans were certainly that.

"Keep the door bolted, just to be sure," I said.

I hurried back to my mare and cantered to Nicholas's *plasty*. At least I could make certain Gwilliam was warm, especially if he needed to flee. Nicholas was much taller than Gwilliam, but he might be willing to hand down some of his old clothes. I could modify them to fit, and Hannah would not be sewing patches onto patches.

I paused at the front door and laid my hand on the smooth wood. It exuded warmth, a hominess and comfort that wrapped around me. As a child I had run through this door many times, following my brother or Nicholas and his siblings in one of our games, but the welcome felt different now. I was working here, out in the stillroom and down at the cottage as well, becoming a part of Nant Bach.

The doorposts gleamed invitingly, polished by generations of family coming and going. It would be glorious to belong somewhere again. I stared back across the sweeping fields, the neat cottages of the tenants, the sheep and cattle grazing on the hills, and up at the sturdy stone house with its glass windows and cozy great hall.

I could come to love this place. My cheeks warmed as I remembered Nicholas's nearness the previous day, and his strong, gentle touch. Could I come to love him, and he to love me? It was one thing to be his friend, when we could focus on our commonalities and ignore those things we disagreed on, but a husband was lord and master over all his house. A wife out of harmony with him would have an uneasy time, and Nicholas and I were at odds over so many things.

I sighed and pushed the door open.

I stopped short at the sight of Nicholas and Hugh standing toe to toe in the great hall, their faces burnished red with anger. Hugh's hand was raised as if to emphasize some point, but their discussion must have been whispered if I had not heard it from outside. They were likely arguing about religion again.

"My answer is no, Hugh," Nicholas said, stepping back. "I'll not reconsider." He turned to me, and I almost withdrew. The old curtain was drawn over his features, with no sign of friendliness in his eyes. "Mistress Pryce?"

"I was here to help in the stillroom, and . . ." I glanced at Hugh. I was relieved to see him well, but I could hardly ask for some of Nicholas's clothes with him standing there. I wanted to tell Hugh about the children, but when I did, I would be asking him about Father Perkins, and I could not do that in front of Nicholas. My separate lives were colliding, threatening to crush me like a pair of grinding millstones.

I looked back at Hugh. "I apologize, Master Richards, but may I speak with Master Bowen alone for a moment?"

Hugh nodded curtly. "I think my business here is finished. Good day to you both."

He slipped past me, pausing long enough to give me a questioning glance. Nicholas settled onto one of the stools by the fireplace, his arms folded and his foot tapping in the rushes.

"Is anything amiss?" I asked quietly.

"Of course not," he said coolly.

I pursed my lips. The day before, he might have told me, but whatever had passed between him and Hugh had thrown him back into his old ways. Would he even be willing to help me? I cleared my throat. "I needed to ask something. If this is not a good time . . ."

He sighed. "'Tis as good as any. How can I be of service?"

I knelt by his side and lowered my voice. "One of the orphans I told you about is a boy. I was able to make over some of my old clothes for the girls, but I have nothing for him." My cheeks tingled with a blush. "I did not know if you might have something . . ."

His expression softened a little. "Hmm. Aye, I might. How old is this boy?"

"About thirteen, but small. I can alter the clothes if they are too big or need mending."

Nicholas nodded and strode from the room.

I stood awkwardly, not certain if I should follow. A harp sat dusty and forgotten in the corner. I had learned to play a little as a child, though my tutor had focused more on singing. I strolled over and plucked at the strings. They were out of tune, but I picked out one of the songs I remembered. When I finished, I found Nicholas staring at me from the doorway, his expression full of sorrow.

I backed away from the instrument. "I'm sorry. I should not have touched it."

"'Twas my brother's," he said softly. "I did not know you played."

I almost snapped that he would have known more about me if he had not stopped writing, but the mention of his brother cooled my tongue. This place was not my home, and I should not have made myself so comfortable. "Only a little."

He walked over slowly and handed me a bundle of clothes: hose, breeches, white linen shirts, a black doublet, and a warm cloak of dark blue wool. After my mistake with the harp, I did not have the courage to ask if they had belonged to him or another member of the household.

"Thank you," I whispered.

He shrugged and walked back to the table. "Good morrow, Mistress Pryce."

So there was to be no more work in the stillroom. Just today, or for good? I clutched the clothes to my chest, uncertain if it was my offense or Hugh's that brought the visit to such an abrupt end. I wanted to apologize again, but he did not glance at me, so I quietly left.

The trees around the cottage waited in shadow, empty, still, and watchful. I did not feel secure until I had bolted the cottage door behind me. It cheered me a little to see Gwilliam and Hannah's smiles when I presented the clothes. Beth ignored me, intent on the lumpy thread she wound onto her spindle. Gwilliam immediately gave Hannah the huge cloak.

"The clothes are too big." He held up the doublet, which could almost wrap twice around his thin shoulders.

"They are very fine, though," Hannah added. "You'll look like a gentleman when we sew them to fit you."

Gwilliam glanced at me. " 'Twould be illegal for me to dress above my station."

I frowned at the doublet and breeches. He was right. Nicholas dressed for his role as one of the *bonheddwyr*, but Gwilliam's family had only been yeomen: comfortably situated, but not of ancient, noble stock like Nicholas. "The fabric is fine, but we want you to have every advantage when you leave. We'll keep the style simple and hopefully no one will notice."

I showed Hannah how best to cut and stitch the clothes. She picked everything up quickly.

"Hannah, can you read?"

She blushed furiously. "Nay, mistress."

"Would you like to learn? You'll need something to do these long winter nights. I do not have many books, but perhaps I could find you a prayer book or some of the New Testament in Welsh." Then, when William Morgan's translation was done, she could read the entire thing.

Hannah paled. "'Tis against the law for me to read the Bible." She glanced down. "I am not highborn enough."

I sighed. I had forgotten. The queen was afraid if just anyone read the Bible, they might ask awkward questions. Only those who had been trained to think her way were to be trusted. "I do not believe Her Majesty in London has the right to tell Hannah in this cottage at Nant Bach what she may read. Would you like to learn?"

Hannah glanced at Gwilliam, who gave her a nod.

She smiled. "Aye, thank you, mistress."

"Please, call me Joan." The impulse surprised me, but the comfort I felt around the children reminded me so much of home, with my parents and brother, it seemed they were part of the same circle. Fostering was an old tradition among the Welsh—a way to extend bonds of kinship and friendship—and in a way I had adopted Gwilliam, Hannah, and Beth as siblings.

"Aye, Joan," she said shyly.

After seeing that they were settled in, I rode to Plas Lloyd. The warm scent from Nicholas's doublet lingered on my skin, making me feel like he was riding beside me. I imagined talking with him about the children. Would he approve of teaching Hannah to read? He loved books and seemed to believe people should take responsibility for their own thoughts and actions, but it was still against the law for Hannah to read the Bible.

I gave a guilty start when I walked into the great hall at Plas Lloyd to find Hugh sitting with Master Lloyd.

"Mistress Pryce!" Hugh stood and greeted me as though we had not seen each other just an hour before. Whatever had caused his argument with Nicholas, the storm had not quite blown over; annoyance still flickered in his eyes.

"Master Richards." I smiled in return, trying to hint with my gaze at the hundreds of questions I wanted to ask. "Are you staying for long?"

"Not tonight, but I'll be visiting with my brother through Christmas. Master Lloyd has been good enough to invite me to your family's Christmas dinner."

"Oh, I'm glad to hear it!"

"I'm inviting Master Nicholas as well," Master Lloyd called from his seat. "I did not think you would want him left out, Joan, since you have been spending so much time with him of late."

"Of course not," I said, though Hugh's mouth tightened at the news. I wondered if I could ferret out the cause of their disagreement.

"I had best be heading back." Hugh grabbed his hat.

"May I walk you out?" I raised an eyebrow. "I would like to hear whatever news you might have."

"Of course," Hugh said, his expression brightening.

In front of the *plasty*, he paused and fidgeted with his hat. "Your lands have proved to be an ideal hiding place. Thank you for suggesting it."

"I'm glad to hear it. Can you tell me aught of Father Davies or Father Perkins?"

"I can do better than that, if luck favors me."

"Oh?"

"They are performing a Mass for Christmas, if we can find a suitable spot."

"A Christmas Mass!" My father had hosted them, gathering all the local Catholics into our family's old chapel. The candles had filled the cold, sacred darkness of Christmas night with warmth. Goose bumps raced the length of my arms remembering the solemn echoing music, the deep men's voices blending with the higher strains of the women. My mother would hold me close, her smell of fresh baked bread and verjuice embracing me as the priest recited the sacred words and presented the Mass, a reminder of God's presence in our lives. At that time, all the world seemed filled with love and hope.

"Only if we can find a suitable place," Hugh warned. "My brother's wife nearly fainted at the suggestion, and Nicholas flat out refused. I have managed to shake the queen's agents for now, but everyone is too jumpy at the idea of a Mass. Is it not worth a little risk, though?"

The nighttime search of Plas Lloyd had taught me how near the danger was, but Hugh, whatever he had been doing, seemed to be living with even more peril. This was another chance to steal our freedom from the queen, and to safeguard our souls in the bargain. It could be years, perhaps even the rest of our lives, before the chance would come again, especially to hold the Mass at Christmas. "Aye, 'tis worth it."

Now I knew the cause of Hugh's argument with Nicholas. Could I convince Nicholas to change his mind, help him understand what a joy it would be? Likely not. Nicholas and I were becoming friends again, but there were some things he refused to understand. "What did Master Lloyd say?"

"He did not refuse me, but he said he could not think of a safe place."

Master Lloyd had an empty chapel in his house, but I could understand why he thought it unsafe, with the queen's men probably still watching the house. My mind went to the little cottage, the closest thing I had to home in this world—a stolen haven. What a joy it would be to bring such a happy occasion there. It was on Nicholas's land, though. As much as I longed for it, it seemed too much like betrayal to go against his wishes.

"What about the cave?" I asked.

" 'Tis not very big," Hugh said, but he looked thoughtful.

"Are you expecting many people?"

"Probably not more than a dozen or so. Everyone is too frightened right now."

"We would fit if we huddled together."

"You may be right. I'll speak to Father Davies about it."

"How will you spread the word? People who want to be there should be able to, but it will be dangerous."

" 'Twill be deadly if we are caught. Do not concern yourself over it; I'll see to it."

He smiled at me, but I could not hide my frown. If I was helping so much already, I could do more. "You should add three more to the list of celebrants."

"Oh?"

I quickly explained about Gwilliam, Hannah, and Beth, especially their need to speak with Father Perkins. I left out the details of where they were hiding or how I was maintaining them. I was not inclined to share my secrets with someone who kept so many from me.

"Of course, Father Perkins will be happy to speak to them," Hugh said, "though 'twill be summer before anyone is ready to travel again. I know he sometimes helps people reach Ireland, and from there 'tis easier to travel to other parts of the world. I have never known Father Perkins to break his word."

"I'll tell the children. They'll be so glad."

Hugh stepped closer and lowered his voice. "What of the latest papers? Have you delivered them all?"

"Not after the queen's agents searched here. I thought it safer to lie low."

"It was wise to wait and watch, but we do not have the luxury of time. Things are in motion. Great things. They'll change everything for Wales, for Catholics. The papers are only a small thing—strengthening the faith of those who waver and doubt—but they'll help. I know you're brave enough to do this, Mistress Joan."

He kept a tight grip on my arm, his voice and eyes radiating excitement. My heart thrilled. Great things. Would we finally be free? Then I could look back someday and tell my children and grandchildren that I had helped in the fight. "Of course. I'll deliver the rest."

"Good. Then I'll see you at Christmas."

He gave me a warm farewell kiss that left my head spinning and rode off. I leaned against the house, utterly confused. My elation faded into a swarm of questions. How was he planning on changing things? When would it happen? Was what I did truly helping? I smacked my hand against the stone wall. What a fool-born scullion I was, falling into a reverie before a handsome face instead of demanding to know more. I had to keep my word, though.

We made a last trip to Conwy before Christmas, and I carried the papers in the lining of my cloak. Hugh's directions led me to a metalworker's shop. The heavy clang of a hammer on brass echoed off the stone buildings lining the narrow street. My hands did not shake nor my feet waver. I nodded to everyone I passed. The danger was so normal now it made no more impact on me than the sea air.

I peered into the metalworker's shop, pretending to admire his buckles and brooches. Then I caught sight of the man working at the anvil. My hands went cold, and I turned away. It was the squint-eyed man who had taken the coins from Master Red-Plume.

I half-stumbled out of sight, my knees trembling. Did Hugh know? The exchange of money could have been a normal business transaction, but if so, why not conduct it in the shop? The squint-eyed man might be misleading Master Red-Plume, but he could just as easily be a spy infiltrating Hugh's network, trying to trap us.

My chest tightened. I could not draw enough air. I threw my cloak back, feeling the weight of the papers. Hugh told me so little; he left me no choice but to trust him or give up. The pages of the book were important to his plan, and I had promised to deliver them. I would not be a coward or the weak link in the chain. Others depended on me. I took a deep breath and stepped into the shop, slipping the papers onto the counter.

The man stared at me as I rushed out, and my skin crawled. Had I done right, or would we be having another midnight visit from the queen's agents soon?

Chapter Sixteen

On Christmas morning, the household arose before dawn to prepare for the *plygain* service. I rubbed the sleep from my eyes and swung out of bed. My teeth chattered as I pulled on my thick wool skirt and bodice in the dim light of the fireplace embers. I bounded down the stairs. Everyone from Master Lloyd to the little scullery maid gathered in the great hall, bundled in their warmest cloaks, full of smiles and quiet chatter and holding a lit candle.

We set off into the predawn air rich with the smell of peat smoke. My candle's flame trembled as my boots crunched over the frosty ground. I drew my cloak tighter and burrowed my tingling nose into the soft, warm wool. Our party trekked to the hill near the church, joining with a stream of neighbors and parish members, their cheeks bitten rosy by the cold and their eyes bright with excitement. The candles gave their faces a warm glow.

As the first light of dawn washed over the sky, we sang our welcome to the holy morning. Age-old songs filled the air with harmonies in the ancient British tongue. The sound raised the hairs on my arms, and I shivered in delight, feeling a part of something larger and more beautiful than anything I could be by myself.

I huddled close to Alice and Mistress Lloyd. Master Lloyd's bass voice boomed behind us. Master Rhys hovered near Alice. His sister gave me a friendly nod, and I smiled at them. Even the sight of Mistress Meredith did not bother me. Nicholas stood alone on the edge of the group, his face pale and downcast in the glow of the dawn. I caught his eye and grinned. He replied with a solemn nod.

After the sun's rays bathed the hillside in chilly morning light, the entire parish filed into the church to listen to the familiar songs and scriptures of the Nativity.

When the service ended, I snuck away into the misty morning with a fabric-wrapped bundle tucked under my arm. Frost glittered on the branches and painted patterns on the stones. My breath fogged around me, adding to the haze. I felt like I had wandered into the fairyland of my childhood stories. I crossed myself three times, as any wise hero in a fairy story would do, and hurried to the cottage.

Hannah and Gwilliam huddled close to the fire, their faces ruddy and grinning. Even Beth, who sat close to Gwilliam and twisted her spindle, seemed to be smiling a little.

"Happy Christmas!" I shut the door against the cold.

"Joan!" Hannah rushed over to embrace me and kiss my cheeks. "You came early! Are we really going to see Father Perkins tonight?"

"Aye, and that may be the best present I can give you, but I still wanted to bring you something this morning."

I held out the package. Hannah squealed and rushed over to the fire to open it. Beth wiggled next to her, a spark of interest in her gaze. Gwilliam leaned in, trying to look nonchalant, though his eyes were bright with excitement.

Hannah pulled a soft-haired doll from the bundle. "For Beth?"

I nodded, and she handed it to her sister. The little girl stroked the doll's hair and held it close, rocking gently. Hannah smiled and pulled out the next gift, a fine wooden comb, inlaid with mother of pearl.

"Far too good for me," she said in a hushed voice.

"Nonsense." I smiled. "Now you'll not have to borrow mine."

She laughed. "Thank you. I think this must be for you, Gwilliam."

This last object had been the hardest to get without rousing suspicion, but as Gwilliam lifted his new dagger, I was glad I made the effort.

"Thank you, Mistress Joan," he said, slipping the knife from its sheath to admire the blade.

"Every gentleman needs a dagger, and your old one is worn out," I said. "The rest is for you to share."

They pulled out some walnuts coated in sugar and three oranges. At that, Beth perked up, grasping for the fruit.

Hannah laughed. "Let me peel it for you first."

I smiled. They were still thin, but they had a healthier glow to their cheeks. By the time winter was over, I would have them fit for their long journey. I paused. Maybe *our* long journey. Every time I consulted my heart about it, I felt only hazy confusion. I had until after winter thawed to decide.

I pulled out my last gift, a couple of simple poems and prayers copied from my book of hours, and a printed Book of Matthew from the New Testament. "Hannah, this is for you as well. We'll start on your lessons soon, but I think Gwilliam knows enough to get you started."

His mouth moved as he worked out the words, and he nodded. "Aye, I can read it. I'll show you, Hannah."

"What of Beth? Do you think she can learn?" Hannah's voice dropped. "People used to say she was a cast-off fairy child or possessed by a devil, but our mother always believed Beth was smart in her own way."

I glanced at the thin child clutching her doll and stroking its hair. I had never heard her speak, though sometimes she straightened up the cottage, putting things into neat rows, and she was learning to make a fine thread on her spindle. "We can try." I sighed. "I wish I could stay all day, but I have to return to Plas Lloyd. I'll fetch you tonight for the Mass."

"Happy Christmas!" Hannah said. "Thank you for everything."

The warmth of the cottage lingered on my walk back, and I reached the *plasty* with a glow on my cheeks.

The family and many neighbors, including Master and Mistress Rhys, gathered around the table. Hugh grinned when he saw me and met me with a friendly kiss. I needed to tell him about the metalsmith and Master Red-Plume, but this was not the place for it. Nicholas rose hesitantly and gave me a quick bow. A harper struck up a series of carols as we sat to eat.

Master Lloyd had used the feast to make his feelings clear, seating me next to Nicholas so I was facing the unblemished side of his face. Nicholas shifted and looked down when I sat by him, his jaw tight. I smiled and leaned over.

"Happy Christmas, Master Nicholas," I said, keeping my voice beneath the harper's songs and the talk around the table.

He looked at me in surprise and smiled. "Happy Christmas, Mistress Joan. Has your day been pleasant so far?" He glanced at my dew-soaked skirts.

I blushed, but at least I could tell him what I had been doing. "I was delivering presents."

"That is a good way to start Christmas. If I had known I might have added a gift of my own."

"You have done enough already," I said quickly. More than he knew, providing us with the borrowed cottage.

He fidgeted with his goblet. "I have something for you."

"Oh, but I did not get you anything."

He shrugged, but his mouth turned down at the corner. I should have thought of it, after everything he had done to help, but I never knew what to expect from him, or what he expected from me. He pulled out a folded document and slipped it to me.

I smoothed out the paper. My eyes raced over the neat writing, one of the pages from William Morgan's unprinted Welsh Bible.

"What a perfect Christmas gift, but how can I accept this?"

Nicholas smiled a little but did not meet my eyes. "'Tis not much of a gift, really. Soon you will be able to buy a printed copy."

"That makes an original page all the more precious."

"I would like you to have it. You seemed quite moved by it."

"I am. Thank you." I folded the paper back up and kept it in my lap.

The servants marched in with the courses: geese, mutton, venison and mincemeat pies, tarts filled with custard, cheese, or apples, trays of figs and pears, and the roast boar coming last. We ate, listening to the ancient songs played on the harp, the same ones my mother used to sing with me. I closed my eyes, pretending she and my father sat at the head of the table. The yule log crackling and popping in the hearth might have been brought in by my father and brother, and the murmurs of conversation were our old friends. I thought I heard their voices, and warmth and peace washed over me. When I opened my eyes, the illusion shattered. Many of the faces around me were strangers. I would not see my family again in this life. I set down my knife and spoon and touched my gold mourning rings.

"Are you well?" Nicholas asked. "You look pale."

"I . . . miss my family," I whispered.

"Oh." He looked down at his plate. "I'm sorry."

"Does it ever get easier?"

He did not answer for a moment, and I wondered if I had intruded too far on his privacy. Finally, he spoke in a low tone. "You'll go days without thinking about them, then maybe a week or two. Something will remind you, and . . . 'tis like an old wound tearing open." He rubbed his mourning band. "After a while, the reminders come less often, cut a little less deeply. I wish I could say it stops hurting, but . . . sometimes I walk into the great hall, thinking I'll find my father or one of my sisters sitting at the table. I imagine I hear the spinning wheels or the harp, but there's no one there. Normally I love Nant Bach, but on days like Christmas that bring the old years so close again . . . 'tis the hardest time."

I nodded and blinked back tears. No wonder he'd looked so stricken when I played the harp.

"Do you pray for them?" I asked and then wished I had not. Prayers for the dead were heresy now, no matter what solace they might offer the living.

But Nicholas's mouth twisted up and he nodded. For all his conformity, he still sought the familiar comforts too. I grabbed his hand under the table and squeezed it. He squeezed back, and we sat like that for several moments in a silent prayer for those we had lost, his strong fingers warm against mine.

"They would want us to be happy," I said, finally releasing his hand.

"I know." He smiled ruefully. "Yet we do not always get what we want in this life; I'm not sure the next is much different."

Before I could think of a reassuring response, Master Lloyd called for the servants to present the subtleties: little shepherds, sheep, wise men, and angels molded in sugar. Only the Holy Family were carved of wood, not meant to be eaten. I slipped a shepherd, sheep, and angel into my pouch for the children in the cottage. Nicholas caught the movement and slid his own sugary angel over to me.

"One for you as well," he whispered.

I accepted it with a smile.

Alice, who was sitting across from me, leaned closer. "I talked to the maidens' guild at church today, and we are planning a masque for Twelfth Night. You'll help, will you not?"

"Of course," I said. It felt like a lifetime since I had danced, and it would be good to have something to look forward in the dark, cold days after Christmas.

"Will you attend, Master Bowen?" Alice asked.

Nicholas looked down. I opened my mouth to encourage him, but he shook his head. "I'm not much of a dancer, I'm afraid."

I tried to hide my scowl. I would have liked to dance with him, and he needed to get away from the lonely halls of Nant Bach.

Alice glanced down the table to where Hugh sat. "Master Richards, I'm sure you'll not disappoint us."

He looked at me. "I love to dance. If my business does not call me away, I'll try to be there."

I smiled. At least I would have some pleasant company. I imagined dancing with Hugh, flirtation in every look and touch, and my heart beat faster.

"And Master Rhys?" Alice's pale cheeks turned rosy when she spoke his name.

"Aye, I would not miss it."

He and Alice grinned at each other. I tried not to look at Nicholas. If he had ever entertained any ideas about Alice, they would be crushed now.

Mistress Rhys rolled her eyes. "Please do not disappoint us, Master Richards. 'Twill not be much of a masque if the only young man there is my brother."

Everyone laughed except Nicholas. He kept his eyes fixed on his plate, his mouth curved into a thoughtful frown.

After dinner, we rose from the table and Master Lloyd handed out gifts to the family, guests, and servants.

Hugh came to stand by me. " 'Twill be time to go soon."

I nodded. "I'll get my cloak. I'm going to meet you there."

"Very well." He smiled and rested his hand on my arm before striding off to make his farewells.

As I edged out of the room, I caught Nicholas watching me. I met his gaze, wondering if he would come to the Mass too. He had refused to allow it to be held on his lands, though. The problem with weaving a life from half-truths and equivocations was there was no way to bring all the threads together into one neat picture. Nicholas seemed to read my uncertainty and glanced away, allowing me to slip out unseen.

Chapter Seventeen

I came back downstairs with an old cloak draped over my shoulders and my leather traveling mask in hand. Master Lloyd waited for me by the door to the buttery. I paused, not certain if he objected to me taking Mass. Would he forbid me from leaving? Ask questions I could not answer?

"Ah, I know where you're going," he said, "and I'll not try to stop you. Indeed, I wish I were going myself. I'm half tempted, but were we to get caught . . ." He shrugged. "Be cautious, child, and say an extra prayer for my welfare."

"Of course, Master Lloyd," I said. "Thank you."

As I hurried to the cottage, I could not help comparing Master Lloyd to Nicholas. Master Lloyd believed what we were doing was right, but he was too afraid to come with us. He was willing to break the law smuggling for extra profits, but not to follow his conscience. At least Nicholas was consistent in his stance. Perhaps Master Lloyd was more the coward, to turn his back on what he thought was right instead of forging his own path and sticking to it.

The children grinned at the Christmas treats. Hannah and Gwilliam tucked theirs away for later, but Beth sucked her sugary angel as we disguised ourselves. The children donned their ragged old clothes, and I tied on my mask. It would look suspicious if anyone saw us, but I could not afford to be recognized. Beth grunted in protest when Hannah told her to leave the spindle behind, but we finally coaxed her outside.

We trekked through the long afternoon shadows to the cave. The space blazed with candlelight, and a table and cloth were set in the back for the Mass. The gold crucifix and cup glinted in the bright light. I caught my breath, and Hannah gasped in wonder. Mass transformed the dirty little cave into a sacred space, a miniature cathedral, not only by its trappings, but also by the reverent quiet of the small group gathered there, a motley handful of gentry and yeoman farmers.

Several other women were there, also masked, and most of the men wore low hoods, but I recognized a few from church. We did not glance at one another. We were sharing a sacred moment, but we had to pretend we were alone. Everyone huddled close, not all fitting inside the cave, but at least able to see and bask in the light.

Father Davies caught my eye, and I nodded. He motioned me over with a smile. I curtseyed to him, and Father Perkins joined us.

"I am glad to see you well," Father Perkins whispered to Gwilliam and Hannah. He ignored Beth, but Father Davies smiled and let her gently touch the end of his crucifix.

"We're safe, thanks to Mistress—" Gwilliam caught himself before betraying my name to any unfriendly ears, but he did not hide the reproach for Father Perkins in his voice.

"It is well you found each other." Father Perkins turned to me. "Are you considering traveling overseas with them?"

I felt Hugh's gaze on me. "Perhaps."

"Think of your duty," Father Perkins said. "God gave you your life, and you ought to return it to his service. Even death is not too much for Him to ask."

"Aye, if it comes to it," Father Davies said more gently, "but life is precious. God does not give us gifts expecting us to throw them aside."

The two priests exchanged an uncomfortable glance. This was part of some longstanding argument, it seemed, and not just about me.

"We need to speak," Father Perkins said to Hugh, leading him aside.

Father Davies smiled at me. "I am glad to see the good work you are doing here. You have tamed your fire?"

I could not lie to a priest. "I do not know. I am still angry. I want to see my country free." I remembered the look on Nicholas's face when he told me of the horrors of war. "I'm uncertain if what I'm doing is right, or if what I want is even possible."

Father Davies nodded and spoke in a hushed tone. "The best minds of our age have the same dilemma. Some Jesuits believe, as Father Perkins, that we must take action against our enemies, do whatever we can to dethrone the queen. Father Garnet is our superior now, though, and he hopes we can find a more peaceful approach to winning England and Wales back to the old faith: that by living devout, honest lives, we can prove that we should be trusted to live our religion in peace. He encourages us to have faith in God's will."

It was an enticing idea, but I struggled to accept that living a quiet, peaceful life would change much of anything. It would just allow the queen and her agents to win.

Father Davies studied me. "We dishonor God by not trusting in Him, Mistress Pryce. What does your heart tell you is right?"

"I do not know. Sometimes what my heart says does not make sense."

"What the heart wants is not always what our head knows is best for us. Then it takes great courage to follow the course we know is right. Other times, though, it takes great faith to follow what our heart whispers, even when we see no sense or hope in it."

"How do I know which time is which?"

"You listen to heart and head. Then you pray, and you be still."

He left me and joined Father Perkins in presenting the Mass. I leaned forward, focused on each familiar Latin phrase. After the raising of the Host, Father Davies recited an account of the Nativity, using the same verses the Protestant priest had that morning. How odd two groups who bled and burned over their differences would celebrate the same sacred day with the same beautiful words. But the Mass filled the hunger in my soul—my longing for a lost world and my lost family—in a way the Protestant service did not. I could almost imagine myself once again in my father's chapel, with everything right in the world.

Hoofbeats shattered the quiet: several riders approaching fast.

Our little group scattered like sheep before wolves. I hesitated, glancing back at the cave. Father Perkins and Father Davies scrambled to gather their sacred vessels and linens. Hugh drew his sword with a wild grin. He caught my anxious gaze.

"Run! I'll make sure our friends are safe."

He was right; I would only be a hindrance. I pulled up my hood and grabbed Hannah's hand. Gwilliam swung Beth into his arms, and we bolted for the trees.

The riders broke formation, charging after the fleeing Catholics. One man hung back, directing the others, his hat recognizable even with its red plume broken off. Would I never be rid of him? I tightened my grip on Hannah's hand and ran harder, my pulse hammering a steady rhythm in my ears. Nay, it was the sound of hoofbeats getting closer.

Blessed Mary, preserve us!

The trees' branches reached out in welcome. I veered to where the trunks were thickest and dove through the tangled limbs. A branch glanced off my mask and drew a stinging cut across my unprotected cheek and ear. I scrambled deeper into a stand of wild hazel and motioned the children to follow. We huddled against the trunks, the thick branches arching over us.

Gwilliam clutched Hannah's hand. Beth whimpered and clung more tightly to his neck.

Racing footsteps crunched past. I peeked out to see one of the men from the Mass gasping as he ran for a nearby hill.

"Stop in the name in the queen!" a voice called behind him.

I jerked back and drew my cloak closer. Gwilliam and Hannah peered through the branches, their eyes wide.

"Get down!" I whispered.

"Nay," Hannah said, "we cannot let them catch him! He'll end up like my parents."

I groaned. Her parents had died in jail, as my father practically had. We could not stand by and watch the queen's agent arrest a fellow Catholic.

Gwilliam shoved Beth into my arms and crawled from our hiding place, dagger in hand. Beth went stiff and then rocked gently in my arms. I bit my tongue to keep from shouting and betraying our position.

Saint David, keep Gwilliam safe!

Gwilliam crept past the bare trunks. The queen's agent tackled the fleeing Catholic, tumbling to the ground with him. The Catholic was an older man with a long, gray beard. The queen's man hauled him to his feet and punched him in the face. Gwilliam raced forward and plunged his dagger into the agent's leg.

The man screamed and collapsed to his knees, glaring at Gwilliam. Gwilliam stood like a figure from a carving, still holding the dagger aloft. The gray-bearded man paused to kick the queen's agent in the gut, then jerked at Gwilliam's arm.

Gwilliam did not look at us but fled deeper into the woods. I tapped Hannah's arm and motioned for her to sneak away from the queen's agent and his shouts for help. Soon the woods would be alive with men searching for us. Searching for Gwilliam.

We stumbled through the trees, slipping on wet leaves and patches of ice. My arms ached from Beth's weight.

"Here!"

Gwilliam motioned to us from behind a fallen tree. I staggered over and slumped beside the mossy trunk, my whole body trembling. Hannah sank down next to me. I handed Beth into her embrace. Gwilliam still clutched his dagger, the point dark with blood.

"I think we've escaped." His tone sounded hollow, and he slowly wiped the dagger clean on a clump of dried grass. The dagger I had given him. He might have killed someone with it, and I was the one who brought him into this danger. It had been his only chance to see Father Perkins, though. I looked again at his pale face. Now, one of the queen's men recognized Gwilliam and would be watching for him. He was no longer just a vagabond child in hiding but a known outlaw.

"We need to get you back to the cottage," I whispered. It was not truly safe, but the illusion was there, and at least it offered a little protection. It was on Nicholas's land, and his reputation might shelter the children still. I had not seen all of our pursuers, but this time I believed that Nicholas had nothing to do with them.

The children got shakily to their feet, and we crept through the woods, watching over our shoulders. We found our way to the cottage without seeing another living creature. Even the birds seemed to be hiding. Did that mean the queen's men were still hunting, or had they captured a big enough prize to let the rest of us go?

"Stay inside," I warned Gwilliam. "I'll try to come tomorrow to bring you news."

He shut the door, and the bolt clanked into place. The day was wearing to a close. I needed to return to Plas Lloyd, where I could make a pretense of innocence, but I could not go back without knowing what had become of the others. I could not help thinking of the squint-eyed metalsmith and wondering if my actions had betrayed us.

I snuck toward the cave, keeping in the evening shadows. The sun slipped behind the hills, snuffing out what little warmth it had offered.

Quiet footsteps rustled on the path. I swung behind an ancient tree and pressed against the smooth bark. Someone passed by slowly, and I held my breath. Once their footsteps moved beyond my hiding place, I peeked out and recognized the tall silhouette.

"Master Hugh!" I called softly.

He whirled, hand on his rapier hilt, and then his shoulders relaxed, and he loped forward to pull me into an embrace.

"You're safe!" he whispered. "I wanted to be sure."

"Aye, and the children are too. What of—"

He held up a warning hand. "Our friends all escaped this time. We were quite fortunate. Some of the queen's men were distracted helping a wounded comrade."

There was a question in his voice, but I chose not to answer. The fewer people who knew what Gwilliam had done, the better.

"I am just glad no one was captured." The comfort of the Mass lingered over me like the fading glow of the sun, but perhaps it was well that there would not be another one for some time. Still, it had been beautiful. Our actions hurt no one until they forced us to defend ourselves. *Curse the queen and her sheep-brained agents!*

"We might not be able to use the cave again now. I have some more papers for you, but you'll have to hide them somewhere else. We are counting on you to keep them safe."

I nodded. I could not risk keeping them in the house. Perhaps I could find a place in the garden. I would miss the cave, though. It would look just as it had before, but it would never feel the same to me, marked now by the events both sacred and frightening that had taken place there.

"Bring them to me, and I'll take care of them," I said.

"Thank you." He shifted and looked up, squinting at the distant mountains. "Tell me, are you truly thinking of going overseas?"

"I am considering it."

"To take orders?"

"I'm not sure that life is for me, but it is becoming so dangerous, I do not know if there is anything left for me here."

Hugh looked down and scuffed his boot on the dirt. "Nothing at all?"

"I'm not sure. Every time I try to see where I'm going, there is only haze."

"Maybe you can be convinced, then, that there's something for you here?"

I stared into his amber eyes, my legs suddenly feeling weak. How much longer could I tolerate living in shadows and half-truths, though? "Perhaps."

"*Perhaps* is all I need. I fight for the things I believe in." He stroked back a stray curl of my hair, and I shivered.

"I know," I whispered. I would fight for what I wanted too, when I was sure what it was.

Chapter Eighteen

I approached Plas Lloyd by way of the privies, trying to act as though I had not been missing for hours. I carried my mask inside my cloak and wore my hood up to conceal the throbbing scratch on my face and ear.

Shouts echoed from the front of the *plasty*. My hands went cold, but I stepped through the door of the buttery as if nothing were amiss. Extra food from the Christmas feast was piled in the room, awaiting the servants and poor tenants. I quickly took off my cloak, wrapping my mask inside it.

One of the serving girls carried another platter into the room. I turned so she would not see the cut on my face. She gave a start when she saw me, then smiled.

"Pardon me, mistress. Hiding from the racket?" she asked.

"Aye, I have a headache enough as it is. Why must they shout?"

"They're like peacocks, always showing off. 'Tis clear enough the master has been here all day, not off causing a ruckus. We've half a dozen neighbors to vouch for it. I suppose the priest hunters have to search everywhere, though."

"Certainly."

"'Twould help if he were a little more regular about attending church." The girl paled a little and curtseyed. "Forgive me. I meant no disrespect. He's a good master."

She hurried out, and I relaxed. The queen's men were probably searching everyone suspected of Catholic sympathies. Master Lloyd was innocent of this offence, and his servants were faithful and loyal. A rare enough trait, but he had earned their respect by his fair treatment. I could only hope the other Catholics at the Mass had good excuses or good servants and friends willing to cover for them.

My presence was not needed, and I did not want to attract attention if Master Red-Plume was directing the search, so I trudged upstairs. At least I was not lying when I claimed a headache. I curled up on my bed with a groan and pulled the cloak over me.

The mask tumbled out, its hollow eyes staring back. I shivered and turned it over. If I stayed in Wales, would I have to spend the rest of my life hiding? I could not be caught with the mask if anyone had seen it. I sat up and tossed it into the fire. The flames licked around it, smoldering the edges black and slowly consuming it.

Nicholas's Christmas gift sat on my pillow where I'd left it. Things had seemed so simple this morning. I unfolded the paper and lost myself in the words of the Bible—perhaps the one thing I did not have to hide—drifting to sleep with the page clutched in my fingers.

The next morning, I applied enough face powder to hide the red scratch and went downstairs as though nothing were wrong. No one said anything about the events of the previous day until the Rhyses arrived with Mistress Meredith.

"It was an uprising, a coup!" Mistress Meredith proclaimed. "And on Christmas. *Que Dieu nous bénisse!* The Papists will never let us have peace."

I huffed quietly. Nit-brained girl.

"There was only one injury," Master Rhys said. "I would hardly call that a coup."

I nodded, then caught myself. Alice cast me a suspicious glance, but I rubbed my neck and concentrated on my sewing.

"Did they catch anyone?" Alice asked.

"Nay," Master Rhys said, "but they are looking for several culprits: a man with graying hair and a long beard; two priests, both lean and clean-shaven; a tall young man, perhaps twenty, with dark hair and beard; and a boy, about thirteen, thin and poorly dressed."

Hugh and Gwilliam! The queen's agents had seen the priests too. At least they did not seem to know about me. I could help the others.

David and Winifred, save us!

I passed the day sewing like a dutiful young lady. With dreams of Italy and freedom still playing in my mind, I decided to create a Roman costume for the masque, remaking an old white chemise into a stola and draping it with a purple sash. Alice was finishing her gown to be Cleopatra. My mask was a simple white affair that would cover my eyes. My identity would not be particularly hidden, but I was weary of secrets.

At dusk, one of the serving girls quietly fetched me to the door of the buttery, a sly grin on her face. Hugh stood in the shadowy yard, looking very young with his beard freshly shaved and his face hidden by a hood.

"They're looking for you," I whispered to Hugh as soon as the maid left us alone.

"I know, but I have things to do, and I will not let them stop me."

I walked with him to the garden, where he showed me a stack of papers wrapped in leather. We found a large bush to bury them under.

"The printing's going well, then," I said, wiping the dirt from my hands.

He looked away for a moment, and I wrinkled my forehead. Was he worried about the raid on the Mass, or was there something else he was hiding?

He cleared his throat. "Aye, everything's fine. We've nearly printed the entire first section. Then we'll need to get copies of it smuggled across the country."

His smile looked forced. Well, we all had enough to worry about, with enemies always waiting and watching, and even our friends liable to turn on us.

"The metalworker you asked me to deliver the pages to," I said, "I do not think you can trust him."

He sighed and pushed his hair back. "Did he do something that made you suspicious?"

"A while ago, I saw him take money from that man who led the attack on the Mass. I was not sure what to think of it, but after the raid—"

Hugh swore quietly. "I was so sure about him." His expression brightened. "We can use this to our advantage, though—feed him false information to pass on. This is a brilliant discovery, Mistress Joan! And at very little cost to us. Thank you!"

I smiled, until I remembered that Gwilliam was now a wanted outlaw. I did not count that cost as small.

He rubbed his eyes. "'Tis always hard knowing whom to trust. There's so much at stake. More than you can guess."

I leaned forward. "I wish I could help more."

"You may get your wish soon. There's much to be done in the days to come if we're to free ourselves from the tyranny of the queen."

"Good," I said. "I suppose you will have to miss the masque, though?"

"I wish I could attend, but I would not want anyone to get in trouble for being close to me. Especially not you."

I wanted to protest that it might be worth it. I was tired of standing with one foot in and one out. Before I could frame my argument, he leaned down to give me a quick kiss.

"I'll see you again when I can."

With a smile, he hurried off into the mist rising from the woods. I touched my lips, still warm from his. I could easily be swept away in his passion, if only he would include me in it.

Over the next week, I kept my head down and avoided drawing attention to myself. I snuck away a couple of times to the cottage, always making certain I was not followed, but the rest of the time I threw myself into preparations for the masque. The maidens' guild hoped to earn enough money from selling ale there to buy new prayer books for the church. At least they would be in Welsh. Maybe we could raise money for copies of the Welsh Bible when it was printed.

The guild was to meet at Plas Lloyd the day before the masque. I rode out in the morning to visit the children, watching for signs of pursuit. I slowed my mare as I approached the cottage. Here was a place I could be happy, pretend that all was simple and comfortable in the world. I worked with Hannah on her reading and again talked Gwilliam out of going outside. The time passed too quickly, and I was riding back to Plas Lloyd.

I gave my mare an extra helping of oats and walked to the front of the *plasty*, but Nicholas stood there, leaning against the doorframe as if in pain. I drew breath to call out to him; then the voices from the *plasty* reached me through an open shutter.

"He may end up excessively rich if he keeps going this way, but think of having to look at that face every day," Alice said.

"Aye, it might not be so bad in the dark, but waking up to it each morning?" Mistress Rhys snickered.

"You might not have to put up with it much anyway. He's so cold, 'tis hard to imagine . . ." Alice trailed off in a giggle.

"There is a reason God gave him a countenance like that," Mistress Meredith said. "He is a selfish, plague-festered monster, as everyone knows."

"I could tolerate quite a bit, though, for as rich as he'll be. Is Joan Pryce to marry him for certain?" Mistress Rhys asked.

"I doubt it," Alice said. "She's been spending time with him, but I think Father told her she must. She much prefers the company of Hugh Richards, and who can blame her?"

More giggles rained through the shutter, setting my teeth on edge. Bleating, hen-brained harpies.

Saint David send cankers to blister their tongues.

Nicholas straightened. I whisked myself out of sight around the corner. Slow footsteps trudged past me.

"Master Nicholas!" I called softly.

He spun and glared at me. I scurried to catch up with him.

"I . . . I'm sorry."

"Sorry for what?" he whispered. "Was anything they said untrue?"

What could I say? It was not his face that bothered me—not anymore—but he did not believe as I did and showed so little passion for life. He gave no sign that he wished to marry me, and I did not think we would ever suit each other as aught but friends.

"You're not a monster," I said, "and no one forces me to visit you. I'm glad we are friends."

He shook his head and trudged for the stables. I watched him go, my temper boiling through my veins, and then I fled in the other direction. I would not sit with those cruel girls. I could not smile in their faces when I wanted to run them through with rapiers made of their own piercing gossip.

I stopped when I reached the stones marking the boundary between Nicholas's land and Master Lloyd's. Was I wrong to be friendly with Nicholas? His reaction to the cruel gossip might have been due to more than the mockery. Had I led him to believe my feelings were changing? Had his changed? He was certainly more open with me now, but he was so restrained compared to Hugh's flirtations that I could not be sure. Besides, I might be leaving. It was unwise to be too attached to anyone here.

Chapter Nineteen

On Twelfth Night, candles blazed in the windows of our neighbor, Master Jones, casting a warm glow into the chilly gray evening. I tugged my wool cloak more snugly over my costume and adjusted my white mask. A secretive smile curved Alice's lips beneath her Cleopatra mask. My stomach tightened as we stepped into the great hall crowded with neighbors from the parish. A fire roared in the hearth, and musicians gathered on the raised platform at the far end of the hall, tuning their instruments in a cacophonous racket. Colorful tapestries brightened the walls, and evergreen boughs crowned the room.

We hung our cloaks among many others, the animal smell of damp wool mingling with the scents of smoke and pine.

"Mistress Lloyd! Mistress Pryce!"

Masked faces swiveled toward us. The hooded and glass eyes looked menacing behind their feathers, beads, and carved leather. I touched the smooth silk of my mask, wishing now that it hid me better. Mistress Rhys strutted over with a grin, and the crowd shifted to let her through. Several men watched her with admiring glances. Peacock feathers from her mask arched over her forehead, and smaller plumes curled down to caress her cheeks.

"You both look beautiful." She grinned. "Everything is just perfect!"

"Where is Mistress Meredith?" Alice asked.

Mistress Rhys laughed. "She decided this was an impious way to celebrate the wise men's visit to the Holy Family. Do not look sorry, Mistress Lloyd. This frees more dancing partners for the rest of us."

She took our arms and paraded us through the great hall. I was the only Roman lady in attendance, but I spotted a Julius Caesar among the men. Several ladies wore the gossamer wings of fairies, and others used the excuse of the party to break the sumptuary laws restricting dress and bedeck themselves as queens and fanciful goddesses. The men were mostly disguised as knights, though I noticed a Poseidon in the group, and even a devil with a black mask to compliment his dark doublet and hose.

We crowded onto the benches lining the hall to watch a troupe of players perform a Christmas pageant, ending with the Holy Family fleeing to Egypt while King Herod killed all the male infants. I shivered. The story was better with just the shepherds and wise men.

The musicians struck up their chords, and Master Rhys, dressed as Mark Antony, swept Alice into the dancing. Two men hurried toward Mistress Rhys and me, but when the first claimed Mistress Rhys's hand, the other sank back into the crowd. Humiliation brightened my cheeks, and I pressed back from the dance floor. I did not know anyone in the parish well, and everyone assumed I was spoken for. No one would be courting me. Just as well. I had to be careful what I said and did. Still, I loved to dance.

"My lady?" a deep voice asked.

I turned to see a knight, his face hidden by his helmet, extending his hand to me. I grinned and accepted it, and he led me into the dance: a slow, courtly pavane.

"Greek or Roman?" he asked, his voice muffled by his visor.

"Roman."

"Perhaps not the best choice these days. Roman sympathies are not very popular."

I paled. If only my mask covered more of my face. The complex steps of the dance gave me a few moments to compose my answer. A girl's costume would not be enough to condemn her, I hoped, but I could not trust someone who seemed to be prying for information.

The festive atmosphere of the masque suddenly seemed raucous, the hidden faces all unfriendly.

"I had not thought much of the difference. I could be Greek if you prefer. Diana or Artemis—it makes little difference to me."

"The goddess of the moon, then? Her Majesty would be flattered."

Of course, Queen Elizabeth associated herself with Diana as the maiden goddess of the moon. I had been thinking of Diana's role as the archer and goddess of the hunt when I designed my costume, but I would not gainsay my mysterious partner now.

"Now it is my turn to guess your identity," I said.

Did he tense a little, or was it just the difficult turn in the dance?

"Very well. And who do you suppose I am?"

"A noble knight, of course. Perhaps one of the best: Arthur, Llewellyn the Great, or Owain Glyndŵr."

"Arthur is noble enough, but Owain was a rebel."

I gritted my teeth. The man's Welsh was good, but no Welshman would dispute the glory of our last native prince. "I was thinking only of his bravery."

"Your guess was closest with Llewellyn, but I am greater, for I am he who conquered his dynasty, Edward Longshanks."

I recoiled. "Sir, that is in bad taste!"

"To honor the first who brought England and Wales into their current harmonious state?"

Harmonious? He was trying to see how far he could push me. I smiled. "I would give the credit for that victory to Henry the Seventh. Was it not he who united in himself Welsh and English blood and started our current dynasty? The fruits of Edward Longshanks were war, but Henry Tudor brought us peace."

He bowed his head in acknowledgment and said nothing more. I stood tall and straight until he left me at the end of the dance; then I sank onto a bench, clasping my hands in my lap to keep them from trembling. Was this man the same who ordered Plas Lloyd searched? Who had followed me in Conwy? How many enemies had I collected in my adventures? The false Edward watched me from the side of the great hall, so when a young gentleman dressed as

Charlemagne asked me to dance a lively galliard, I forced a smiled and accepted as though nothing were wrong.

The whole time I danced, I felt someone's gaze on me. I glanced up, expecting to see the false Edward again. Instead, it was the devil tracking my movements. The mask covered his face completely, but something about the way he stood seemed friendly and familiar. Could it be that Hugh had come in disguise? I stood straight and, despite my fatigue, forced myself to keep my steps light and quick, the match of my partner.

When the dance ended, my partner returned me to my place. The man in the devil mask appeared at my side. I had expected it—perhaps even hoped it—but still my heart beat faster. He did not speak, just offered his black-gloved hand. I studied his face, but the mask obscured his features and shaded his eyes so I could not identify him as Hugh. I placed my hand against the smooth, warm leather of his glove. He wordlessly encircled my fingers in a strong grip and led me to the floor for another galliard.

He stepped close, and the smell of his leather doublet wrapped around me. His hand pressed against my back, warm and sure, guiding me as we leapt and turned through the crowded room. My skin tingled where his hand rested, his fingers pressing into my thin linen costume. He spun me, keeping his hand close so his fingers trailed over my waist, then pulled me near again. My breath came faster, and my face flushed.

The tempo of the dance increased, and some couples dropped to the sidelines. My legs ached, but I tightened my hold on the devil's gloved hand. He guided me with a firm grip, never missing the beat, releasing me then pulling me so near I could feel the fast rise and fall of his chest. His touch sent thrills racing over me even through his gloves. He leaned close enough to kiss me if his mask had not prevented it. I tilted my face to his, trying to meet his shadowed gaze. He spun me again, setting curls flying loose from my pinned braids.

The dance ended with me encircled in his strong arms, his heat washing over me, my skin alive to his touch. I leaned against his chest, struggling to catch my breath.

It was he who finally stepped back and returned me to my place with bow. My racing heart twinged as I let go of his arm. I did not dare speak Hugh's name in case knowledge of his presence put him in danger, and I could not be positive it was him behind the mask.

"Will you not speak?" I whispered as he moved to leave.

He paused and gave a quick headshake. I reached out, and he turned back. He gently traced the faint red scratch on my cheek with his thumb. I shivered and closed my eyes. Then his warm touch was gone.

I sagged onto the bench and leaned my head against the wall. The musicians played a bransle, and the dancers joined hands in a line snaking through the room. The devil disappeared into the shadows on the edge of the hall, but my heart would not stop pounding. My head felt light, as if I had not eaten all day. The room, filled with milling, swaying bodies, was stifling and dangerously hot.

Upstairs, servants were laying a feast for after the ball. When all the guests went up to eat, we would remove our masks and laugh at the confusion. Would the false Edward be there? Would the devil? Nay, I was certain both would disappear before the repast, leaving the whole evening like some strange dream. I longed for the return of normalcy, and for something cool to drink. I rose unsteadily and snuck over to the back staircase. It was poor manners to seek drink or food before it was offered, but I needed a moment of quiet.

I started up the dim stairs, pressing my hand against the plastered wall for support. An echo to my footsteps sounded in the narrow staircase. I paused and looked behind. Nothing moved in the gloom. My back prickled with goose bumps. I glanced up toward the gallery and the waiting refreshments, but being alone had lost its appeal. I turned to go back down.

The false Edward rushed out of the shadows below me.

I screamed. He covered my mouth, swinging me around with my back against his chest and forcing me up the stairs. I dragged my boots, tripping over each stair. He lifted me with one arm. I bit hard into his gloved palm, tasting blood and leather.

He swore and smashed my head against the wall. I sank to the stairs, my ears ringing. The staircase swam into haziness. I tried to slide away. He grabbed a chunk of my hair and slammed my head into the edge of the stair. Black spots spun across my vision.

"Do not scream again. I need information from you. I would rather not have to kill you, but you would not be the first pretty miss to die tumbling down the stairs."

"You dungheap worm," I spat.

He slapped me, and my head rocked to the side. "Do you want to try the sharpness of your tongue against my dagger?"

I could not draw enough breath for a reply. It would be better to die silent than as a traitor to my friends.

"Who else is involved in smuggling the papers?" the man asked. "What are you scheming against my queen?"

I shook my head. He gripped my hair and yanked my head back, wrenching my neck. A whimper caught in my throat.

"Where is the outlaw priest William Davies? I know he was a guest at your father's *plasty*." I could hear the sneer in his voice. "Master Pryce was willing to tell me whatever I wanted to buy his way out of jail, especially when I reminded him you could join him there. It was most unfortunate that he died before handing me the priest."

The stairway seemed to collapse around me, dropping me into nothingness. Had my father's betrayal of his faith gone so far that he would throw his friends to the wolves?

"'Twas you who searched his house, my room," I said, my words a little slurred. "Vile pig."

He smacked my head against the stairs again. Another blow might be enough to kill me. I prayed he would hit too hard, end it quickly.

He grunted and lurched forward, landing beside me. I blinked at the dark figure on the stairs just below us. The man in the devil mask! The false Edward kicked out. The devil grabbed his leg and yanked him down. Edward's helmet fell off, revealing Master Red-Plume.

The English lout braced himself and kicked the devil in the knee with his free leg. The devil stumbled but caught himself against the wall. Master Red-Plume drew his dagger.

"Watch out!" I cried hoarsely.

Master Red-Plume turned to strike me. I flinched. The devil

jabbed him in the kidney. Master Red-Plume swore, and his dagger clattered to the stairs. He fumbled after it, but I kicked it out of reach.

The devil snatched the dagger and lunged. Master Red-Plume rolled aside and scrambled to his feet, scurrying up the stairs. The devil snarled behind his mask and moved to follow, but stopped when he reached me. He reached a gentle hand to touch my face. I grasped it, as if it could stop me from slipping into the black that hovered at the edges of my sight.

Voices sounded from below.

"You had better run too," I mumbled, "unless you want to answer questions."

He nodded once and ran up the stairs after Master Red-Plume.

Frantic hands and voices pressed around me. My head pounded and my stomach churned. I listened for any noises above, but my assailant and my rescuer vanished like ghosts.

"Mistress Pryce? What happened?" asked a worried voice I thought belonged to Master Jones.

What could I say? Master Red-Plume had allies in the parish. I could not guess who they were, and I did not want to draw their attention.

I wet my lips. "I wanted some air—I was too hot—I think I fainted and hit my head."

"Bring some wine," Master Jones ordered one of the men standing behind him. "Find Master Lloyd."

"I do not want to ruin the masque," I said.

"Well, 'tis over for you, at least," he said gently. "We'll see you home."

Chapter Twenty

The Lloyds kept me in bed for several days on the orders of the local surgeon. He bled me until my arm was dotted with sore, purple bruises, and he ordered the maids to pour foul broths down my throat. I gagged on each one, which brought my headaches screaming back. I was paying for my lies now, but I had to keep my secrets; they were not mine alone to share.

"Joan, there's a gift for you," Mistress Lloyd announced after the latest visit of the surgeon.

"A gift? All I want is sleep," I mumbled. Each appointment with the surgeon left me weaker. Master Red-Plume may have killed me after all.

"Are you certain? This might wash the foul taste from your mouth."

I pushed myself up and squinted. The dim light stung my eyes, making my head throb and my stomach turn. "What is it?"

"A cask of cider from Master Nicholas." She gave me a sly smile. "There's a note as well."

I unfolded the paper, my hands shaking from weariness.

Mistress Pryce,

I am sorry to hear of your illness. Please accept this with my wishes for your speedy recovery.

Your servant,
Nicholas Bowen

I carefully refolded the note. He was the only one who had sent me anything. The rest of my neighbors apparently thought little of my well-being. Of course, I had not gone out of my way to be friendly to any of them. Still, Hugh might have sent me a message, especially if he was the masked devil. Had he escaped safely? What happened to Master Red-Plume? He knew who I was and could arrest me on a whim.

"Would you like to try the cider?" Mistress Lloyd asked.

I licked my cracked lips. "Aye, please. Did Master Bowen bring it himself?"

"He did."

"Is he still here?"

Mistress Lloyd brought a pewter cup and helped me sit up to drink. "He has gone."

"Oh." The ache of disappointment surprised me. I did not have the strength to go down and visit with him anyway. "Please send him a note. Tell him I thank him for his kindness."

I sipped the cider, thick and cool with a rich, woodsy flavor from the cask. It soothed my throat and filled me with warm memories of autumn, working beside Nicholas in the stillroom, his rare, friendly smiles and his sturdy, dependable seriousness. I took another sip and let the sweetness fill me until I could almost believe myself back there again, safe and happy. I had not realized how much I missed those moments.

"Thank you."

I forced myself to stay sitting, first to finish the cup and then to work on my embroidery. I could not keep my thoughts off Master Red-Plume. He might have left me free in order to draw out the other conspirators. The priests were more valuable prizes than a rebellious girl. I was no more than a pawn in this game. If Master Red-Plume spoke the truth, he had threatened me to manipulate my father too, forcing him to give up his faith and his friends. Would I have betrayed a priest to save my father? Would God forgive my father for his treachery? My worry kindled a horrible throbbing behind my eyes. I had to lie back occasionally to rest, but each time I pushed myself up, the pain faded more quickly.

When the surgeon returned the next day, he pronounced my color better, and frowned when he decided he did not have to bleed me again.

Shortly after, a maid bundled me in dressing gowns and blankets and helped me downstairs so I could join Alice next to the fire in the great hall. Cold crept in under doors and between shutters and stalked along the floor to bite our feet, despite our stockings and slippers. The wind snarled past the house, shaking windows and moaning through the fireplace, making the orange flames dance.

I pulled my blanket closer and watched out the window as the wind pushed and sculpted the snow, leaving feathery patterns, as though some giant bird had beat its wings against the cold ground. Were the children safe in the cottage? It was snug enough, and they had wood and food, but they were probably worried. I longed to talk with Hannah and the others, but even if I could bundle up enough, the snow on the ground would betray my secrets. I hoped the children would not venture out.

I flexed my fingers and picked up a chilly brass needle. Back to work. At least I could dream of Italy while I stitched. Warm fields stretched out before my imagination, laden with grapes and figs, alive with the warmth of sunshine and freedom.

Alice sat next to me, her dreamy smile mirroring my own.

"You seem cheerful," I said.

She shrugged but could not suppress her grin.

I cleared my throat. "I suppose you had a good time at the ball."

Her cheeks pinked.

"Dancing with Master Rhys?" My needle made a faint pop as it pierced the linen.

"Do you think it's terrible?" Alice whispered.

"Terrible?" I wrinkled my forehead. "What do you mean?"

She stopped her stitching. "I loved John Bowen. A part of me always will, but I'm tired of mourning. I feel hollow and empty all the time. Yet when Master Rhys smiles at me . . ."

"Oh, Alice!" I grasped her hand. "'Tis good that you're happy again. John Bowen would not want you to mourn your life away. He was always smiling, from what I recall."

As Nicholas had been in those days. Was it worse to be so sad when you had once known what happiness was? Or was the happiness like an ember, keeping away a little part of the cold? My heart still ached to think of my family, but I was glad I had the memories of them, knowing I had not always been so utterly alone.

"Thank you." Alice squeezed my hand. "I just want to be happy. A home, husband, and children, and my heart will rest at ease."

"Then I'm sure you will find your happiness. It must be a gift, to have a content heart."

It was certainly a gift I did not possess. I was jealous of it. I wanted the same things she did, but I did not think they alone would bring me peace. My heart was always seeking, like a bird that could not find a roost.

After a week of bleak whiteness, the snow gave way to rain and turned the ground to muck. Still, it was enough to rouse the parish. After dinner, some of the Lloyds' poorer tenants braved the miserable, gray weather to take away the remnants of meals, and we finally had visitors again.

Each time someone came to the door, my shoulders tensed. Master Red-Plume might be near. His agents could drag me out into that bleak cold, never to return. If I was still long enough, they might think I had been scared off and would not be smuggling any more papers.

I ached to think my father had lived out his last days under this fear to spare me, and I worried over it as I sewed. Had Master Red-Plume always been watching, even then? My father had refused last rites. My needle paused mid-stitch. I had taken his final stubbornness as a betrayal of his faith, but if he had known Father Davies was in danger, he might have forbidden a priest's visit to spare his friend. Father Davies was willing to take the risk, but my father was trying to protect everyone he cared about as his life slipped away. A renewed admiration for him grew from my concern and sorrow.

It was the Rhyses who came to Plas Lloyd most often, nearly every day. I shrank from any company, though my secrets were safely hidden.

"Your needlework is so fine, Mistress Pryce." Mistress Rhys's voice made me jump. "Where did you learn that pattern?"

I traced my finger over the stitched green leaves decorating my wedding linens. "From my mother."

"Oh." Mistress Rhys looked down. "My mother died when I was very young. My aunt taught me to embroider"—she smiled a little—"but she's better at buying fine things than making them."

"I'm sorry about your mother."

Mistress Rhys nodded and stared at the fire, her sorrow an echo of my own. We might not agree about many things, but we both understood the pain of losing a mother.

"Would you like me to teach you?" I asked softly.

Nearly every day after that, Alice flirted with Master Rhys while I taught his sister to embroider. Alice blossomed anew in the cold winter afternoons, her cheeks pink, her smile bright and happy. I paled and withered under the weight of my fear and uncertainty.

I finally found a morning to lace up my boots, bundle in my cloak, and venture out into the misty rain. I could not imagine any of the queen's agents having the job of watching Plas Lloyd at all hours of the day, but to be cautious, I wandered a roundabout route, stopping in the stables to visit the horses and warm my tingling fingers for a few minutes, then dodging my way along the hedgerows, always checking over my shoulder until I reached the cottage.

Rain dripped from the thatch, and lazy trails of smoke wandered through the hole in the roof. I knocked on the door and stomped, trying to warm my tingling feet until Gwilliam called, "Who is it?"

"'Tis Joan. Please let me in before I freeze!"

"Joan!" Hannah squealed, rushing to embrace me. Even Beth glanced at me for a moment before going back to twirling a piece of yarn around the spindle.

"We were worried about you," Hannah said.

"And I about you." After a moment's debate, I told them a tamer version of the events at the masque.

"And the devil man saved you?" Hannah sighed. "It sounds like a romance story. Do you think you'll marry him?"

I laughed a little. "'Twould help if he were not hiding from me." I kept my speculations about his identity to myself. "I'm afraid here

155

in Wales there are too many things standing between me and the men I might marry. Perhaps overseas I could find someone who believes as I do, and who I do not have to keep secrets from."

Hannah glanced at Gwilliam. He reddened and looked away. It would not be long before he and Hannah were old enough to marry, if he had some way of supporting her. Apprentices could not marry until they were done with their training, though. The trial of their love story might be the long years of waiting, like Jacob serving fourteen years for Rachel. If I went overseas, I could help them before finding my way to Rome.

Beth cuddled close to Hannah and picked up the pages from the Welsh Book of Matthew Hannah had been reading. She tugged Hannah's sleeve and pointed to one of them.

Hannah's eyes widened. "Joan, Gwilliam! Listen to what Beth was pointing at: 'What therefore God hath joined together, let not man put asunder.'" She looked at her sister. "Do you understand this, Beth?"

Beth stared at Hannah for a moment, then went back to twirling her yarn. Hannah looked to Gwilliam and me, her eyes wide and hopeful.

"You've been reading to her and trying to teach her every day," Gwilliam said. "She may have learned more than we realized."

"But she read it herself and understood it, did she not?" Hannah said, her expression pleading.

"Try another one," I said softly. I flipped the page and smiled as I read the words. "Beth, do you know what Jesus said about children?"

I held the book out to her. Her forehead wrinkled briefly, and I kept my gaze on her face, though she would not meet my eyes. Instead, she studied the page for a moment and pointed.

Hannah read the verse quietly, "'Suffer little children, and forbid them not, to come unto me: for such is the kingdom of heaven.'"

She looked at me with tears in her eyes. "She understands. She can read."

"Aye, I believe she can." I stared at Beth in awe. What else could she do, if given the chance? Her best opportunities lay outside of Wales. The queen did not wish her poor subjects to read. Her fear held back Beth and so many others, smothering their potential.

Hannah laughed, wiping her tears, and grinned at Gwilliam. "Maybe we can teach her to talk to us this way. She does not have to be so hard to reach anymore."

He smiled too, and we gathered around Beth, gently coaxing her to point to words. She tired of the game and went to sit alone with her spindle, but that did nothing to dampen our hope.

We visited for as long as I dared. My joy drained away as soon as I left for Plas Lloyd, constantly watching for spying eyes. My nerves jangled by the time I reached the great hall, and I jumped to find Mistress Meredith sitting with the others, a smug expression on her face. Everyone else looked pale. They gave me wary looks, and Master Lloyd's expression was stern. What did they know?

I swallowed and slipped into the room, forcing a smile. "Good morrow."

"Good morrow, indeed, Mistress Pryce," Mistress Meredith said with a wolfish smile. "Have you heard the news?"

"Nay." I glanced at the others, but they did not meet my eyes.

"Mary, Queen of Scots, has been executed."

"Executed!"

"*Mais oui*. Beheaded," Mistress Meredith said.

I clutched at my throat. "Queen Elizabeth would not execute her own cousin."

"She would if her cousin was a scheming, honorless Papist. Let it be a warning to all traitors."

"Mistress Meredith!" Master Rhys glared at her. "We all want to see the queen safe, but there is nothing to celebrate in Her Majesty's council executing a woman and a sister queen."

I sank onto a stool and picked up my needlework, though I could hardly focus on it. Mistress Rhys sat quietly beside me, not touching her own embroidery.

"Woman or not," Mistress Meredith said, "it is all any Papist deserves. There have been more arrests all around Wales." She met the uncomfortable glances of the others. "At least the queen does not burn Papists as her half-sister did to Protestants, or slaughter them in the streets."

I jumped, pricking myself with the needle.

Mistress Meredith's voice rose. "My mother was a Huguenot, forced to flee France because of her Protestant beliefs. Her brother stayed behind with his wife and children. In the St. Bartholomew's Day Massacre, his own neighbors broke into his house. They murdered him, his wife, and their children—even the baby—and threw their bodies into the street like garbage, laughing and celebrating over the corpses." Her voice caught. "That is what Papists do. That is why we will never be safe as long as they are lurking in Wales."

My hands shook, and I clutched the pillowcase meant to be part of my wedding linens. My throbbing finger left a bloody spot on the soft, cream-colored fabric. True, Mary Tudor, the Catholic queen, had put Protestants to the flame. Now, her Protestant sister cut up Catholics while still alive. The massacre of the Huguenots was like a scene out of Hell; I could not comprehend it. Each generation grew more vicious. Could anger turn me into such a monster that I would enjoy the pains of others? Perhaps that was what Father Davies had been trying to warn me of.

"We need no more talk of bloodshed," Master Lloyd said.

Silence settled over the room. They killed the Queen of Scots. They would hunt Catholics to extermination, and being a woman was not the protection I had thought. I nearly died at the masque, and I was not safe now. Master Red-Plume knew who and what I was. The message from London reached us all the way out here on the coasts of Wales. If I stayed in my country and could not conform, my life would be forfeit.

When the air lost its bitter bite, Mistress Lloyd prepared for a trip to Conwy. I did not take any papers with me. Master Red-Plume or his associates might be watching, and my chest was heavy with thoughts of Queen Mary. I shopped halfheartedly, picking up a book of sonnets for Hannah and Beth and trying to decide if there was anything I could get Gwilliam that would help him overseas.

We passed a group of men working on the walls. Were they afraid the Welsh were going to rise up against them? It seemed the country was tame enough, eating out of the queen's hand. I watched for a moment. Nay, the men were not strengthening the walls. They were pulling part of them down. A shiver raced up my back.

"Mistress Lloyd, what are they doing?"

She squinted at the workmen. "Getting stone for the new houses."

"New houses? For Englishmen?"

"Mostly for Welshmen. Many people want to live in the town. There's more opportunity here."

She walked away, but I stared a moment longer. The walls of Conwy were coming down, and to build houses for Welshmen. Did that mean they no longer thought we were a threat? Was Wales defeated? Or were we gaining the trust of our monarch, winning our freedom?

Not freedom for everyone, though. They would set the Protestants free while tightening the noose around the Catholics. I was not welcome in my own country. I shuffled after the Lloyds.

We passed Mistress Meredith, who shared food with a poor mother and her children. I looked away before she caught me watching, sensing she did not do it for a public display. What an odd mix of anger and sympathy. A heart that hurt deeply might also see more opportunities to love, except where its injury had made it blind.

"Mistress Pryce!"

I jumped, but I had nothing to hide. Nicholas's crooked smile shone from beneath his hat as he stepped out of a goldsmith's shop, slipping something into his leather pouch. He hurried toward me through the crowd.

I smiled. "Master Bowen. 'Tis good to see you again. It seems a long time." I winced. The last time I saw him, the parish girls were insulting him.

"Since . . . after Christmas." He fidgeted with the starched ruff of his shirt, his gaze resting on me for a moment then darting away. "Um, I have some smoked fish. I believe they were part of our bargain."

"Oh! I'll have to find a reason to go riding to get them from you. The weather's been so bad . . ."

"Aye, it has," he said quickly. "I wanted to come, but I was not certain . . ."

We stood there for a moment, not quite making eye contact. Nicholas's hand drifted to the pouch at his belt.

"I was sorry to hear you were ill," he said. "I hope you're fully recovered?"

"No thanks to the doctor and his leeches." I grimaced, and he chuckled. "I appreciated the cider. It turned out very well."

"That was all thanks to you. I drink your health every time I taste it."

I blushed. "Thank you. You have been so kind. I'll not forget it."

His smile faded. "What do you mean?"

I had said too much. I felt so comfortable with Nicholas, I had almost forgotten how many secrets I kept from him. "Just that . . ." I sighed. I wanted one friend whom I could talk to. What I planned was illegal, but I did not think he would betray me. I could say just enough that he would understand, when the time came.

"I have been dreaming of Italy again."

His expression fell. "Oh?"

"It might seem silly to you, but I long to be warm when everything is dreary and . . . and to find somewhere where I do not have to hide."

"I see." He looked at the gray clouds drifting over the walls of Conwy. "I have to admit I cannot imagine being anywhere but home, but 'tis not silly to want to see more. You always had dreams of other places."

"I dream of home too," I said softly. "The only home I ever knew was taken from me, though, and I do not know where I belong."

He stepped forward and reached for my arm but pulled his hand back before his fingertips brushed my sleeve. "I hope you find what you seek, Mistress Joan," he said in a low voice.

He turned away. I almost called him back, but the words caught on the lump in my throat, so I watched him slowly wind his way through the crowd, ignoring the stares of strangers who recoiled from his face.

An ache built in my heart, a lonely emptiness I did not understand, almost as keen as when my father died. I clutched after my dreams of Italy, but they melted when I touched them. Winter's imaginings no longer warmed me. A fresh breeze from inland caressed my cheek and brushed aside the scent of the sea. Was I ready to bid farewell forever to the gentle hills and green valleys? To the chorus of Welsh hymns on Christmas morning? It did not matter what I wanted, for as long as Master Red-Plume hunted me, I would not be safe in Wales. Outcast, sojourner, I did not belong anywhere. There was nowhere that I could be free. I strained to see beyond the gray walls of Conwy, but if Wales held the key to finding my peace, she kept her secrets close like everyone else.

Chapter Twenty-one

The days grew longer, and green crept back into the garden and over the hills. Buds swelled on the twisted blackthorn branches, revealing hints of white petals, like pearls adorning the dark, thorny twigs. Each morning I awoke with an itching restlessness, unable to focus on my spinning or needlework.

I dared not dig up Hugh's papers in the garden, so I had to hope our hiding place was enough to keep them safe and dry. I heard nothing from Hugh or Nicholas. Hugh's tokens still clung to the tree, but the winter winds tore them to faded gray tatters. Only Gwilliam, Hannah, and Beth provided me with any company, and we talked of little but what we would like to do overseas.

One night in April, a tap at my shutters roused me from sleep. I rolled over and listened. Something thumped the side of the house. The wooden shutters rattled again. I threw on my dressing gown and swung my feet from the warmth of the covers. The cold stung my toes as I crept to the window. I opened the shutter a crack and peeked out.

Two hooded figures stood in the garden below—grown men, one leaning heavily on the other. My chest tightened, and I moved the shutter, but it creaked.

"Mistress Pryce!" Hugh's voice was barely more than a whisper on the wind.

"Master Richards? What—"

"We need help; please come down."

I swung the shutter closed and fumbled for my boots. My fingers paused on the laces. Could this be a trap? Might they be forcing Hugh to call me? Nay, I did not believe he would betray me, and there were easier ways to draw me out.

I snuck down the stairs, creeping past the quiet great hall, where the male servants slept, and out the door of the buttery.

"Master Richards?" I whispered. My breath blended with the creeping arms of mist reaching up from the fields.

"Mistress Pryce!" That voice belonged to Father Perkins.

I raced toward it, stumbling in the moonless predawn gloom. Hugh sat on a turf bench in the garden, clutching his side. Father Perkins bent over him.

"What happened?"

"He was cut," Father Perkins said. "Can you get something to clean it?"

Hugh gave me a rueful look, his face lined with pain. I hurried to the stillroom for some clean linen and verjuice and brought out a candle. In the flickering light of the beeswax taper, blood darkened Hugh's hands. I grimaced and cleaned the wound, but the cut went deep and fresh blood welled from it. I pressed a cloth to it, and it soaked through. I suspected it came from a sword thrust, but of course they were not going to tell me.

"You need to see a physician. I cannot stop the bleeding."

"We cannot go to anyone," Hugh said quietly. "We have been caught."

I inhaled sharply and glanced at Father Perkins. He nodded. "They discovered the cave where we had the printing press. One of the men, through God's grace, was friendly with Robert Pugh and did not want to see him hanged, so he gave us warning as they closed in."

"We took what we could and ran." Hugh slumped, holding his head in his hands and smearing blood across his forehead. "We lost the printing press and most of the copies of the book. Our work is ruined."

A lump formed in my throat. The book destroyed, the heart of our secret network torn out and stilled, and Hugh bleeding out his life in Master Lloyd's garden.

"They are looking for us," Father Perkins said. "I do not care what happens to me, but we cannot let them get the books."

I scowled at him and knelt in front of Hugh. "You're not going to live long enough to worry about being caught if we do not have someone with more experience look at this wound," I whispered to him.

"Would Master Lloyd give us shelter?" Hugh asked. He coughed and winced in pain.

I glanced at the sleeping *plasty*. The queen's men already suspected Master Lloyd, and he had a constant flow of Protestant visitors. This might be the opportunity Master Red-Plume hoped for by leaving me free: a trap for Hugh and Father Perkins.

"Nay, we need somewhere more private, less suspect." I gripped Hugh's sleeve. "What about Master Nicholas?"

"Nicholas Bowen?" Father Perkins cut in. "He's a heretic, only interested in himself."

"He would not let a friend bleed to death," I snapped. "Does human decency not go deeper than how one says his prayers?"

Hugh raised his head. "Aye, but 'tis a risk for him."

I glanced at the blood-soaked rag in my hand. Hugh would die if he did not get help. Nicholas was his friend, and he did not want to see any more bloodshed. He would want this chance to save Hugh's life.

"He would not turn his back on a friend," I whispered, "and his reputation makes Nant Bach safer."

"I see little other choice," Father Perkins said reluctantly. "Perhaps God blessed your friend with a rebellious heart for just this time."

"What about the papers?" Hugh asked, his voice raspy.

"Where are they?" I asked.

"In one of the casks in our wagon, over there," Father Perkins said.

"You brought it this far; I'll make it secure."

Father Perkins helped Hugh into the soft hay in the back of the wagon. I hoisted myself next to him, and Father Perkins took the reins.

"We have to get the papers out of the area," Father Perkins whispered as he guided the wagon through the mist. "Everyone here has been compromised."

"Where do they need to go?"

"To Saint Winifred's Well. My associates there will not be connected back to us."

"Oh." I sat back against the wagon seat. That was a journey of a couple of days, not as simple as a shopping trip to Conwy. "Why not just hide them?"

"They are the fruit of all our work and sacrifice," Father Perkins said. "They were not meant to be hidden away where the queen's men may ferret them out. We want the light to shine to all of Wales."

He was right. We had risked our lives for this cause. No sense in letting our work fall into Master Red-Plume's grubby hands. Did the whole of Wales not have the right to read the first book printed on our native soil? The queen's agents knew who I was, but I had not seen any trace of them for some time. If I got away without them following me, the papers and I should be safe.

"I'll find a way to take them," I said. "I can pose as a pilgrim."

"Do you know how to drive?" the priest asked.

"Nay." I bit my lip. This might be an adventure I could not undertake alone. I did not want to put the children in any more peril, but with spring approaching and the queen's men on the hunt, their hiding place was less secure. If we were together, we could watch out for each other and find our way overseas if necessary.

I raised my head. "If you take me to Nant Bach by the back way, I'll fetch the children. I think Gwilliam knows about horses—he's a yeoman's son—and we'll look less suspicious traveling together. We can say we are seeking a cure for Beth." The miraculous waters of the well might do some good for her troubled mind.

"Pilgrimages are still illegal," Father Perkins said.

"Few have the heart to stop them, though," Hugh said, struggling to rise on his elbow. "It could work."

" 'Tis very dangerous," Father Perkins said. "Not just for Mistress Pryce, but for the books as well."

"I understand," I said, "but this is important. When it is done, I can leave the country."

"Very well," Father Perkins relented and changed course. He exchanged a glance with Hugh, who gave a quick nod. "You'll need to go by way of the Pughs' home at Plas Penrhyn. There are papers hidden there . . . Mistress Pryce, we are putting everything in your hands. One document in particular is critical to our plans. The future of Wales depends on it."

My heart beat faster. "I will not fail you."

He nodded once and gave me precise instructions on how to find the papers hidden in a priest hole beside the fireplace at Plas Penrhyn, as well as where to meet his associate near Saint Winifred's Well.

"There is a fissure running beneath Plas Penrhyn and opening up near Little Orme—the cliffs overlooking the sea, where we had the printing press," he said. "You can enter it through a hidden opening in the courtyard. That is your safest route to escape the *plasty*."

I repeated his instructions back to him until he was satisfied that I had them memorized. Hugh showed me how to open the secret compartment in the cask. We neared the cottage. The wagon creaked loudly in the nighttime quiet of the woods.

"Wait here."

I hopped out and hurried through the oaks to the cottage. Gwilliam answered my summons, his eyes bleary with sleep. Behind him, Hannah and Beth lay huddled close to the remnants of the fire.

"Mistress Joan, what is it?" Gwilliam asked.

"We are going on a journey. When we return, 'twill be time to go overseas."

He smiled, the sleep melting from his face. "Wake up, Hannah, wake up, Beth! We are going!"

The girls stirred. "Where?" Hannah asked.

"I'll explain on the way," I said, "but we'll be leaving Wales soon."

Beth showed no reaction except to clutch her doll closer, but Hannah's face brightened. "Do we need to take our things?"

"We'll probably be back before we set sail. Your belongings are safer here than with us at an inn or sleeping on the road. If you have anything you cannot bear to be without, though, take it in case we have to flee. Gwilliam, can you drive a wagon?"

"Aye, I have done it before."

"Good. Let's go."

Their enthusiasm reignited mine as we hurried to the wagon. Hannah curtseyed to Father Perkins and stared shyly at Hugh, who was pale in the predawn light. Father Perkins let Gwilliam drive while I explained the plan to the children. Gwilliam handled the wagon well enough, bringing us close to Nicholas's *plasty*.

"Leave us here," Father Perkins whispered. "If things go wrong, you and the books will still be safely away."

"Do you know the old Roman road near Plas Penrhyn?" Hugh asked.

I shook my head, but Gwilliam nodded. "We used to walk that way."

"Good. 'Tis less likely to be watched than the main roads. Stay on it as much as you can, especially near Plas Penrhyn."

Gwilliam nodded. Father Perkins helped Hugh climb down and bade us farewell. I watched them limp away, my heart heavy with concern for Hugh. Gwilliam turned the wagon, and we began the journey.

"Stop near Plas Lloyd," I whispered.

He pulled the horse to a halt just out of sight of the *plasty*. I left them and rushed back inside for my best skirt and bodice and my worst ones—it might pay to be able to change my appearance— as well as my blankets and all the coins I had available, hopefully enough to buy us lodging at an inn so we did not have to sleep on the road.

Then I wrote a note to Master Lloyd. I did not want to lie, so I explained that I had been called on a pilgrimage, that I was traveling in good company with other young women, and that I would return soon. He might make the connection between my sudden spree of religious devotion and the hunt for the fugitives, but at worst he would throw me out of his house, and I already saw no choice but to flee the country. I almost took my mother's jewels, to be safe, but the chance of them being stolen on the road seemed higher than the likelihood that Master Lloyd would withhold them from me. The only thing I could not bear to leave behind was my mother's rosary, which I tucked into my skirt.

I tiptoed downstairs as the household stirred, and fled for the garden to get the last of Hugh's papers. Then I hurried to the wagon. The hills to the east glowed with dawn. I clambered into the driver's seat next to Gwilliam and handed the blankets to the shivering girls.

"Go," I whispered, and we rolled on toward Plas Penrhyn.

Chapter Twenty-two

The old Roman road cut through the oak-filled lowlands near Plas Penrhyn. Gwilliam guided the skittish horse beneath the canopy of clawing branches. A rustle from the trees broke the quiet. I clutched the edge of the seat, the rough board biting my fingers. A bird burst from the brambles, and the horse threw its head up.

"Whoa!" Gwilliam's voice sounded too loud in the stillness.

I glanced at the four casks poking out from the hay behind me and pulled a bit more hay over the top. One held in its false bottom the remnants of all our work, and my death were I caught with it.

Gwilliam wore Hugh's rapier sheathed at his side, though the sight of it turned my stomach. Wearing a sword meant you were prepared to draw it, and Gwilliam was no swordsman.

I had changed into my poorest bodice, hoping to look like a yeoman's daughter going to market with my siblings rather than a gentlewoman. Hannah and Beth slept in the prickly hay while we made our way down the lonely road.

We approached Plas Penrhyn, but patrols of soldiers combed the grounds near the stone building.

"Keep moving," I said to Gwilliam. "If we show too much interest, 'twill look suspicious."

"What are you going to do?" he asked.

"We'll move on down the road, then I'll sneak back at night and get the other papers."

We continued a few minutes, winding up the steep hill of Little

Orme to find a place off the road where we could camp with the wagon. The thick woods sheltered us from the queen's spies. At least the presence of so many armed men would keep bandits away.

As the sun dipped below the oak-crowned hills, I put Gwilliam's cloak over my light gray bodice—the deep blue hopefully blending with the darkness—and borrowed his dagger. The weapon did not bring the reassurance I expected, and I prayed I would not have reason to use it. Gwilliam, Hannah, and Beth settled in the back of the wagon. I hated leaving them, but Hugh and Father Perkins said that document hidden at Plas Penrhyn was essential. With a prayer repeating in my mind, I started out, shadowing the road. I wished I knew where the fissure running to the house opened, but Father Perkins had not been able to direct me to it clearly.

Mist rolled in from the nearby sea.

Thank you, David and Winifred.

The hazy shroud distorted the sounds of my movements and cloaked me from watching eyes. I would not be able to see them either, but I thought my chances better this way.

Hoofbeats echoed in the dark. I froze. The fog obscured the sound, so it could have been coming from anywhere. Maybe the fairies were out for a midnight ride. Maybe it was bandits. Maybe the queen's agents were searching even now, drawing closer. I fumbled for the dagger, but the sound of horses passed into the night.

Plas Penrhyn loomed out of the fog, its glass windows dark and its tall stone walls pushing back against the mist. The two sides of the *plasty* reached out around the front courtyard as if offering to protect me in their embrace. I stepped into the open, too much like a doe in an archer's sights.

A light flickered in the dark, and I paused. Lantern or fairy light? It bobbed and circled, moving away from the *plasty*. Normally, I was skeptical of fairy stories, but tonight I thought it might be a good omen. The fairies were said to favor the old faith.

The foggy darkness remained quiet. I crept forward, hardly daring to breathe until I reached the front courtyard. I paused briefly to try to find the entrance to the fissure in the dark. A sound from beyond the house made me jump, and I hurried up the steps to the newer wing. The fissure could wait. I leaned against the oak-planked door studded with nails, listening for any sounds of movement. I could not be sure no one was inside, waiting to catch Robert Pugh or his associates if they dared return.

I rested my hand on the cold brass handle. There was nothing to do but open it and see what waited for me on the other side.

The hinge screamed in the darkness, the shrill sound ringing across the mist. I gritted my teeth and slipped inside, stumbling into the hollow black of the great hall. I tripped over something and froze. It did not move, and I dared not touch it. Might it be a body? I could not make myself find out. Instead, I tiptoed across the musty-smelling room to the cold fireplace.

A breeze slithered through the room, whispering over the tapestries. Something clicked. A footfall on the stairs? A distant door? My palms turned clammy, and I fumbled around the cold fireplace, looking for the entrance to the priest hole. Another click from the far side of the room. A rustle on the floor.

Blessed Mary, where is the door?

Had Father Perkins told me wrong? My fingers trembled as they traced the wood paneling. My heart beat so loud and fast anyone else in the room would have to hear it.

Tap. Rustle. Tap.

My mouth went dry.

Something moved beneath my fingers. I almost cried out in relief. I pushed, and the entrance to the hidden room whispered open. A stale, wasted smell wafted over me. I gagged but lifted my skirts and crouched to step inside. Almost immediately I pushed against another stone wall. The room was hardly wider than a man's shoulders, but it stretched out to my left.

Tap. Tap.

I scrambled for the door and pushed it shut. Total darkness engulfed me. My heart pounded. I leaned my head back against the cold stones. The wall muffled the tiny sounds from outside. I hardly dared move, but my feet went numb as I sat on them. I blinked, trying to force myself to see something, anything, but it was as dark with my eyes open as with them shut.

I pressed my hands against the walls, the ceiling. The space was so tiny I could hardly move. I did not even dare shift for fear of pulling the door open in full view of whatever might be out there in the dark room. The walls closed around me, and I wondered if they would crush me, suffocate me. I thought of my father, buried in a tiny box beneath the heavy weight of his native soil. This space would hardly be a bigger tomb.

A breeze brushed across my face, much sweeter than the musty air inside. There was a breathing hole, then. I would not suffocate. I closed my eyes, pretending I sat in my bedroom with my book of hours, though the weight of the walls still pressed around me.

Muffled voices drifted in along with the air.

"I'm sure I heard something."

"It could have been a cat or a rat."

Oh, please, Blessed Mary, no rats.

"Maybe, but I'm of a mind to search the whole house again anyway. The new Lord President is not so forgiving as his predecessor. Necks may stretch for letting those Papists escape, and I would rather mine were not one of them."

I pressed against the wall, scarcely daring to breathe. Did they know about the secret room? There was nothing I could do or say to protest my innocence if they found me here. I wrapped my chilled fingers in my wool skirt and closed my eyes to pray.

I may have dozed off. I thought I heard voices nearby, and I jolted up with a little gasp, then stifled the sound in my hand. After a while the house grew quiet. I did not trust it to be empty, but eventually the men would give up and go away. In the meantime, I needed to find the papers.

I fumbled in the darkness, tracing the edges of the room. It stretched away from the fireplace but remained too low to stand and too narrow to stretch my arms. My cold muscles ached, and I rolled my shoulders, trying to shake off the stiffness and the chill. Farther along the wall, I found the loose stone that Father Perkins had described. My fingers throbbed as the cold edges bit into them, but I flexed my stiff joints and tried again, pulling out the stone with an echoing scrape.

The stone slipped, but I shifted my grip before it could crash to the ground. I sat in the darkness, listening for sounds of alarm, my heart pounding. The darkness around me grew quiet again. I rocked the stone to the side and carefully set it down, moving my fingers at the last minute to avoid crushing them. I fumbled in the dark hole and found sheaves of papers, a book, a cross, a little box, a sloshing wineskin, and some candles.

The only thing I was supposed to take was the papers. I caressed the cross and laid it back in its hiding place. Cradling the papers to my chest, I scooted the stone back into place and half-crawled over to the corner to wait for some sign that it was safe to come out. The fog would probably last through the night, but the sun would burn it away, and then I would have no cover. Once I was away from the *plasty* I would not look so suspicious—just the daughter of a farmer or fisherman out for a walk—but as long as I was here, I was guilty. I worked the door open a crack.

After the perfect darkness of my hiding spot, the room looked bright, and I thought my chance had passed. It was just the brightness of the moon reflecting off the mist, though. I crawled out, so stiff I could hardly straighten, and limped toward the front door and the escape through the hidden fissure. My hand froze on the latch. Nay, the front door squeaked, and I might not find the fissure before the men found me.

I crept back toward where the buttery or kitchen might be, placing my hand against the wall to feel my way forward in the dimness. The familiar smells of herbs and verjuice drew me to the stillroom. I trod carefully across the narrow space, bumping into a butter churn and broom before finding the door that would lead to the outside kitchen. I wished I had my own cloak now. I could have stowed the papers inside the lining. Hopefully the dark blue would hide me from unfriendly eyes.

The door swung open with no sound to betray me, and I snuck outside as quiet as a ghost. The stirring breeze rent the veil of mist into tattered shreds, but I walked slowly through the thickest parts.

"Is someone there?"

I stopped. The voice sounded distant, but it was hard to tell in the fog. The trees were close, but I dared not sprint for them. If the men saw me, I could not outrun them.

More lights bobbed in the distance.

"What's out there?" a voice asked, closer this time.

"Will-o'-the-wisps. Tricks of the devil. Pay them no heed."

Footsteps faded into the haze. I wished I could grab the mist and wrap it tight around me like my cloak.

I stepped forward, almost against my own will. Then I took another step, and another, bringing the woods ever closer. Finally, I dashed forward, trying to tiptoe into the shelter of the trees, though leaves crunched under my boots. I let out a shaky breath and pushed through to the old Roman road, walking alongside it, jumping at every rustle of the woods.

The wagon appeared out of the mist like home port welcoming a lost ship. The horse flicked its ears at me and gave a snort. I stumbled forward. Gwilliam hurried over to meet me, catching my arm.

"Are we safe?"

"Aye, but it was close."

"Hide the papers, then you can get some sleep."

I inhaled the sweet smell of hay. Now that the immediate danger was passed, my eyelids felt impossibly heavy. "Nay, you have to drive the wagon, so you should sleep while I watch."

"You sleep first," Gwilliam said, "then it will be my turn."

I nodded and let Gwilliam take the papers, all except one. The rest looked like licenses to travel and documents to establish identity, but the paper on top was folded and sealed with wax. That must be the one Father Perkins referred to, the one that everything else depended upon. I slipped it into my bodice between my chemise and my corset. There it was as safe as my life and my blood could make it. I crawled into the back of the wagon next to the warm, sleeping forms of Hannah and Beth and collapsed into slumber.

Chapter Twenty-three

I woke to the glare of the morning sun piercing the canopy of leaves. Gwilliam had let me sleep. I sat up, a scolding on my tongue, but he snored on the ground next to the wheel. Hannah perched on the seat of the wagon, mending a sleeve. She smiled at me as I climbed up next to her.

"How long have you been awake?" I whispered.

"Gwilliam woke me just before dawn so he could sleep a little."

"I hate to disturb him, but we need to move on."

"I know. He told me to only let him sleep a couple of hours, but you both looked so tired."

I sighed. "Well, we cannot afford to be caught here."

I roused Gwilliam. He rubbed his eyes and chided Hannah good-naturedly for being too kind. We turned the wagon back onto the Roman path and followed it until it crossed the main road heading east toward St. Winifred's Well. The jarring of the wagon's wheels over the rutted road made enough noise to discourage talk. Occasionally we passed thin, ragged peasants trudging off to seek work or beg for food. The road would not be a safe place to sleep tonight with so many desperate people around. We had to find a *plasty* willing to give us shelter. Hopefully Welsh hospitality would not fail us. I was glad for the fine clothes I could change into; it would help convince them to treat us well.

We reached a cluster of houses and shops along the road, and the smell of roasting meat and onions drifted from the inn. Beth perked up, and Hannah stared longingly at the wood-framed building.

"We can stop," I said.

Gwilliam grinned and turned us toward the smell of food. We left the horse and wagon in the hands of an ostler and stretched our stiff muscles as we wandered into the dimly-lit inn. A few locals cast unwelcoming glances in our direction as I quietly asked for some bread and stew. We settled into a table in the corner to eat in silence.

Just as I sopped up the last of the watery stew with my bread, a pair of gentlemen with rapiers burst into the room.

"Whose wagon is that in the yard?" one of the men bellowed.

I ducked my head. I thought we had done everything right. What had given us away? I glanced around the room, but there were too many men between us and the doors to escape unseen.

Gwilliam jumped to his feet. "'Tis mine, my lord. Have I done something wrong?"

I grabbed Gwilliam's sleeve. I would not let him take the punishment for my mistake. The men came to stand on either side of us.

"Who are you, boy? What is your business here?" one of them asked.

"Gwilliam ap Thomas, sir. My father sent me and my sisters to visit our cousins while Mother is ill."

"Leave the children in peace, Master Vaughn," called one of the locals, a tall man with fiery red hair. "They cannot mean any harm."

Vaughn swung around to face down the room. "Do you know these children, then? Will you vouch for them?"

"I do not know them, but I've had a belly full of watching you bully everyone who stops looking for a warm meal. Their coins are as good as anyone's."

"Stupid lout." Vaughn sneered. "There are Papist fugitives on the loose. A conspiracy is afoot, and if we do not stop it—"

"Then what?" The redheaded man stepped up to Master Vaughn, swaying a little with drink. "People will stop paying lip service to your heretic queen?"

"Papist traitor," Vaughn spat.

"I'm a loyal Welshman. 'Tis you who are the traitor."

Vaughn snarled and drew his rapier. The redheaded man did the same, and in a flash of quick movements, the room bristled with blades. I grabbed Hannah and Beth and pulled them under the table as the first scraping blows of metal on metal reverberated through the room. Gwilliam ducked next to us as the men clashed. The woman who had served our stew shrieked and brought a pewter mug down on a man's head, sending him crumpling to the ground.

Someone crashed into our table and thumped onto the floor. It was our redheaded defender. He stared at me with glassy eyes, his mouth moving soundlessly. Blood drooled past his lips. I covered my mouth. He groaned and grew still, his unblinking eyes still fixed on my face, all his bravado gone.

I gagged and turned away.

Mary, save us!

Hannah choked out a sob, cradling Beth's head so her sister could not see. Pale and wide-eyed, Gwilliam put an arm around Hannah.

I shook myself and stared across the room. Several people lay groaning on the floor. The rush of clanking blades and shouting ebbed.

"We need to get out."

Gwilliam nodded. I gave a parting glance to the dead man and crossed myself with a silent promise to pray for his soul.

We half-dragged Hannah and Beth from the room and raced for the wagon. Gwilliam whipped the horse into a canter, nearly breaking the wagon apart as we bounced down the road. I clutched the side, unable to see anything except the memory of the man's life draining out before me.

"Mistress Joan?" Gwilliam called.

I glanced at him, and for a moment I saw the dying man's face overlaying his, the light snuffed out in his gaze. I rubbed my eyes. "Aye, Gwilliam?"

"What do we do if they find us?"

My hand jumped to my bodice, where I carried the paper that Father Perkins said was the key to all their plans. My skin turned clammy, and I glanced back, but no one followed us.

"I think we escaped for now. Slow down before the wagon flies apart. Remember, we are just frightened young people fleeing a fight that has nothing to do with us."

Gwilliam brought the horse back to a walk.

I hugged my knees to my chest, still imagining shouts and the clanging of swords. I had thought I understood what Nicholas feared. I thought I understood the costs of war, of freedom. Now, though, I knew that man's death would hover on the edge of my consciousness as long as I lived. How many fires had Nicholas seen extinguished in men's eyes? Did their ghosts walk with him, haunting every step?

"Let's rest the horse," I mumbled when we'd put a long stretch of road between us and the inn.

We found a place off the road to stop. Hannah and Beth huddled back against the casks while I helped Gwilliam feed and water the horses. Beth cried out, a wail of frustration.

"Joan?" Hannah's voice cracked.

"Is Beth hurt?" I hurried back to the wagon.

"What's in these casks?" Hannah asked.

"Besides the papers? Just wine."

"No, look what Beth found."

I scrambled over the pile of hay. Beth held her hand out, black smudges coating her fingers. She'd opened a secret compartment I had not noticed in one of the other casks, and dark powder spilled out of it.

"Take her and wash off her hand," I said to Hannah, who nodded and guided her sister away.

I rubbed the black powder between my fingers. It had a faint, sulfurous smell. Now that I looked more closely, I could see that all four casks had secret compartments.

"Gwilliam?" I called.

"What's happened?" he asked, climbing up next to me.

I showed him the gritty black powder. "Do you know what this is?"

He rubbed it between his fingers. " 'Tis gunpowder."

"You're certain?"

"Aye, one of my brothers is a soldier. He taught me to shoot his musket."

We looked at the two unopened casks. Was it any of our concern what they contained? Hugh and Father Perkins were probably trying to protect us, allow us to claim innocence if we were caught. I was the one taking the risk, though, along with Gwilliam, Hannah, and Beth. If we were found with something illegal, we would be punished for it, no matter how we protested our innocence. Was there anything that I would not be willing to carry for Hugh and Father Perkins?

I remembered Mary, Queen of Scots, executed because of a letter smuggled in a cask. Aye, there were some things I was not willing to do, especially when the children were with me.

"We need to open them," I told Gwilliam.

He nodded.

We pried the other two compartments open. They were also filled with gunpowder.

"Are they making it themselves, or did they steal it?" Gwilliam asked softly.

"I do not know."

"What could they want with it? Are they selling it to the Spanish?"

"Maybe," I said.

I pulled the sealed paper from my bodice. I had respected its privacy up to now, but I was tired of secrets and half-truths. I carefully slid my fingernail under the seal to lift it, but the wax circle cracked. I winced. I could not hide my prying now. The paper listed the names of English great houses. I recognized some of them as places Queen Elizabeth often stayed on her royal progress through the countryside. Maybe a warning of places for priests to avoid.

The sour smell of gunpowder seeped over the wagon. I looked at the paper again. They knew where to watch for Elizabeth, and they spoke of freeing Wales from her tyranny.

My hands went cold. They were going to blow up one of the houses on the list, kill the queen. Not just her, but her court and the innocent people in the house. Women, children, servants. The gunpowder would make no distinction between oppressor and oppressed, guilty and innocent. They would all die together.

"Clean up the spilled gunpowder," I said. "Bury it—make sure no one will find it."

I stepped away from the wagon. This was the plan Hugh had hinted at. Elizabeth and her court would be replaced by some king more favorable to Catholics. No more priest hunters or midnight raids. If the new monarch disappointed us, there would be gunpowder for him too. Catholics would be free.

If the plot failed, though, Catholics would pay the price, and so would Wales. Even if it succeeded, the Protestants would retaliate. The fighting would not end with this blow. Were we like the pelican, shedding our blood to save our children? Or, we were just cutting out our own hearts? With each generation, the wounds grew deeper. Eventually everything would explode, just like at the inn or the massacre on St. Bartholomew's Day. Protestant against Catholic, English against Welsh. It would be Nicholas's dark vision come true.

I turned away.

"Where are you going?" Gwilliam asked.

"I . . . I need to think."

I raced through the trees, my mind so jumbled I hardly noticed the branches snagging my skirts. This decision was too large for me alone, but whom could I ask for guidance? I did not believe that Father Davies would condone assassination. How was I to know, though, when those around me kept their secrets close? Everyone seemed to be shouting in my ears.

Our time has finally come!

'Tis all gone, drowned in fire and smoke and blood.

There's no treachery more vile.

Trust in God.

Papist traitor.

Threw their bodies into the street like garbage.

The future of Wales depends on it.

I stumbled into a clearing where a little stone chapel stood falling into ruin. Probably a casualty of King Henry's lust and greed. I cautiously walked through the empty doorway. Even in its desecrated state, I dared not approach the sacred space around the altar, reserved for priests. Instead, I knelt among the drifts of leaves.

Once, this building had been full of beauty. Statues of saints stood along the nave, reminders that heavenly friends always waited to aid petitioners in their search for God. Fine linens and gold had decorated the apse around the altar, and intricate carvings adorned the screens and walls. Now, the saints were smashed, hands broken off, faces battered beyond recognition. The roof had collapsed, and bird droppings stained the scarred walls.

Saint David, is this what you want for Wales? Is it what God wants?

I looked up again at the pale blue sky framed by the broken walls. The voices of priests, family, and neighbors all quieted. My saints withdrew to a distance, and I felt myself very alone. Just me, the endless sky, and the God who ruled over it all. Everything was still. Instead of loneliness, a sense of freedom lightened my heart, and my thoughts grew clear.

My country did not need a war. Hate was easy, insidious, poisonous. There were times to fight, but what I needed now was the courage to seek peace, to forge a path where it was possible to be a loyal Catholic and a loyal subject. They called me a traitor, but I would not let their fear and anger define me.

I could see Queen Elizabeth now as a woman like me, trying to survive in dangerous times. I did not love her, but I would play no part in killing her. The next time I went to church, I would pray for our queen, that her lonely heart would feel mercy for all her subjects.

Father Perkins would get more gunpowder eventually, but it would not be by my hands. I would take the papers, but nothing else. If Hugh wanted to be angry with me, that was well. I was more angry with him.

Finally, my heart and head were in agreement. Peace settled in my chest, warming me and washing away all my uncertainty, my fears, my anxiety. I poured out a prayer of gratitude. Wiping my eyes, I slowly backed out of that sacred place and retraced my path to the wagon.

"We are not taking the casks with the gunpowder," I told Gwilliam.

"What do we do with them?"

"Dump out the gunpowder, mix it with the wine, and bury it."

Gwilliam rested his hand on the cask. "Gunpowder is valuable, maybe worth enough to help pay for passage overseas."

I hesitated, but shook my head. "Whom would we sell it to? Someone else who meant no good with it, or a spy who would arrest you for it. No, we'll trust God to provide a way."

Gwilliam set his lips in a tight line but did not argue. We poured out the precious gunpowder and the wine and stirred them into the ground, staining the earth a deep red. I cleaned my hands and face and changed into my fine gown before we set out again. As the sun slipped toward the horizon, we came across a great *plasty* with glass windows and people and animals milling in the yard. Gwilliam stopped, and I climbed down, approaching a well-dressed woman.

"*Noswaith dda*," I greeted her.

She narrowed her eyes and replied in English, "What?"

I cleared my throat and conjured up my English. "Forgive me, Mistress. I am traveling to take my younger sister to St. Winifred's Well, looking for a cure, and I need a place to sleep for the night."

"What ails her?" the woman asked warily.

"A disease of the mind, present since birth."

The woman stared at Beth, who clutched her doll and rocked in the wagon. The Englishwoman met my gaze, and her expression softened with sympathy. "Not much room in the house, but you can sleep in the barn. I hate to put young ladies out there, but we have too many guests as it is. Mind your horse eats its own hay and none of ours. There's not much food this year, but I'll have one of the servants find something for you to eat."

"Thank you, Mistress," I said. No matter our religion or language, we all understood the pain of watching a loved one suffer. Wales could do without the English's arrogance, but they did not deserve to be killed. Feeling warm again at my decision to leave the gunpowder behind, I motioned Gwilliam to bring the wagon around.

Chapter Twenty-four

The road widened as we approached St. Winifred's the next afternoon. Other pilgrims trudged along beside us. I wanted to offer them space in our wagon, but we could not risk anyone discovering the papers in the remaining cask. We found an inn with a room we could share and paid to stable our horse and wagon.

"We need to deliver the cask," I whispered to the children, surveying the crowd milling around the inn. Father Perkins thought we would be safe here, but if the shrine drew Catholics, it could also be teeming with Her Majesty's spies.

"May we go to the well first?" Hannah took Beth's hand and gave her an anxious glance.

Gwilliam nodded. "That way we'll have been there if we need to leave quickly."

"Please," Hannah whispered.

I shut my eyes. The inn's racket of neighing horses, clinking dishes, and chattering guests set my nerves on edge. Still, I could not deny Beth this chance.

"Very well," I said.

Saint Winifred, preserve us.

We joined the other pilgrims on the path leading down to the shrine, and the throng pressed us forward. Many around us limped on crutches or shook with racking coughs. Others carried their loved ones on their backs or led them by the hands: blind men and women

183

stumbling over the rutted road or those like Beth whose eyes spoke of a mind that did not see the world as others did. I said a silent prayer for each of them, but especially for Beth. Would there be a miracle for her at the shrine?

The little chapel surrounding the well rose before us: a stone building with arched doors and glass windows. It still stood in defiance of Henry VIII's destruction of the shrines and the ban on pilgrimages. The fact that King Henry's grandmother helped fund the chapel might have spared it, but now it was one of the last great monuments to our ancient tradition of saints and shrines.

St. Winifred's spring rose from beneath the chapel and flowed out an arched front opening as a rushing torrent. We gathered with the other pilgrims, waiting our turn to enter the shrine. Finally, the crowd shifted forward and we stepped inside.

Light from the windows shimmered off the clear blue-green spring in its star-shaped stone pool and reflected onto the walls. In front of the spring, the water gathered in another narrow pool with steps for the pilgrims to enter. There, those who had been healed etched their names in stone as a permanent testament to God's grace.

Beth watched the dancing light, her eyes wide with wonder. She smiled with a brightness I had never seen from her before. Perhaps this was the start of her miracle.

The scuffing of boots, lapping of the water, and occasional twitter of birds were the only sounds breaking the reverent silence, though a dozen people stood in the room, waiting for their turn to enter the pool. We stepped forward and took off our outer layers of clothing. Shivering in my chemise, I walked down the steps into the little pool. I gasped at the cold and waded across, stepping out again to fetch my clothes and watch Beth. Hannah guided her into the water and coaxed her to cross it three times.

I worried that Beth would rebel at the idea of soaking in the pool, but she stared into the water with fascination. She laughed awkwardly and splashed, watching the shimmering ripples bounce from one end of the little pool to the other. Hope lit Hannah's face as she watched her sister, and the gentle lapping of the water washed away the edge of my worries.

Other pilgrims waited at the edge of the pool, shuffling impatiently.

"Come," I whispered reluctantly.

Beth grunted and struggled against us as we pulled her out of the water. She squirmed her way to the floor and rocked, her shoulders curled in. Hannah and I exchanged a concerned look.

"Beth, would you like to see where the water comes from?" Hannah asked gently.

Beth slowly relaxed and let us dress her. We threaded our way past other damp pilgrims to lean over the star-shaped pool and watch the water bubble up from the spot where Winifred had been killed by an enraged suitor for her decision to become a nun, then restored to life by her saintly uncle Beuno.

I studied the faces around me out of the corner of my eye. Surely these people were not all Catholic, and some of them were undoubtedly English, yet here we stood, united by our longing for peace and healing, and by our reverence for the beauty of that place created by God and man. Nicholas was right. This was what Wales needed more of.

Gwilliam came to stand next to us, his dark hair wet and slicked back. He slipped one hand over Hannah's and put the other on Beth's shoulder. The shrine around the well was cool, but warmth washed over me.

The crowd shifted to make room for newcomers. I gave Hannah's shoulder a gentle squeeze. She nodded and guided Gwilliam and Beth after me. We paused at a pump to sip some of the cold, sacred water. As we entered the sunlight, Beth's gaze fell again to the ground, and she walked on in her shuffling gait.

Hannah's expression fell as she watched her sister, and she blinked back tears. Whatever change Beth had felt seemed to have been left by the sacred spring. Gwilliam looked at me in alarm.

"Nothing changed," Hannah said.

"I'm sorry the water did not heal her." My heart ached for Hannah and Beth. Injustice and hardship beset us on every side, but certainly God or St. Winifred could have spared a small miracle for a little girl.

We walked along the river flowing out of the sacred spring. Local people brought their clothes to wash in the cold water, the mundane and holy mingled side by side in daily work. Why did the spring cure some and not others? They said it was not just the water, but also faith that brought the miracle. Did we not trust God enough? Was there something more we needed to sacrifice? I flinched at the thought of giving up anything more and felt the weight of my own unworthiness.

Hannah looked at her sister. "She did seem happy to be there."

"Maybe she does not need to be healed," Gwilliam said, kicking a rock down the dirt path. "Maybe she's just different, and that's how she's supposed to be."

Hannah slowly smiled, and I looked again at Beth. She kept her eyes down, but her expression was peaceful. Perhaps it was only pride that made me think she ought to see the world in the same way that Hannah, Gwilliam, or I did. Pride that said I had the answers for her, for Wales, or for anyone. It seemed it was a shortcoming I had in abundance.

"I think you may be right," I said softly.

Gwilliam shrugged, but a smile tugged the corners of his mouth. "Do we deliver the cask now?"

I squinted at the setting sun. "We'll be spending the night here anyway. We can do that as we leave tomorrow. Hopefully we'll draw less attention that way."

The others nodded. I bought dinner in the inn, and we gorged ourselves on the hot, delicious meal. What a difference it made, to have warm food in one's belly after long, tense days on the road. We sat in contented silence and listened to the harper sing about Wales's ancient greatness.

I smiled thinking of the secret pages hidden in our cask. Maybe Wales was going to have new glories: its own books, reason for the people to learn to read the language, to continue speaking it in the face of English snobbery and interference. As the harper strummed bold chords and sang of heroes, I imagined I was fighting for my country too, but in a way that made it stronger instead of bleeding it dry.

The sense that someone was watching pulled me from my dreams. I looked around but saw nothing suspicious. I rolled my shoulder blades, trying to relieve the tingling sense that someone was staring. When I looked again, I saw a man's face vanish behind his tankard of ale. The hairs on the back of my neck rose. He looked like Master Red-Plume. Had he tracked us, or was it a coincidence, perhaps even my imagination? Between the fight at the inn and the household of the Englishwoman who had given us shelter, there were many who might identify us to an enemy.

I almost pulled Gwilliam up to go immediately and deliver the cask, but that would give us away. The best we could hope to do was look casual and try to slip past the man while he was not looking.

As soon as we finished eating, I insisted we retire to our room. Hannah and Beth shared the bed, while Gwilliam and I slept on straw pallets on the floor. I woke up in the morning grateful to find I had not been eaten alive by bed bugs or fleas, with a new sympathy for servants who slept thus every night.

I peered down into the courtyard. The man from last night stood near the stables, watching everyone who came and went. I chewed my lip. How long would he wait? Probably long enough that our money would run out, and the more time we spent at St. Winifred's, the more chance we had of running into trouble, especially with those papers in our possession.

"What is it?" Gwilliam asked sleepily, buttoning his doublet.

"We are going to need a distraction. I think that man's been watching us, maybe following us."

Gwilliam frowned. "We could start a fire in the courtyard."

"And risk burning down the inn? Nay, not that."

"Is he Welsh or English?"

"English, most likely."

"Perfect." He grinned. "How about a fight, then?"

"Gwilliam! If you start a fight with him, you may get arrested."

"Only if I'm the one doing the fighting." His eyes brightened as he surveyed the courtyard below. "I have an idea."

"Please, be careful."

"I will, but make certain everyone's ready to leave soon."

He rushed out of the room. I woke the girls, then hovered beside the open window to watch below. After a few minutes, Gwilliam sauntered past the Englishman and into the stable, looking every bit like a young gentleman in Nicholas's modified clothes. The man turned to watch Gwilliam but stayed at his post by the door.

A moment later, a huge man, as solid as a barrel, stormed out, rapier in hand. He yelled at the Englishman, who scrambled back, waving his hands and shouting something unintelligible. Other guests came to their windows, whistling and cheering, and the men in the courtyard gathered together excitedly, probably making bets.

I grimaced, hoping this did not end badly for anyone, except maybe Master Red-Plume, if it was he.

"Come, Hannah, Beth. We need to leave."

We hurried downstairs. In the courtyard, people laughed and cheered over the clang of swords. So much for peace in Wales, at least this morning.

As we reached the entrance to the courtyard, two constables arrived to break up the fight and escort the shouting Englishman away. It was Master Red-Plume for certain. I ducked my face, but I felt his gaze pass over me, and his protests quieted for a moment. I swallowed. We had not seen the last of him. He would be free soon, no doubt, and he might have other associates waiting. We would need to flee Wales, and quickly.

Gwilliam had the horse and wagon ready. We climbed in, and he snapped the reins. I gripped the wooden seat, waiting for the sounds of pursuit, but we rolled free of the inn yard.

"How did you do it?" I whispered to Gwilliam.

"I found the biggest Welshman I could and told him the Englishman in the doorway was saying unkind things about Welsh women." He grinned wickedly. "Well, I did not put it in quite those words."

"Gwilliam!"

"Too bad the innkeeper and the constables saved him."

I could not bring myself to disagree. I did not want to see anyone run through, but what Master Red-Plume planned for me and my friends was much worse. I directed Gwilliam to the house Father

Perkins had described. A surly-looking housekeeper opened the door.

"I have some wine for the master of the house, compliments of Master Perkins."

The woman regarded me with narrow eyes. I resisted the urge to fidget and wondered if I had made a mistake.

"Alan!" she shouted over her shoulder. "Get some lads to unload the casks."

Two boys in household livery came running, and Gwilliam helped them move the cask.

"Only one?" the woman asked. "I thought there was supposed to be four."

"Only one," I said firmly.

"Hmph. Good day to you then." She shut the door.

I exhaled. Was it over, just like that? She did not even offer us food, though I suppose that was wise for all of us. Still, I had expected something more. I wanted to know what would happen to the papers, make certain they were well protected. Any inquiries would look suspicious, though, if she had her own agent of the queen to deal with.

I turned away, my task done, and climbed heavily into the wagon.

"Finished?" Gwilliam asked.

I nodded. "Now, we return to Plas Lloyd."

Chapter Twenty-five

We took the same route back, our moods much lighter. We avoided the Englishwoman's house where we had stayed in the barn. I did not want to think ill of her, but I was still concerned that we were being followed or watched. Instead, we stayed at the home of a wealthy yeoman farmer. They seemed pleased to offer hospitality like one of the *bonheddwyr*. Hannah, Beth, and I shared a room with the daughters of the house, while Gwilliam slept in the great hall with the menservants.

We traveled the next day until it grew dark. There were no houses nearby to beg for shelter.

"I think we are only a couple of hours from Plas Lloyd," I whispered to Gwilliam. "Do we dare travel after dusk?"

"These woods are dangerous—full of bandits."

Dangerous to travel through, dangerous to sleep in.

"The moon is nearly full. Let's press on."

We did, though the jangle of the wagon filled the darkness. Sometimes I thought I heard an echo to the noise, an extra set of hoofbeats. Could Master Red-Plume have found our trail? Unless he was chasing a bigger prize, he might have followed the same path to try to catch us.

"Pull off the road," I whispered to Gwilliam.

He frowned but guided the wagon over when we reached a level spot beside the road. He moved the horse behind a stand of trees and offered her a handful of hay as he petted her silky nose. I motioned for him to stay and crept forward. Aye, the quiet sound of hoofbeats continued up the road, moving slowly. There were several of them. Spies or bandits? I almost preferred the latter.

I withdrew into the shadows and held my breath. The hoofbeats paused. Could they see our tracks amidst so many others? I glanced back. Gwilliam's hand moved for Hugh's rapier, but I shook my head.

The hoofbeats moved past us, fading into silence. I sighed and sagged against the trunk of a tree. We waited quietly as the stars marked the creeping passage of time, but nothing stirred on the road.

"Let's move quickly." I pulled up my hood. "We do not know if they'll be back."

The jarring ride was worse in the dark, every rut and hole catching our wheels until I thought my teeth would rattle out of my head. Hannah and Beth managed to sleep, but I could not relax, imagining hoofbeats galloping behind us and eyes watching from the trees. When we finally reached Plas Lloyd, the light from behind the shutters called to me like a beacon to a lost sailor.

"What do we do with the wagon?" Gwilliam asked.

"Hide it near the cottage. We'll turn the horse loose with Master Nicholas's for now."

They left me at the *plasty* and drove off. I stepped into the front door, trying to look as casual as if I had just been for a walk in the garden instead of gone for nearly a week.

Master Lloyd stared into the fire, his face drawn. I had caused him worry. Of course I had; he was responsible for me. He looked up, and his worry hardened into anger.

"Joan Pryce!"

I stood still and bowed my head, ready to accept whatever punishment fell to me. Master Lloyd glowered for what seemed an eternity, then quietly said, "Ah, I'm glad to see you safe. Go rest; we'll talk later. You'll be punished enough, I think, without anything I could do to you."

With those foreboding words, he turned back to the fire. The servants watched me over their cleaning and mending, some looking sympathetic and others almost angry.

"What happened?" I whispered, but no one answered.

My stomach sat like a lump of ice as I climbed to my cold room, stripped off my dirty clothes, and curled up on the bare mattress. Exhaustion overwhelmed me.

Late in the morning, I awoke chilled and thickheaded, but I dressed and hurried down the stairs. Alice sat in the great hall, refusing to look at me. Mistress Lloyd shook her head sadly.

When she left the room, Alice glared at me.

"I do not know what you were thinking, running off and only leaving a note behind. You have spoiled your reputation and brought trouble to all of us. Englishmen have been poking their noses around, asking questions, throwing everything into chaos."

I took no thought for my reputation—I knew I had done nothing to tarnish it, and I would be leaving everyone who knew me behind—but I had not considered Alice's or the Lloyds'. "I'm sorry. 'Twas thoughtless of me."

"You're lucky Master Rhys is so understanding, or I would . . ." Alice pressed her lips together. "Well, whatever you have been involved in, you'll feel the sting of it. Nicholas Bowen turned your friend over to the constables three days ago."

It hit me like a blow to the face. I must have misheard. "What?"

"Aye, he's proven his loyalty to the realm, while you were out trying to bring the downfall of your family and your future. I guess we should be grateful you were not around to be implicated, though it may still happen. I have the feeling Master Bowen knows more than he's said."

Nicholas would not betray me. He could not have turned his guest and his friend over to the constables when he knew what would become of them. There had to be a mistake.

I fled before I could hear any more of this terrible gossip. I slammed the front door open and raced to the stables, calling for my mare.

The stable boy fidgeted. "I'm sorry. We're under orders. You're not supposed to go riding."

I snarled at him and raced outside. I would run all the way to Nicholas's. He would tell me the truth. I stumbled along the way, my limbs unnaturally heavy, but I forced myself to keep running. Tears whipped across my cheeks as I pushed into the wind. I faltered to a stop at Nicholas's *plasty*. A few of the servants in the yard recognized me, but instead of friendly greetings, they turned away. My heart caught. It could not be true.

I banged in to the great hall, heedless of the flustered steward. Nicholas rose from his chair, his scarred face mottled red and white. Everything I had feared was written in the mixture of guilt and anger in his expression.

"How dare you?" I asked. "I trusted you, and you betrayed me!"

"*I* betrayed *you?*" Nicholas hissed, motioning the servants out. "What were you thinking? Do you have any idea the consequences if I were caught harboring a priest? Hanging's only the beginning of it."

I paled, recalling the tales of men cut apart while alive. "You would not have been caught."

"I could not take that chance."

"The laws of hospitality, the customs of our people—"

"I'm sorry you're upset, but what's done is done."

I shook my head, tears stinging my eyes. I had trusted him. Poor Father Perkins. And Hugh. He would die in prison with that wound. Nicholas had condemned a friend who put his life in his hands. "You have no idea what you have done."

"I understand perfectly what I have done."

He did not, of course. He could not, and he had no interest in knowing. Master Red-Plume was following the children and me. Nicholas had just killed our friends and ruined our best hope for escape, but what was that to him? I turned and fled the *plasty*, racing to the only refuge I knew.

I stumbled, tearing my skirt, cutting my hand on the rocky ground. I wrapped my bleeding palm in the ripped fabric and limped forward, crying in relief when the cottage loomed before me. Master Red-Plume did not know of this place. The children and I would be safe here for now. Somehow, we would find our own way to Ireland

and then overseas, even if I had to sell everything I owned and row us there myself.

My face felt hot, but I shivered as I unlatched the door. I needed something to eat. Nay, something for my parched mouth and throat. Something to put out the fire that burned inside my head.

Hannah sat near the fire, crying. Beth lay beside her, pale and motionless except for the raspy sound of her breath. On his pallet in the corner, Gwilliam moaned and tossed, his face flushed red, his eyes unseeing. My chest tightened, and I coughed.

"Joan?" Hannah whispered, her voice hoarse. "Is it you?"

"Aye." My terror swept away all other thoughts. "What happened?"

"Beth got sick first, then Gwilliam. And I . . ." She shut her eyes, and her face blanched white.

I rushed to her side. Her forehead was burning hot, but she shook until her teeth chattered.

"Lie down, Hannah," I said, my voice trembling.

"I need to take care of Beth."

I glanced at the little girl on the pallet, as pallid as a corpse. Just a few days before she'd been the happiest I'd ever seen her. Was it some final gift before God took her life? Was this a punishment for my rebellious behavior?

"I'll take care of her," I whispered around the scratchiness in my throat. "You need rest."

Hannah sank to her pallet, tears streaking her face. I moved like a person in a dream, trying to force weak cider into the children's mouths, wiping their sweaty foreheads, mumbling words of comfort I did not hear or understand. If only I had access to a stillroom, I might have done something for the fever, but all I had was in that little cottage, filled with fever-hot, sweating, shaking bodies and raspy breaths.

They all slipped into a numb, fevered sleep. I shifted Beth, but her limbs felt unreasonably heavy and did not bend as they should, her small body difficult for me to move. I went back and forth between the children until my joints stiffened so I could hardly hold the cloth. Finally, unable to stay upright, I sank on the pallet next to Hannah and let the darkness swallow me too.

Chapter Twenty-six

Hounds bayed in the distance. The hounds of Annwn, Lord of the Dead, coming for us. Maybe it was not just Wales, but this world that had nothing left for me.

The creak of the door reached me through a fog of delirium. Hounds whined and snuffled across the floor. I sensed a presence over me, tall and warm through the chills, though I could see only shadowy figures. I knew Death made no bargains, but I had to try.

"Please, not the children. 'Tis my fault. Take me, but leave them."

"Oh, Joan. Not you too," whispered an anguished voice.

Strong arms lifted me from my pallet. I struggled weakly then relented, leaning into the soft leather doublet. Somehow, I thought when Death came for me, he would strip me of my mortal frame and set me free from my suffering. I shivered more violently.

"The children?" I asked through cracked lips.

"They'll be taken care of. Sleep."

And so I did.

I awoke on a soft feather bed, but still my body ached as though I'd been running for days. My mouth was dry, my lips cracked. I stirred and found myself almost too weak to turn over. I forced myself up. Hannah? Beth? Gwilliam? The room was large, with a fire in the hearth, the glass windows propped open, and painted cloths and carpets draped over the wooden chests. The only other person in the room was a thin, wrinkled old woman. She was so frail looking I wondered if the sweet-smelling breeze might crumble her.

I sank back down. "Where?" The word scratched my throat. Where was I? Where were the children?

The woman set aside her knitting and tottered to my side to place a gentle hand on my forehead. "Your fever has broken." She smiled a toothless grin. "The master will want to know."

"Who?" I tried, but she toddled off like a ragdoll brought to life.

I laid my head back and stared at the ceiling carved with elaborate geometric designs. Tracing the endless knots of circles and diamonds made my eyes hurt, so I shut them. Sleep was creeping up on me when the door whispered open.

"Are you certain she awoke? She still looks very pale."

Nicholas's voice. I was not sure I wanted to open my eyes.

"She sat up and tried to speak," the old woman said. "'Twill be some time before she gets her strength back."

"You have done well. I'll ask you to stay on until she's fully recovered."

"Of course, Master Bowen."

This was Nicholas's home. This fine room . . . My head throbbed again. Had he put me in his own chambers? Embarrassment and gratitude made me want to crawl beneath the blankets. Since I could not hide, I opened my eyes.

Nicholas was watching me, his expression unreadable. Our eyes met, and a hundred questions danced between us.

"Mistress Pryce, do you understand me?" His voice was soft, concerned.

A lump formed in my throat, and I nodded. "How?"

"How did I find you?" His voice turned chilly. "Master Lloyd came looking for you when you did not return. I set my hounds on your trail. You're fortunate we'd had a couple of days without rain."

I squeezed my eyes shut. He had discovered us trespassing on his property. What must he think of me? I wanted to offer to pay for the year's rent of the cottage, as well as the cost of bringing me here and hiring this woman to care for me. I could not deny I owed it to him, even if it meant I had less to take with me overseas.

If he planned to turn me over to the queen's agents, the money would do me little good anyway.

"The children?" I asked, my throat aching.

Nicholas refused to meet my gaze. My heart seized. I would not cry in front of him, yet I was too weak to fight the tears brimming in my eyes. He glanced at the old woman. "Leave us, please."

She left the room without comment, pulling the door shut behind her. I swallowed and huddled under the covers. Nicholas was too much a gentleman to risk my reputation for anything that was not serious.

Nicholas lowered himself to the bedside, his face even with mine, but still he would not look at me.

Blessed Mary, please not the children. If you were going to take someone, it should have been me.

He cleared his throat. "The older two are out of danger. The younger—"

"Beth," I cried, struggling to sit up. "Not Beth!"

"She's alive!" he said quickly, reaching for me, then pulling his hand away.

I choked on a sob and lay back.

Thank you, Mary. Thank you, God.

Nicholas dropped his voice. "I do not want to upset you, but I think you're out of danger, and you have a right to know. I do not know if she'll ever be well. The fever may have damaged her mind. She'll not speak. She sometimes stares without seeing and rocks back and forth . . ."

I almost laughed, and it came out as a cough. Nicholas paused, and I shook my head. "That's Beth. How she is."

"She's always been like that?"

I nodded. "Tried Winifred's Well."

"That's where you went?"

I hesitated. I should not have given him any hint about where we'd taken the papers, but it was too late now. I nodded again.

He looked down. "Was her cure the only reason you went?"

I curled my fingers into the soft down blanket. It did not seem right to lie to the man who had saved my life and the children's, but I could not tell him the truth either.

He sighed. "I need to know what to do with the children. I've not asked them any questions, but at some point I must. I cannot afford to allow vagrants to live in my cottages."

"I'm sorry," I whispered. A coughing fit seized me, and I wheezed helplessly.

He watched with concern as I caught my breath, and then he said softly, "I could find work for them."

I blinked away fresh tears. "You would do that?"

"It does not benefit anyone to allow honest, able-bodied youths to starve or drift into crime. I could find a position for the girls and an apprenticeship for the boy."

I stared at him. He was placing great faith in my word to put such effort into unknown children instead of turning them over to the parish. The queen's men might recognize Gwilliam, though, if he came out of hiding. He had to leave. Were Nicholas to arrange an apprenticeship for Gwilliam only to have him slip away in the night or be arrested, it would reflect badly on him. I could not do that to Nicholas after he rescued us.

"Gwilliam has family overseas," I rasped out. "He wants to join them. The girls too."

Nicholas blinked a few times, but otherwise hid his surprise at my confession. I did not have to say they were Catholic; I could tell by the concern in his eyes that he understood.

"Acquiring a license for three orphans to leave the country would be almost impossible." He absentmindedly twisted the edge of the down-filled blanket. "I'm not so well connected in London."

My heart jumped. He sounded almost ashamed. "I had not meant that you should," I said, letting his answer guide how much I revealed. "God will provide."

Nicholas's gaze jumped to mine, and his eyes narrowed slightly. "I do not think God acts unaided. This is a dangerous game, Mistress Pryce. Even women can be executed."

How well I knew it, but Gwilliam was not safe in Wales, and neither was I. "God will provide," I repeated.

Nicholas pressed his lips together. "I can find them work around Nant Bach." He met my eyes again. "For as long as they need it, but I expect no trouble to come to me because of it."

"I understand." They would have to be careful, but it would only be temporary.

Nicholas stood and walked slowly to the door.

"Thank you," I whispered. Only his brief pause told me he had heard.

I slept again for some time, but in another day I began to feel thirsty, then hungry. Everything I asked for appeared, though I did not see Nicholas again. Just as well. As soon as I was strong enough, I would need to leave, and when I did, there would be nowhere to go but overseas. I had burned my bridges and left nothing behind for me here in Wales. I could not forget that, because of Nicholas, our best hope of escaping was now in prison, probably awaiting execution.

And poor Hugh. I swallowed against the lump in my throat. He made his choice, knowing what he risked. A little anger lingered behind my sorrow when I remembered that he had involved me in a deadly conspiracy without my knowledge.

My best hope was that Robert Pugh or Father Davies was still at large. I had no idea how to find them. The priest near St. Winifred's Well might help. It would be some time before we could make that journey again, though, and I did not know if Nicholas had confiscated our wagon.

Finally, my worries prompted me to rise from bed. My nurse helped me take a few shaky steps to a stool. I sank down near the window and glanced out, catching my breath at the view. From this height, Nicholas's lands stretched away from me, rolling hills dotted with sheep, horses, and cattle, the fields divided into uneven strips by thick stands of thorn and oak. Pink and white drifts of apple blossoms spread over the orchard like clouds. A sweet scent blew in from the meadows: the smell of spring, new life, green things growing. Could Rome's ancient streets offer any sights so lovely?

Groups of poorly clad people crossed the yard below me, arms laden with the leftovers of some huge meal. Had Nicholas been feasting? His tenants must be glad for it.

"Thank heavens 'twas not the plague like Master Bowen thought," the nurse said. "Otherwise you would not be here to enjoy this view."

"The plague?" I turned quickly, and a wave of dizziness made the room tilt. "He thought we had the plague, and he still brought us here?"

"Aye. He sent everyone else out of this part of the house, closed it off."

"And you were willing to come?"

"I'm a poor old woman. It seemed a risk worth taking for the price he offered."

Why would Nicholas take the risk, though, and after losing his family to the plague? I remembered the words from my fevered dream. *Not you too.*

He thought I had the plague, and he risked his life bringing me here. Yet he was almost as cold and distant to me as he had been before. Maybe he had seen too much death to be frightened of it again, and simply did not want to see us suffer. Then why was he so angry about the risk imposed by Hugh and Father Perkins? Was it just that he wanted to meet his end on his own terms? Compared to being drawn and quartered, the plague was a friendly angel of death.

"Are the children well?" I asked the nurse.

She nodded, eyes sparkling. "I'll fetch them if you'd like."

"Please!"

It took a little time, but Gwilliam appeared in the doorway, looking pale and thin, though his eyes were bright. Hannah stood behind him, clutching Beth's hand.

"Mistress Joan!" Gwilliam hurried to my side. Hannah smiled and embraced me, her arms shaky around my shoulders.

"We were so afraid," she whispered.

"I know," I said, "but everything will be fine now. You may need to work for Master Bowen for a short time, but he'll be a good master."

"Are we still going to find my family?" Gwilliam asked.

"Aye, though I admit I do not know how to locate the friends who will help us do that. Still, I promise we'll find a way."

"Why not ask Master Richards?" Gwilliam asked.

I blanched. How could I tell them that their friends were gone, and that it was Nicholas's doing?

"Your room is so much bigger than mine and Beth's," Hannah interrupted, admiring the carpets and tapestries.

"I think my room is right below yours," Gwilliam said, peering out the window. "And Hannah and Beth are in a room beneath Master Bowen's. He has four rooms just in this wing of the house. 'Tis hard to believe. My parents only had two bedrooms altogether."

I tilted my head. "Is this not Master Bowen's chamber?"

"Nay, his is the next one over. 'Tis even bigger than this one and has a table all covered with books and even a couple of chairs with cushions and backs." He gave me a cautious look. "I explored a little. I hope it was not rude."

"It was a little. We are his guests. You should respect his privacy."

Still, I looked around my chamber with new curiosity. He was wealthy, but this was extravagant for a guest room. It ought to have been a room for his family, but they were all dead. Of course, this chamber might have been intended for his wife—the mistress of the house. My hollow cheeks burned at the realization.

Not all wealthy men had separate chambers for their wives. When Nicholas had it built, had he meant it for whomever he married, or had he been thinking of me? It could be a room for a woman he thought might not wish to share his bed, to look at his face each morning. Or, perhaps, for a wife he had not relished the thought of spending too much time with. Maybe one he thought he could not trust. Well, I had proven that right. I had played a fool's part.

The room had been built several years ago, when we were not speaking to each other. When pressed by Master Lloyd at our reunion, Nicholas had claimed that he would obey my wishes in the matter of our betrothal, but he certainly had not shown any fondness for me at the time. Then again, I had hardly given him reason to, staring at him in horror as I had. If I had reacted differently, would he have as well? An ache of loneliness and loss gripped my chest. I shook my head. It hardly mattered now. The walls between us were beyond surmounting.

Chapter Twenty-seven

From my window, I watched Nicholas and Gwilliam guide their horses toward the fields of Nant Bach. Nicholas spoke and gestured, and Gwilliam nodded thoughtfully. I smiled a little to see Nicholas in the role of mentor for my young friend, but when Nicholas flashed one of his rare grins at something Gwilliam said, I looked away. Nicholas had not asked me to leave—indeed, he still avoided speaking to me as much as possible—but I doubted he would ever smile at me again.

My weary legs shook when I stood, but I forced myself to walk each day in the gallery overlooking the great hall. There, I hovered like a ghost, watching the life of Nant Bach unfold below me. Compared to its previous crypt-like stillness, it buzzed, a beehive of activity. When Nicholas was not overseeing the work on the estate, he was at the service of his tenants: giving advice, resolving disputes, worrying with them over their families, their livestock, and their crops. Even when he dined alone, the meals were generous, and servants carried away the extra to the poor who came to the back door. Something had finally cracked the shell of Nicholas's indifference. Toward everyone except me, that was.

"'Tis a wonder Master Bowen has time to breathe," I said to the woman who came to fetch the laundry. I sat in my room. In the yard below, Nicholas inspected the spring lambs.

She rested her basket on one hip and nodded. "He always took his ties to the land seriously, and I've never seen a master more generous and concerned than he's been of late. To think we nearly lost it all."

"He should not have endangered himself to help me, I suppose," I said quietly.

"Well, I'll not judge that. Master Bowen cannot stand to see suffering, and he did it as safe as he could. Nay, I meant that horrible priest who tried to hide here."

I winced inwardly. If she knew who had sent the priest, she probably would not have spoken so freely. "What do you mean?"

"He came here to get help for Master Richards, but he would not be quiet about opposing the queen, though Master Bowen and Master Richards both warned him to silence. Master Bowen could have been arrested, and all of us turned out."

"Surely Master Bowen's uncle would not be so cruel as to turn everyone onto the streets if he took over Nant Bach."

She gave me an odd look. "If Master Bowen was caught with the priest, they would not have just killed him. They would have stripped the estate from his family and given it to some English lord in favor with the queen."

I sat back. Father Perkins must have known that. What had he been thinking, to endanger Nicholas's life, his dependents, and everything he had worked for that way? Even if he had given no Christian thought to Nicholas and his kindness in taking them in, he should have seen the danger of thrusting a stalwart English Protestant into the midst of this community, with priests coming and going.

I hardly heard when the washerwoman bid me good day and went about her work. Instead, I snuck a look at Nicholas outside.

He was willing to risk his life to help a foolish young woman who might have the plague, but he guarded his estate with the ferocity of a parent for a child. He would not have liked turning Father Perkins in, but he did what he had to. It was a different sort of bravery than Hugh's, and maybe harder to sustain: the day-to-day courage to do the best he knew how, with no one else to rely on. No wonder he was furious with me.

I pulled my cloak tighter. It did not matter anymore. As soon as I was well, I would be away and stop endangering him and Nant Bach. Still, I shifted in my seat, suddenly feeling as if I were sitting in a muddy skirt, staining the ancient furniture.

My guilt over Father Perkins plagued me and drove away my sleep for the next few nights. Would I forever be making foolish choices? My nurse complained that I grew pale again and did not eat as I should. I would not be at peace until I had apologized to Nicholas.

I started downstairs for the great hall, clinging to the bannister to support my unsteady steps. I heard familiar voices below.

"You say you love your country, but you're going to destroy it," Nicholas said.

"I want to make it free!" Hugh's voice rang out.

I caught my breath. Hugh was there, arguing with Nicholas as if he had nothing to fear from him. I tightened my grip on the railing. I had assumed Nicholas turned Hugh in as well because Alice had spoken of my friend, and I had heard and seen nothing of him. But the washerwoman said Hugh was also trying to quiet Father Perkins, and Gwilliam had mentioned him . . . I thought it was only wishful thinking.

"Free from what?" Nicholas asked. "You would only trade one evil for another."

I took a few more steps down and peered into the great hall. Nicholas and Hugh sat together on stools before the fireplace while Gwilliam sharpened a knife and servants carried away the remnants of a generous repast. Clearly, this was not a private moment. Hannah and Beth worked at the spinning wheels. Hannah noticed me on the stairs and flashed a quick smile. Beth ignored everything but the fine thread she spun.

Nicholas leaned forward, lacing his fingers together. "I have seen war. I know its face as well as my own. Better, perhaps, because the face I see in the mirror is not mine. War means suffering." He lowered his voice. "And hate spreads in war even faster than pestilence. You do not understand what you ask for. No one who loves his country wants to see it at war."

"Nor do they want to see it oppressed!" Hugh shouted, then

paled and clutched his side. "Ah, Master Nicholas, you have the upper hand on me. I do not have the strength to fight now."

"May God always keep you as weak as a kitten, then," Nicholas said with his quirky half smile.

"Nicholas, you truly are the devil, just as they say," Hugh said with a weak chuckle.

"The devil?" Hannah glanced at me then back at Hugh, and her eyes brightened. "Oh, do you mean Master Bowen was the devil at the masque?"

Nicholas's face tightened, and his gaze jumped to me.

Hugh looked at Nicholas in surprise. "The masque? I did not think you liked to dance."

I stood rooted on the steps. The devil at the masque. The man who saved me. Who danced so passionately with me. Nicholas and Hugh were of a height, of a build. It could as easily have been one as the other. I tried not to stare at him, but he sat frozen in place, watching me.

Hugh followed his gaze. "Mistress Joan! I'm so glad to see you able to come downstairs! I would have gone up to see you, but Nicholas assured me it would be improper, and besides, I do not think this wound will let me brave the stairs for some time."

"I'm glad to see you well." I smiled weakly. "It looks like you will recover."

"Aye, and 'twill not be soon enough for me." He glanced at Nicholas. "Why do you look so uncomfortable? Do you think your old nickname disgraces you in front of the ladies?" He gave Hannah a wink. "They say when Master Bowen was a solider in Ireland, he marched into battle as cold as iron. And then, with that face of his . . . the English soldiers called him the Welsh Devil, and some of our countrymen took up the nickname too. He was *Y Diafol*."

I tried to read Nicholas's expression, but he turned away to pet one of his dogs. His guilt betrayed him. I wanted to ask him why. Why he had not made himself known, why he hid such passion behind a cold exterior.

That felt like a lifetime ago, though, before our choices and our words had put such a barrier between us. Nay, the barrier had always been there. Only when we wore masks, hid from each other and ourselves, could we be together. Now that it was too late, I finally began to understand him, his hidden courage and passion. If circumstances had been different, how deeply and fiercely I could have loved my betrothed.

"Mistress Joan, are you still unwell?" Hugh asked.

"What? Oh, perhaps a little." I made my way down the stairs and sat heavily on a stool.

"I asked if you'd decided what you're going to do. I know you mentioned leaving, but perhaps you'll stay after all? There's still work to be done for Wales." His voice was hopeful, and it fanned my lingering anger at him and his schemes.

"I have discovered that I prefer forging my own path, and I want it to be a peaceful one. I am weary of secrets." I met Hugh's eyes, and he had the grace to look guilty. I glanced at Nicholas, but he still focused on his dog.

Hugh leaned forward. "I had word from our mutual friend, Sir William. He said some of his associates near St. Winifred's Well were troubled that their goods went missing. Perhaps you could shed some light on the mystery?"

Gwilliam glanced up from his work, his eyes wide. "Sir" was the traditional title for a priest. Sir William must have been Father Davies. Well, I knew they would find out about the gunpowder eventually.

"I have done nothing that was not for the greater good of Wales." I could equivocate as well as the rest of them.

"The greater good?" Hugh's eyes flashed, and he dropped his voice to a whisper. "You do not think freedom is in Wales's best interest? No one is going to give it to us, Mistress Joan. If we do not fight for the things we believe in, we will lose them. Aye, if we do not fight, perhaps we deserve to."

My cheeks warmed. "I know we have to hold to the beliefs that are dear to us—we have to stand firm in our convictions." I hesitated, my thoughts becoming tangled with uncertainty, until I remembered the sweet peace I had felt in the ruined chapel. I went on more quietly, "I do not have all the answers, Master Hugh, but I believe that there must be a way to be true to myself without destroying others. I do not want the things that are beautiful and precious to me stained with hate."

Nicholas's hand paused. He could not have known much of their plan or he would have felt bound to report it, but at least he would know that I no longer shared in their desire for violence.

I met Hugh's gaze. "I am surprised Sir William does not agree."

Hugh glanced down, suddenly looking weary. "He does, in fact. He believes God's will has been done. He knows of Gwilliam's desire to find his family, and he told me the opportunity should come up in a week's time."

So soon? It was the opportunity I wanted—that I needed to be safe—but I glanced at Nicholas. He understood well enough what we were speaking of. If he would just meet my gaze, let me see something of what was going on in his mind. Did he want me to leave? Was there anything left between us that might be worth saving?

He did not look up.

"Will you be joining them?" Hugh asked.

I glanced at Hannah. Her encouraging smile eased a little of the ache in my heart.

"I love Wales," I said softly, "but I'm afraid the home and the peace I seek may not be here. I'll go with the children and see if I can find it elsewhere."

Chapter Twenty-eight

I sat at the table in my borrowed room, with a stack of letters surrounding me. The most pressing was from Master Lloyd, who voiced no objections to my plans to go abroad, but asked how he should dispose of my lands. He had already sent a servant to Nant Bach with my personal belongings and whatever of my funds he could gather—a respectable sum for starting a new life—but this final act would cut my last tie to Wales, my family, and my past.

The paper awaited my decision, its blankness staring back at me. Finally, I drew a deep breath and dipped the quill in the ink.

I, Joan Pryce, do hereby authorize Nicholas Bowen of Nant Bach, and his heirs after, to act as my agent.

Once the first words were written, the rest came more easily, detailing the holdings my mother had bequeathed to me to make my future secure. In a separate letter, I asked Master Lloyd to say nothing about it until after I was gone. I wanted no awkward scenes with Nicholas, but the income from the lands would, in a small measure, make up for the trouble I had caused him. No one could manage them better. In a way, I was still fulfilling our fathers' wishes to see the properties united.

"Joan!" Hannah burst into my room, her cheeks burnished red from running. "Look what I made!"

She showed me a full skein of soft, brown yarn.

"'Tis fine work," I said. "You've developed a deft hand for it."

" 'Twill help when we're overseas, will it not? And you should see Beth's threads. I have to force her to eat, she hates leaving her spinning wheel so."

"Aye, it will make a difference. You've a skill now that can earn some coins."

"I want to show Master Bowen." She tugged at my hand. "Come with me. 'Tis lovely outside."

The children had taken to Nicholas so easily, quickly overcoming their shyness at his scarred face, and he seemed to enjoy their simple trust and affection. I longed to join them outside, but every time I tried to talk to Nicholas, he found a reason to be elsewhere. I glanced at my letters.

"I'd best stay here."

She kissed me on the cheek and nearly bounced from the room. Soon, her happy voice echoed in the yard below. I peeked out and saw Nicholas admiring her handiwork. The sunlight played over his fair hair, and he smiled as he spoke to Hannah. I hoped he saw my peace offering in my decision to leave him my lands.

I turned away from the bright scene and, for the second time in a year, focused on packing my belongings. Some of them I would have to leave behind because we had so little space. I opened my small leather trunk with my mother's jewels, my pages from the Welsh book, and Nicholas's gift of Welsh scripture. I caressed this last paper longingly. I would probably never see those words in print. A Welsh Protestant Bible was unlikely to find its way to Rome.

Then there were Nicholas's letters. I hardly knew what to do with them. It seemed, if I was starting a new life, I ought to leave them behind, but I did not have the heart to burn them, and leaving them with anyone else would be awkward. I tucked them away in the trunk. Maybe carrying this memory of the past would keep me from repeating my mistakes.

On the evening appointed for our departure, Father Davies came for us under cover of dusk, dressed as a fisherman and driving a cart. Tears stung my eyes at the sight of him, bringing as he did reminders of so much: my father, my old home, the time when I thought everything was simple.

"Mistress Joan, child, have these last months been so very hard?" he asked gently.

"They have," I whispered as Gwilliam loaded our trunks onto the cart. "I feel as if I have done everything wrong. I came here thinking I would discover God's purpose for me, and all I have found is that I am a very foolish girl."

He smiled sadly. "That is often the first step to wisdom. Sometimes we do not get the answers we seek until the moment of crisis." He lowered his voice as we climbed into our places. "We must keep sharp eyes out. Someone has been on my trail for several days—a man with a broken red feather in his hat."

My breath caught. "Master Red-Plume!"

"Is this an enemy you know?"

I nodded, my mouth suddenly dry.

He smiled wryly. "Well, I have many enemies. We must be cautious, but try not to act nervous. Remember, we're just a family of fishermen."

Hannah put an arm around Beth, who cradled her doll and a distaff wound with wool—a gift from Nicholas to ease her distress over leaving the spinning wheel behind. Yet he had not said a word of farewell to me.

We started down the road without a glance back, though I looked all around me, trying to memorize each hill and valley and copse of trees that I would never see again.

Hoofbeats approached rapidly behind us. Father Davies moved his cart aside, but the horseman slowed as he approached. Father Davies's hands tightened on the reins, but his face kept its calm. Nicholas reined in beside us.

"May I have a moment with Mistress Pryce?"

"Of course," Father Davies said, "but not too long. The tides will not wait."

Nicholas nodded and slid gracefully to the ground. My pulse quickened. Had he forgiven me? Had he come to ask me to stay? As soon as I wondered it, warmth grew in my chest like a stoked fire, spreading to my chilly toes. I longed for him to caress my face as he had at the masque, gentle yet passionate. We had learned once to be friends again. If only we could talk freely and openly, putting aside our past and our differences, perhaps we could find a way to be happy together. I would even brave Master Red-Plume for the chance to try.

"Master Nicholas?" I asked, my heart beating so loudly I could scarce hear my own whispered voice.

But there was no warmth in his expression. "I did not want to leave on bad terms," he said coolly. "I brought you a parting gift."

His cold tone extinguished my hope. He held out his hand, but I shook my head.

"I owe you so much," I said softly. "When I think of—"

"You'll need money, Mistress Pryce," he interrupted. "Take it."

He pressed something small and cool into my hand. A ring. I held it up and gasped at the cut emerald shining in the gold band. What could he mean, giving me such a treasure, and in such a manner?

"This must be worth a fortune. I cannot accept it." I thrust it back.

He folded his arms. "'Tis yours. It always has been."

Before I could argue further, he swung onto his horse and spurred it away. I turned the ring over to examine it. On either side of the emerald were dragons, enameled red for Wales, one holding a cross and the other an hourglass. Inside the band were inscribed the words *Nicholas* and *Joan*.

It was my wedding band. I clutched it to my chest. Tears stung my eyes. He had given it to me only to help send me away. How long had he owned it, though? Had he ever intended to offer it to me? If only I could have seen behind his mask long enough to understand. I took a step in the direction he'd gone.

"Mistress Joan, we must go," Father Davies said quietly.

I slipped the ring onto the chain around my neck along with my crucifix and pulled myself back into the wagon, so heavy with regret I sagged back against the seat.

After a long, silent ride, we came to the beach near Plas Penrhyn, where the queen's men likely still kept watch. We left the wagon and climbed down the steep slope to a shore scattered with rocks. A rowboat tottered in the waves that licked the sand. In the distance, a white sail bobbed against the dark of the water, waiting to take us to Ireland and overseas. To our new lives. Away from Nicholas. Away from any hope of ever understanding.

I shivered in the cool, salty breeze, listening over the hushing of the waves for the sounds of pursuit. I glanced at the hills rising on either side of me with their reassuring strength and picked up a small, polished stone from the beach. If I found my heart uneasy in every other place I went, there was no turning back. The heartache would haunt me for the rest of my life, among whatever green vineyards or soaring cathedrals I found myself.

My gaze fell on one of the fisherman, and I recognized him, though I blinked several times to make certain I was not imagining things. It was Father Perkins. I dared not call out and betray him, but there could be no mistake. He saw me and gave a curt nod.

"Father Davies?" I whispered. "How . . ."

"Our friend over there? We received word that his guard would be rather lax on a particular night. He was allowed to escape the country on the condition that he does not return to it."

"You received word? How?"

He looked at me in surprise. "It was your friend, Master Bowen."

"Nicholas Bowen *saved* Father Perkins?"

"After he had him arrested, aye."

Once I might have branded such an act cowardice. Now, I saw it was the most honorable way Nicholas could find to deal with a complicated, confusing situation, one that I had also tried and failed to navigate with grace.

Would Nicholas find himself in trouble for what he had done? Would I even know? I looked back across the rolling green hills and the marshes of the headland. A light bobbed in the distance. Fairies again? They would not go with me to Rome. They were eternally part of the landscape of Wales.

I shook my head. I was lying to myself. It was not just the beautiful hills or the worry over Nicholas that made my heart hesitate. It was love. I closed my eyes and imagined Nicholas's arms around me again. That was the only embrace that would ease the pain in my heart. But did he want me? At times he was tender, concerned, but he had pushed me away. He had claimed the decision about our betrothal was mine, but I did not want someone who did not want me. And what of my beliefs? I had learned to see things through different eyes, but I could not change what was in my heart.

No wonder it ached. Love tore it in different directions.

I stepped back from the little crowd. A small step, nothing significant, but I felt the tear of separation. My heart beat faster. I might not get another chance to go overseas. If Nicholas did not want me, I would be left alone in Wales, probably married to some man more interested in my dowry than anything to do with me. I might have to keep the secrets and dreams of my heart buried all my life, until even the memories were shriveled and dry.

The one dream sat certain in front of me—as certain as anything could be—rolling in the shallow waves. The other waited somewhere in the green hills, in the chest of a man whose dear, frightening face hid his thoughts and feelings.

I took another step back.

"Mistress Pryce?" Father Perkins, in his fisherman's garb, came to guide me to the boat.

"I'm not sure I can do this," I said.

"The danger will soon be over. Have faith."

Faith. The word sent a jolt through me. Was that not what brought the miracles, the healing? Something whispered that, whatever happened, my path did not lie across those vast, black waters.

"I have to stay, Father. I think I'm needed here."

I waited for the disapproval in his sharp eyes, but as his gaze swept my face and then turned to the sea, I saw instead a canny sort of approval.

"Perhaps you are." He glanced up at the cliffs behind me. "The caves of Little Orme have been a place of refuge for us. Here we dared to try to change Wales. I will miss it."

I nodded and found a rock to lean against as the others loaded their possessions into the little boat. The children rushed to me.

"Are you not coming?" Hannah asked.

Her thin arms bit sharply into my sides, and tears slipped down my cheeks. I would never see her grow up, watch her blossom into a young woman. Would they be safe on their own, without me? Perhaps I could not stay in Wales after all.

Faith, my heart whispered, and my fear unwound. They would be in God's hands. I imagined the future I would not see: Hannah's cheeks pink, her limbs filled out from being well fed, her eyes bright with the knowledge enriching her mind. I also thought I glimpsed someone at her side who looked very much like Gwilliam grown into the brave young man I had seen protecting the others, and Beth safe and content along with them. I wept that I would never again see them in person, nor stitch some item for Hannah's dowry. With a sharp ache, I pulled out my mother's rosary. I ran my fingers once more over the smooth amber beads.

"Take this," I whispered.

Hannah hesitated and met my eyes. Her glance fell to the ring hanging at my throat, and she smiled a little. "I hope you'll be happy, Joan." She wrapped her fingers around the rosary and embraced me once more. "I'll use it to pray for you every day. Then I'll always feel like you're close."

Gwilliam tugged her away, tears in his eyes as he raised a hand in farewell. Beth stared at me, and I forced a smile as she turned to follow the others.

"You had best be going," Father Davies said gently. "If we are being pursued, you will not wish to be caught here."

I nodded and hefted my trunk to hurry away, but I cast a glance back at the boat resting on the sand. I needed to see them go. I found a safe place to leave the trunk and climbed a path winding up the rocky hills surrounding the beach, hoping the huge stones would shelter me from curious eyes. From my vantage, I could see the sweep of the sea and the rock-strewn shore, as well as my friends preparing to push the boat into the water.

The bobbing glow in the distance caught my attention. It looked closer, less like a fairy light and more like a lantern. Fishermen came out at all odd hours to ply their trade; I hardly understood the mysteries of tides and winds that were their daily discourse. The sea remained as deep and unfathomable to me as a starless night, no matter how close I lived to it. Still, Father Davies said someone with a broken red feather was tracking him.

I hurried back down the path, ducking around some of the large rocks to see if I could spy the intruder or see which direction he was heading. The man's soft steps came nearer. His lantern cast strange, grasping shadows on either side of my hiding place. I shrank from the phantom hands. The light moved, and I peeked out again.

The glow showed enough to prove this man was no fisherman. He wore fine clothes, and his rapier's hilt glinted in the lantern's flame as he studied the sand. In the dim light, I recognized the profile of Master Red-Plume.

Chapter Twenty-nine

Master Red-Plume straightened and looked toward the shore. Toward where my friends launched their boat. Had he seen them in the gloom? I looked around desperately and picked up a rock to hurl at him. The blow glanced off his back. He shouted, and I raced away into the darkness. His footsteps pounded after me.

Blessed Mary, preserve me. I am an idiot.

I swung behind an outcrop of rocks and pressed my back against the damp stone. Master Red-Plume's footsteps paused. My heart thudded. What would he do? Arrest me, torture me at his leisure? He took a step closer, his breath coming fast. I inhaled slowly and bit my lips closed.

His boots shuffled farther away.

I exhaled softly and glanced at the steep hills. Their caves had sheltered the Welsh printing press; they might offer me protection as well. Open drifts of grass separated me from the wooded rise. I tiptoed toward another large boulder, staying off the soft ground to avoid leaving footprints. A group of huge stones loomed in front of me. I sprinted for them and found a path leading up.

Tiny rocks rattled down the trail below me. I paused. The sound came again, close behind me. I ducked and pushed upward, climbing the steep hill. The trail wound around a bend, and a wide grassy patch stretched before me, broken by large, flat rocks. There was nowhere to hide out there. I scrambled into the thick trees beside the trail and held my breath.

Master Red-Plume's boots scuffed against the stones below me. I picked up a rock the size of my fist. Did I have the courage to smash a man on the head with it? If I failed to kill him, his retaliation would be that much more brutal.

The footsteps paused close to my hiding place. Very carefully, I set down my large stone and picked up a smaller one. I took a deep breath and heaved the pebble across the open field. It clattered in the darkness.

Master Red-Plume raced toward the sound.

I gathered my skirts and rushed down the other way as quietly as I could. Below me, the beach stretched away, and to my right waited the safety of the marshland and woods. I veered right and fled down the trail.

My soft boot slipped on the loose pebbles, and my ankle turned. I tumbled over the hard ground and rolled through a blur of grass and rocks down the steep slope to the beach.

"Stop!"

Master Red-Plume's voice echoed across the bay. He repeated the command in Welsh.

I forced myself to sit up, wincing at the throbbing in my ankle. Footsteps raced down the path, so I pushed myself to my feet. Pain shot up my leg, and I fell to my knees.

Waves rolled over the shore in front of me. The white sail of the boat carrying my friends to Ireland stood out in the distance against the blackness. I crawled toward the water. Maybe if I could get out far enough, Master Red-Plume would not be able to pursue me, and my friends or an early morning fisherman could rescue me. Of course, I did not swim.

A piece of driftwood lay on the beach. I grabbed it and shucked off my petticoats, dragging myself into the sea. The cold waves shoved me back. I gasped and scrambled past them.

"You! Woman! What are you doing?"

Master Red-Plume stood on the beach behind me. After a moment's hesitation, he took off his boots.

Please, blessed Mary, do not let him know how to swim.

As soon as I was deep enough to float, I clung to the driftwood and let my legs trail behind me. The cold water numbed the throbbing pain. Master Red-Plume splashed out into the waves, hesitating at the icy cold. My teeth chattered violently. The tide moved me away from him, but he plunged deeper.

"What's going on here?" a new voice called.

My heart skipped. It sounded like Nicholas. Was the rush of the sea playing tricks on me?

"A madwoman threw herself into the water," Master Red-Plume said. "I was trying to rescue her."

"How uncharacteristically noble of you."

I lifted my head to see the moonlit beach. Nicholas tossed aside his cloak, doublet, sword, and boots and splashed out into the water, swimming past Master Red-Plume with confident strokes. If he rescued me, what then?

He would reach me soon enough, so I kicked my uninjured leg, trying to steer myself in his direction. His good eye widened when he saw me.

"Mistress Joan! He's chasing you?"

"Aye," I said through chattering teeth.

Nicholas's face turned deathly still. He reached for me. I shrank away, but his grip was gentle as he hauled me toward shore. When the shallowness forced me to stand, I whimpered at the fresh wave of pain. Nicholas lifted me, dripping and shivering, into his arms, and I huddled against his chest, his warmth spreading over me like a cloak against the early morning chill.

Three men walked up behind Master Red-Plume. They were dressed like fishermen, but they could just as easily have been spies.

"Hand the woman over to me," Master Red-Plume demanded.

Nicholas tightened his grip. "I will not. She's been hurt."

"I'll see to it that her wounds are tended."

"I doubt that. The last time I saw you in her company, you were abusing her rather severely." Nicholas carefully set me on the sand and picked up his sword.

Master Red-Plume drew his own weapon. Nicholas lashed out with his blade, drawing the tip across Master Red-Plume's wrist. The Englishman shouted and dropped his rapier. The fishermen chuckled.

I caught a glimpse of the scarred side of Nicholas's face, patchy red with rage and almost inhuman in its coldness. *Y Diafol.* But his opponent was the real devil.

The English cur looked to the other three men. "I am an agent of Her Majesty, and I have reason to suspect this girl has vital information relating to treason against our queen. Turn her over to me immediately."

Nicholas's sword point remained fixed on Master Red-Plume's heart. "This woman is betrothed to me. I claim responsibility for her and will answer any questions you may have. I think you'll find I'm a gentleman in good standing, well respected in this shire and a faithful subject of Her Majesty."

I stared at Nicholas, heat and cold pounding through me with each heartbeat. He'd just taken responsibility for me, even knowing what I had been involved in. Did he mean it, or was he only using his reputation to protect me?

The onlookers nodded. "Aye," one of them said. "That's Nicholas Bowen. No mistaking a face like that."

Master Red-Plume's eyes narrowed. "Then perhaps Master Bowen would care to explain what his betrothed was doing out here on the shore in the middle of the night when I have reason to suspect a group of dangerous rebels were meeting here."

"Joan, were you plotting any rebellion here this evening?" Nicholas asked, his tone light. "Did you hear anyone tonight speaking of doing bodily harm to Her Majesty?"

He had phrased the question carefully so I did not have to lie. "Nay, Master Nicholas, nothing of the sort."

He shrugged. "I'm satisfied that she's involved in no rebellion. As for the rest of her actions, they are between her and me."

Master Red-Plume's face glowed livid red in the light of the approaching dawn. There was nothing more he could do. I was a woman, and I was no longer a *feme sole*, a free woman; I was a *feme covert*, a protected one. A man of good standing claimed to be my betrothed and vouched for me. Master Red-Plume's only action could be against that man, who clearly had people willing to side with him, especially against an Englishman.

"If you take even one false step, Master Bowen, I'll be waiting for you."

"I pride myself on being very surefooted."

The fishermen laughed.

Master Red-Plume snatched his sword from the sand and thrust at Nicholas, who brought his blade up to block. The swords scraped together, and the Englishman's tip slashed the air by Nicholas's arm.

Master Red-Plume pressed the charge, barreling into Nicholas and sending him sprawling back onto the rock-strewn beach. Nicholas's sword tumbled out of reach. I crawled after it across the damp sand. Master Red-Plume regained his footing and lunged for Nicholas's heart.

"No!" I shouted.

Nicholas swept his forearm up to deflect the blow. Master Red-Plume drew the sword back, slicing a red line along Nicholas's arm. I winced. Nicholas kicked out, connecting with Master Red-Plume's groin. The Englishman grunted and staggered back. I reached Nicholas's rapier.

"Nicholas," I called, tossing it toward him.

Master Red-Plume lunged. Nicholas rolled out of the way and jumped to his feet, sword in hand. The Englishman charged. Nicholas caught the man's blade with his own, deflecting it, and spun with him. His elbow made a solid smack when he slammed it into Master Red-Plume's head.

The Englishman dropped like a stunned bull. He groaned and tried to raise his rapier. With a vicious blow, Nicholas knocked the sword from the Englishman's shaky hand.

"Attacking an innocent subject of Her Majesty in front of witnesses?" Nicholas asked, his sword tip a finger's breadth from the Englishman's throat. "Do you think your masters in London will support you if I complain to a magistrate?"

The fishermen nodded and muttered to each other. Master Red-Plume glared, then grabbed his boots and stumbled to his feet to limp off through the sand. The fishermen laughed and walked on to their boats, leaving Nicholas and me alone on the beach.

Nicholas knelt beside me, his ferocity dissolved into concern. "Mistress Joan! You're hurt?"

Mistress Joan again. I had liked hearing just Joan for a moment, but it was only part of his ruse. "Your arm—"

"'Tis nothing. The bleeding has already slowed. What happened to you?"

"I fell, running from . . . that man. I could not let him catch me again, after last time . . ." I blushed at the acknowledgment of the incident at the masque, but he showed no reaction.

"So you threw yourself on the mercy of the sea?"

"I had nowhere else to go."

"What about your friends? Are they safe?"

"Indeed. They are gone."

"They left you!" He gave the empty beach an indignant look.

"Nay, I left them. I found, when the time came, I could not leave Wales. I'll miss Hannah terribly, and Gwilliam and Beth, but I looked back and realized my heart was here."

Nicholas reached out as if he would touch my wet hair, but instead grabbed his cloak and wrapped it around me. It was still warm, a bit like an embrace, but he did not touch me himself. Instead, he traced lines in the sand. "What I said . . . I only did that to save you. I hope it did not cause you any alarm."

A lump swelled in my throat. So I was to have none of my dreams. At least I was not deserting my country. "I understand. You're a good friend. I was fortunate you were here. What brought you to the shore at this hour?" I bit my lip, realizing if he had meant to meet with smugglers, I might have ruined his schemes.

"I . . ." He turned his face from me and was silent for so long I wondered if he was very angry.

"I'm sorry if I interfered with some business of yours," I said. "I have done nothing but cause you trouble. I'll find a way to pay you back for trespassing on your property all winter."

"You owe me nothing," he said quietly. "You did not interfere. As I rode back from . . . seeing you, I encountered some men gathering to hunt a Catholic outlaw matching Father Davies's description. I offered to assist them and then rode after you as soon as I could to make certain you were safe."

I stared at him, my heart fluttering like a startled dove. "You came to help us? But I thought . . ."

"What? That I hate Catholics? Nay, I still sympathize with the old faith. I only hate the thought of war."

"Oh." Of course, his coming here had nothing to do with me personally. He simply could not bear to see more blood spilled.

"You know I love Nant Bach," he said. "I thought it was all I had left in this world, so I focused on nothing else, making it my refuge. You reminded me I could do more, though. I was being selfish in my self-pity, turning my back on people who needed my help. I know of the good works Father Davies does in our shire. If I let him get captured tonight, it would put an end to all of that. I could not have that on my conscience."

"You saved all of us," I said.

"I admit Father Davies was not my main concern." He drew a deep breath. "Tonight, when I thought of you gone from Wales forever, Nant Bach seemed too empty. Then, when I learned you might be captured, I was terrified I would be too late for you . . ."

My heart felt like it would pound free of my chest. I reached out, placing my palm over his scarred cheek, and turned his face to mine. "You were not too late."

He rested his warm hand over mine. "Mistress Joan?"

"I said I left my heart in Wales. I meant that I left it with you."

"You cannot possibly mean . . ." He swallowed. "If you wish to be the mistress of Nant Bach, I'll gladly offer you the role to keep you safe. I know you feel some kindness toward me, but I do not want anything offered out of pity, even by a friend."

"I do not pity you, Nicholas. I love you."

He stared and shook his head slightly, as if in disbelief.

I pulled his face nearer to mine and traced my finger over his shattered cheek, across his twisted lips. He shivered and closed his eyes. I kept mine open until my lips met his. He pulled me close and kissed me back with every bit as much passion as he had shown dancing at the masque. The heat of it chased away the chill seeping through my damp clothes and left me breathless.

He pulled back and stroked my damp hair, a smile shining on his face. "Oh, Joan. Is this another dream? You looked at me with such shock when we first met again, I thought you must be disgusted by me."

"Only surprised, and then frightened by your coldness."

He grabbed my hands. "I dared not let myself hope you would want me, but when they searched Nant Bach, they said you had letters from me. I could hardly believe you had kept them. It gave me hope that I might have some chance with you still, and the more I spent time with you, the more I desired that to be true."

"That's why you came to the masque?"

"I was afraid I was losing you to Hugh Richards. 'Twas a foolish thing to do, but I wanted the chance to be close to you, even if just for the evening, as part of the fiction of the masquerade. When you spoke of leaving Wales, and again tonight, when I came to . . . to give you the ring, I almost asked you to stay, but I doubted myself . . . doubted I could make you happy. I have hurt so much, I did not think I could bear to be hurt again, to lose again. This night, though, I realized I could lose something precious by inaction as easily as I could by seeking it out and failing. I had to try, to fight. I would always count myself a coward if I did not."

"You are no coward," I whispered. "This whole time I have been so lonely, so confused." He made a sound of dismay, and I added, "But I finally realized I was happiest with you."

Nicholas regarded me for a long time, then pulled me close. We turned to stare out across the sea as the sun rose. A fire of companionship glowed between us, casting warmth over the scene and touching everything with an aura of gold.

Finally, he smiled a little. "I have lived my life in such a way that the woman I marry may be allowed a little . . . eccentricity in her religious practices. After all, her husband is loyal and faithful to the realm." He cleared his throat. "Would you take me for your husband, scarred and heretical as I am?"

I smiled and traced his cheek again. "Aye, Nicholas Bowen, I would take you for my husband. And what of you?"

"I love you, Joan Pryce. I'll take you for my wife."

The words were legal and binding this time, but instead of constraining me, they set my heart free.

Nicholas grinned. "The sooner the better. I know an old priest who performs marriages in the Catholic style for those who desire it. We'll talk to him today, have the banns read in church, and be married in a fortnight. There's also a chance, if I keep my reputation clean, that we can get licenses to travel abroad someday."

"To visit Gwilliam, Hannah, and Beth?"

"And even Rome. A belated wedding trip."

I smiled and kissed him again. The sea whispered my joy as we watched its waves roll into the distance.

Two weeks later we were married at the church, but in a Catholic ceremony with only Master and Mistress Lloyd and the old priest to witness it. At the churchyard gates, Nicholas swept me into his arms and carried me to his carriage.

"I have a wedding present for you," he said.

I laughed. "You've already given me everything I wanted."

"Well, you'll be needing these." He set me down and handed me a ring of brass keys. "A gift for the mistress of Nant Bach."

I accepted them with a grin. "Thank you, my lord."

"That's not quite all." From the carriage, he produced a small package wrapped in paper.

I tore it open and ran my fingers over the smooth leather cover of a new book. "The Welsh Bible? I thought it was not printed yet."

"Read it," he urged.

I flipped it open and gasped. It was the Welsh book, *Y Drych Cristianogawl*. My book. "How is this possible?"

"Some local men helped the queen's agents when they raided the cave where the book was printed. They burned most of the pages, but saved a few copies as evidence. I was able to slip a set away and have them bound."

I raised an eyebrow. "That was illegal."

"How could I let them destroy a piece of history?" He was smiling.

My history. Wales's history. I turned to the end. The last pages were blank. There was work still to do for Wales, and I was here to see it done. "Thank you, Nicholas. I'll treasure it, as will our children, and theirs."

I pulled him close and kissed him, slowly and tenderly.

He rested his forehead against mine and grinned. "Shall we go?"

"Aye." I blushed and hugged the book to my chest as he helped me into the carriage. Down the road, the green hills and fields of Nant Bach waited to welcome us. We were going home.

Discussion Questions

1 What kinds of bravery did the characters in this novel display? Who do you think had the most courage? Why?

2 Did Joan make the right choice about the gunpowder? What determines when we need to fight and when we need to seek peace?

3 Joan concludes that hate breeds hate, and that she can break the cycle by refusing to hate in return or to be defined by others' stereotypes. Do you agree with her? How would you react to people who hate you because of your background or beliefs?

4 Joan's story is set during a time when women had few rights. How did this restrict Joan? How did she work within those constraints to keep her agency—her ability to determine her own destiny?

5 During the Reformation, the idea of religious freedom as we understand it didn't exist. Most governments believed that conformity to the state religion was necessary for peace. Many people, like Joan, were faced with a choice between their religious convictions and their country. How would you have reacted in their situation? What personal freedoms still need protection today, and how would you find a balance between the rights of individuals and society?

Author's Note

This is a work of fiction, but many of the people and events mentioned in it are real.

Mary, Queen of Scots, was executed as described in the story for her suspected involvement in the Babington Plot, one of many Catholic conspiracies to overthrow Elizabeth. The plot that Joan interrupts is fictional, but it draws inspiration from the Gunpowder Plot of 1605, in which a group of Catholics attempted to blow up Parliament and King James (son of Mary, Queen of Scots, and therefore Elizabeth I's successor; he proved to be no more friendly to Catholics than Elizabeth, despite his family's Catholic history).

The Catholic book, *Y Drych Cristianogawl*, is also real, and the account of its printing on a secret press in a cave in Little Orme near Conwy is accepted by most historians, though the lack of written records makes it difficult to prove. This would make it the first book printed in Wales. It is known that in April 1587, a group of fugitive Catholics escaped from a seaside cave at Little Orme on the property of Robert Pugh, and that they left behind a printing press. Only four copies of *Y Drych Cristianogawl* survive, and the one complete copy is located in the National Library of Wales.

Wales has a long history of conflict with England. The Welsh were in Britain before the English, who drove them from England into the mountains of Wales, where these ancient Britons withstood English incursions for centuries. The English gave the Britons the name "Welsh," which comes from the Saxon word for "stranger," labelling the Britons as strangers in their own land. Edward I (Longshanks) brought most of the country under his control, but the Welsh resisted their conquerors, as national heroes like Owain Glyndŵr fought against English control for centuries. The Welsh language never died out (probably thanks to the written works available in Welsh, including the prayer book and Bible, as well as the strong bardic tradition that kept old stories and patriotism alive), and though English became common in Wales, the native language is enjoying a resurgence today.

The Tudor dynasty, starting with Henry VII and his notorious son, Henry VIII, managed to integrate Wales into England better than previous rulers had. Tudor is a Welsh name, and the Tudor monarchs had Welsh blood. Though Wales did not get complete freedom, and its citizens were still looked down upon by the English, it did get some concessions from the Tudors, including Welsh prayer books and Bibles. For this reason, many Welsh Catholics felt deeply torn between their loyalty to their faith and to a monarch who was of Welsh descent. Though Joan looks on the queen as her enemy, Elizabeth was, in fact, a strong, clever monarch who did much good for England and Wales despite some of her odd personality quirks and the harsh legal system of the time.

Many readers have asked me about the kiss of greeting the characters exchange. It is a kiss on the lips: a common practice in Renaissance England and Wales. It would not seem strange to Joan because she grew up with it, though most of us would probably find it a little too friendly.

The plague was a terrifying disease because germs had not yet been discovered and no one understood how it spread. As with Nicholas's family, those who were infected would sometimes be locked in quarantine until they recovered or died, and they usually died.

Poverty was also a horrible killer. Without the charitable institutions of the Catholic Church, vast numbers of people starved to death on the streets or turned to crime out of desperation and were executed. The homeless could be whipped, branded, have their ears cut, or be hanged as felons. Shortly after the events of this book, a law was passed making it illegal to give shelter or aid to any of the wandering poor (though rest assured that Nicholas and Joan will ignore this particular law, as did other compassionate landowners). By the end of Elizabeth's reign, however, more reasonable Poor Laws were put into effect, raising taxes to provide for the poor.

Elizabethan women did not have legal rights as we understand them. They were little more than property owned by a man: a father, brother, guardian, or husband. Widows were one exception. They might be allowed to continue their deceased husband's business and manage his estate in the name of providing for their children. Brewing was one of the few occupations a middle class woman might pursue. While it was a challenging era to be a woman, they were not always passive victims of the system. They had social power, especially when they banded together, and were often treated as partners by their husbands. Then, as now, some lived in happy situations and some did not. Because of their nebulous legal standing and long tradition of faith, Catholic women were often the strongest allies of Catholic priests and played an important role in keeping their religion alive in England and Wales.

I have made the details of the lives of my characters as realistic as possible based on what we know from plays, poems, letters, and material evidence from the sixteenth century. There are some things we simply don't know or understand about this era, and it is possible that I made some mistakes or oversights. I hope readers will forgive these and still enjoy the rest of story.

Joan, Nicholas, Hugh, Father Perkins, the Lloyds and their neighbors, and Gwilliam, Hannah, and Beth are inventions of my imagination, but they represent real responses of Catholics and Protestants to the religious upheaval of the sixteenth century, a time of great learning and discovery as well as cruelty and violence.

Father William Davies was a real person. In 1592, about five years after the events of this book, he was caught sneaking four young men from Wales to Ireland. He was imprisoned and then executed in 1593 by being hanged, drawn, and quartered. His superior, Father Henry Garnet, was an advocate for seeking a peaceful resolution to the conflict between Catholics and Protestants. In 1605, he learned of the Gunpowder Plot under the seal of the confessional. Feeling bound by the privacy of confession, he did not inform authorities, but begged the young men and even the Pope to put a stop to the plot. They ignored his advice. When the Gunpowder Plot failed, Father Henry Garnet was arrested and executed as a conspirator. His skin was used to bind a book detailing his crimes.

The elusive Robert Pugh was also a real person. I was sorry that he was in hiding at the time of this story and unable to make an appearance, but in a way this book is a tribute to him and others like him who strove to walk the fine line between loyalty to their country and loyalty to their conscience. The cave where *Y Drych Cristianogawl* was printed was on his property, and he helped in the printing. His home, Plas Penrhyn, is still standing—now functioning as a bar and restaurant—with a priest hole reached by climbing into the chimney dated to 1590, according to an antique plaque on the fireplace. I have made the assumption that there was an earlier priest hole before the fireplace was remodeled, as these hiding places were essential to the survival of priests. There is also an underground fissure running below the house, and tradition claims it has an opening somewhere in the ancient building, but its exact location is a mystery.

Robert Pugh spent most of his life living as a fugitive, yet he never participated in any of the many plots against Queen Elizabeth. His grandson Gwilym Pugh was a soldier and surgeon in the service of King Charles I during the English Civil War, as well as a Catholic poet and priest, proving that one could be a loyal subject and a loyal Catholic.

While no single person or group can take all the credit for the religious freedom enjoyed in many Western nations today, those Catholics who refused to succumb to the stereotypes and propaganda against them played a role, as did those who fled to the colony of Maryland. Maryland was founded by a Catholic, Lord Baltimore, as a haven for his co-religionists, and the Maryland Toleration Act of 1649 was one of the first laws requiring religious tolerance in what would become the United States of America. This period of relative tolerance was brief, and Catholics endured a great deal of prejudice and persecution in American history, but they helped plant the seed of a concept that seemed impossible to people at the time: that as divisive as religious devotion *can* be, it does not *have* to be a force dividing nations or people.

Acknowledgments

Thank you to the many people who helped make this book possible:

My critique groups, the Cache Valley Chapter of the League of Utah Writers and UPSSEFW, gave me support and insight throughout the writing process, as did my awesome online writers communities, especially the Neurotic Writers Support Group and Authors' Think Tank. I'm also grateful for the feedback from my beta readers: Jeff Bateman, Karen Brooksby, Sherrie Lynn Clarke, Ashley Crookston, Aubrey Dickens, Arielle Hadfield, Danette Hansen, Sherry Howard, Sarah Isert, Autumn Kirkham, Jeanette Kirkham, Kaylee Kirkham, and Leslie Anne Miranda.

The inspiration for this novel came during research for my master's thesis, and I've had a lot of help along the way from people who know much more than I do. If there are any historical mistakes in this novel, they are my own. I appreciate the guidance of my thesis advisors, Drs. Phebe Jensen, Norman Jones, Robert Mueller, and Leonard Rosenband at Utah State University. I've also had the opportunity to pick the brains of Timothy Cutts at the National Library of Wales, the wonderful staffs at Plas Mawr in Conwy and St. Winifred's Well in Holywell, and Guy Marsh at Penrhyn Old Hall.

Many thanks to the team at Cedar Fort for bringing this book to life: to Emma Parker for believing in this story from the beginning,

ACKNOWLEDGMENTS

and to Heather Baggs, Justin Greer, Kelly Martinez, Michelle May, and everyone else who did an incredible amount of work behind the scenes. There will be cake.

Most importantly, thank you to my family: to my parents who read me stories as a child, and to my wonderful children and my amazing husband, Dan, who makes it all possible.

About the Author

E. B. Wheeler grew up in Georgia and California. She earned her BA in history from BYU and has graduate degrees in history and landscape architecture from Utah State University. With Welsh ancestors on one side of her family and crypto-Catholics on the other, she's been fascinated by the story of Welsh Catholics since writing about them in her master's thesis. She's the award-winning author of *The Haunting of Springett Hall* and several essays, magazine articles, and short stories. She lives in northern Utah with her family. In the rare moments when she's not chasing her kids around or writing, she enjoys gardening, playing harp and hammered dulcimer, knitting and weaving, archery, and, of course, reading.